A Seeking Heart

Mountain Lake, Minnesota Trilogy

A Seeking Heart

A Heart Surrenders

When a Heart Cries

A Seeking Heart

by Kim Vogel Sawyer

"And ye shall seek me, and find me,
when ye shall search for me with all your heart."
Jeremiah 29:13 KJV

A Seeking Heart

Hendrickson Publishers Marketing, LLC
P. O. Box 3473
Peabody, Massachusetts 01961-3473

ISBN 978-1-59856-903-2

Third Hendrickson Edition Printing — June 2012

Dedicated lovingly to Mom and Daddy—
thank you for making sure
my heart never felt the need to go seeking
for love and acceptance.

A Note to Readers

Thank you for choosing to spend time with Samantha and Adam and the residents of Mountain Lake. This story is particularly dear to me because it is loosely based on my family history. I still remember with deep appreciation my visit to the Mountain Lake community years ago.

The Mennonite Brethren referenced in the Mountain Lake, Minnesota Trilogy originally resided in Germany. Persecuted for their faith, which included resistance to taking human lives even in times of war, they accepted the invitation of Catherine the Great to settle on the *steppes*, those grassy plains of Russia, and live their beliefs without government interference. They built colonies and settled the untamed land, living peacefully for a century before new political leaders once again demanded their sons serve in the military and otherwise intruded upon their peaceful village life. Consequently, a number of the families chose to leave Russia and immigrate to the United States of America, where they could practice their religion freely, without fear of those terrifying knocks on the door from soldiers with official documents and weapons.

My great-grandparents, Bernard and Maria Klaassen, were part of a large number of German Mennonites who left Russia in the 1870s to start a new life in America. They established a farmstead near Mountain Lake where they raised their nine children, including my grandmother, Elizabeth. My grandmother's caring, giving spirit is captured here in the character of Laura, and it gives me great pleasure to honor her tender heart and deep faith.

May God bless you richly as you journey with Him,

Kim Vogel Sawyer

Contents

Chapter One 1

Chapter Two 11

Chapter Three 17

Chapter Four 25

Chapter Five 33

Chapter Six 41

Chapter Seven 51

Chapter Eight 65

Chapter Nine 79

Chapter Ten 89

Chapter Eleven 99

Chapter Twelve 107

Chapter Thirteen 115

Chapter Fourteen 123

Chapter Fifteen 129

Chapter Sixteen 135

Chapter Seventeen 145

Chapter Eighteen 155

Chapter Nineteen 169

Chapter Twenty 177

Chapter Twenty-One 187

Chapter Twenty-Two 195

Chapter Twenty-Three 203

Chapter Twenty-Four 213

Chapter Twenty-Five 217

Chapter Twenty-Six 225

Chapter Twenty-Seven 235

Chapter Twenty-Eight 245

Chapter Twenty-Nine 253

Chapter Thirty 263

Chapter Thirty-One 269

Laura Klaassen's Scripture Cake 273

Acknowledgments 274

Klaassen Family Tree

Simon James Klaassen (1873) m. Laura Doerksen (1877), 1893
  Daniel Simon (1894) m. Rose Willems (1892), 1913
    Christina Rose (1915)
    Katrina Marie (1916)
  Hannah Joy (1895–1895)
  Franklin Thomas (1896)
  Elizabeth Laurene (1898) m. Jacob Aaron Stoesz (1897), 1915
  Adam Earnest (1899)
  Josephine Ellen (1900)
  Arnold Hiram (1903)
  Rebecca Arlene (1906)
  Theodore Henry (1909)
  Sarah Louise (1911)
Hiram Klaassen (1872) m. Hulda Schmidt (1872), 1898

O'Brien Family Tree

Burton O'Brien (1870) m. Olivia Ruth Stanton (1873–1900),
  1891
  David Burton (1894)
  Samantha Olivia (1900)

Chapter One

August 1917

*O*n the outskirts of Mountain Lake, Minnesota, a young girl was seated beneath a gnarled, century-old cottonwood. It was one of the few trees left standing when the farmers cleared the land to plant their Turkey Red wheat some seventy-five years past. But she didn't know that, not yet. She rested her back against the bark, the tree's shade a welcome respite from the stifling August heat. The gentle whisper of the wind through the leaves was as pleasing as a lullaby to the weary traveler.

She *was* tired. *Bone-tired*, her Gran would have said. She had come a long distance, sometimes hitching rides in the backs of rattling wagons and once having the luxury of a leather seat in a Model T. But mostly she walked. Her feet carried blisters and calluses representing the many miles covered, and now she pushed them into the soft soil beneath the tree to cool them. Her inner thighs were sore, chafed by the four-sizes-too-large overalls she had donned for her journey, and her wrists were grubby and dirt streaked from constantly rolling up the sleeves of the loose flannel shirt. Her attire was most inappropriate for the heat of the summer, yet she had carefully chosen each item before setting out. Her attempt was to pass as a young farm boy rather than the seventeen-year-old young lady she was. She had her reasons.

The abominable itching of her scalp bothered her more than anything else. She'd tucked her nearly waist-length hair up into a worn brown suede hat discarded by her father years ago. She longed to pull it off, shake out her hair, and scratch her skull until it tingled, but she didn't dare. She might not be able to cram it all back. So she satisfied herself by shifting the hat around on her head. It offered some relief.

Moving her position against the tree, she closed her eyes and released a deep sigh. Her belly rumbled, and she rubbed at her empty midsection. "I know, I know," she mumbled, "I should find something to eat. Soon." She grimaced as her stomach cramped painfully.

It was noon yesterday when she had eaten last, and then only a handful of soda crackers and a wormy apple she'd snitched from the Blue Earth Mercantile's apple barrel when no one was looking. The problem was that her meager cash supply was fearfully low, with her hunger immeasurably high. She crossed her arms over her belly and pressed in, hoping to still the hunger pangs and wondering what she should do.

Truth of the matter was she'd been formulating a plan under her battered suede hat ever since she'd passed a neat farm house about a mile and a half back. The white-washed two-story, its big wrap-around porch and bright marigolds lining the pathways from the house to the dirt road, bespoke of no little wealth. And judging from the number of dungarees, work shirts, and stockings hanging on lines between the barn and outhouse, it also indicated a whole passel of youngsters— too many for one rural farmer in Mountain Lake, Minnesota, to keep track of, the girl reasoned.

Luckily the owner had painted his name on the road side of the barn in neat block letters for all to see: KLAASSEN FARM. It seemed to her as though the man was offering to become her benefactor. She stayed seated, though, pushing the plan back and forth in her mind. Hungry as she was, the thought of stealing rankled. Oh, she'd done her fair share of pilfering, like the crackers and apple, and if you came right down to it, she'd actually stolen the clothes she was wearing from the trunk in the cellar back home. But thievery still didn't set easily on her shoulders. A necessity rather than a choice, she concluded with a sigh.

Another rumbling, this time not from her stomach, brought her bolt upright, prepared for flight. From around the bend came a boxy wagon, its high sides painted celery green and pulled by two large, well-muscled horses, though they also looked like they might be well along in years. Atop the wagon seat, holding loosely onto the reins with elbows resting lazily on his knees, was a figure in a gray plaid shirt, its sleeves rolled above the elbows, faded blue britches, and a fringe of brown hair below the straw hat.

He must have spotted her and nodded a greeting. "Howdy, boy." His smile seemed relaxed, unthreatening.

She gave a barely perceptible nod in return and turned away, heart pounding. The young man clucked to the horses and continued on. She watched around the tree, her heart bumping its apprehension inside her chest, until the wagon disappeared over a gentle rise in the road, headed back the way she had come. When only a cloud of dust remained, she collapsed against the tree trunk.

He thinks I'm a boy. . . . Knowing her disguise was working gave her the confidence she needed to go ahead with her plan. She waited a few minutes to be certain the wagon and its driver were well ahead of her, then pushed to her feet. She reached for her boots, but couldn't bear the thought of confining her poor feet inside those instruments of torture again. She tied the rawhide laces together and slung them over her shoulder. With a sigh—and another loud growl from her middle—she began following the wagon tracks back toward the town.

❦

"Whoa, there, Bet, Tick," Adam Klaassen called as he pulled the team up in front of Tucker's Lumber and Hardware Store. With practiced motions he wrapped the reins around the brake and leaped off the wagon, his landing a soft *fump* in the dirt street. He whipped the straw hat from his head and banged it against his pant leg a time or two to loosen the dust, ran his fingers through his hair, then slapped the hat back on his head.

Three long strides put him on the stoop to Tucker's store, and he squeaked the screen door open. He stood in the doorway a moment, allowing his sight to adjust from the bright sunshine to the gloom of the store's interior. Although the building boasted two large windows, one on either side of the wooden entry door, the owner didn't seem to find time or impetus to clean them. The accumulated dust and grime, whirled up from the street by the near-constant wind, adequately blocked the light from the shop.

Adam stepped a few feet into the building. "Mr. Tucker?" He glanced around at the wild disarray that made up Nip Tucker's stock. Barrels of nails, makeshift shelves holding a variety of tools, and stacks of lumber in various lengths created a mindboggling maze of disorganization. Adam moved closer to the tall, dusty counter at the rear of the store and called the owner's name again.

Adam cocked an ear at rustling from behind the counter, followed by the squeak of tin upon tin, and finally a resounding burp. He held back a grin as Nip's huge frame straightened from his attempt at concealment. Nip slipped a slim tin canister into the hip pocket of his enormous overalls before leaning beefy hands on the counter. He greeted Adam with a face-splitting smile, revealing a gap from a missing tooth.

No one knew Nip's real name, but his nickname came from his habit of partaking frequently of the tin canister he tried to conceal in his ample pocket. Despite Nip's obvious weakness for the tobacco chew he kept in his mouth, he was an honest businessman and well liked in the community by townspeople and farmers alike.

"Well, howdy-do, Adam." Nip's broad face remained locked in a cheerful grin. The man had more smile lines than anyone else Adam knew. His fuzzy white hair stood in tufts around an oversized head, and with his round belly and red-veined nose, he resembled a jolly, giant carved elf from the Old Country.

"Howdy to you, Mr. Tucker." Adam smiled back and leaned his elbows on the unkempt counter. "Pa sent me in for some two-penny nails and a leather piece, say"—he gestured— "so big."

"That I c'n do, I shorely c'n do it." Nip stuck out his lower lip and scratched at raspy chin whiskers. "Let's see now . . . two-penny nails." He ambled around the counter and waddled between aisles of barrels, giving each an inquisitive peek. The man could have done with more room between them, but the store's size and the quantity of stock were realities he couldn't change.

Adam knew the minute Nip found what he was looking for by a happy hiccup. As Nip made his way back to the counter for a paper sack, Adam wondered at the near-miraculous ability of Nip to find anything he wanted. Adam had never been able to spot any kind of organizational system in the cluttered shop. Yet, to his knowledge, Nip had never disappointed a customer.

Nip dropped two huge handfuls of nails in the sack, then carefully weighed them, squinting at the rusty scale with great concentration. "Pound an' a quarter." He peered at Adam over his shoulder. "That enough?"

"Ought 'a be."

"An' a strip o' leather, so big?" Nip held out those large hands.

Adam nodded. "Yep. It's for a hinge on the chicken coop. Pa says the busy rooster just plum wore out the other one."

The men shared a snort of laughter. Nip located a pocket-knife in the depths of his overalls and whacked off a four-inch piece of leather from a much longer strip. He dropped it in the sack with the nails and handed the bag to Adam.

"Can you add this to our tab?" Adam rolled down the bag's opening. "Pa will be in at the end of the month to settle with you."

Nip flapped a big paw in agreement. "No problem, Adam. Your pa's always good for it."

"Thanks a lot." Adam headed for the door with his purchase. He pushed at the door, but before he could step outside Nip called to him.

"Adam, hold up a minute, would'ja? Wonder if you'd mind playin' delivery boy for me." He huffed his way around the counter, waving a thick roll of gray mesh with one hand and toting a clanking burlap bag in the other. "Lank Schroeder ordered up a passel o' drawer pulls for them bureaus he's always building, and I got this here screen to replace that what's tore on the back door of your uncle's store. Could'ja run these things over to the furniture place an' the mercantile fer me?"

Adam noted the time and effort it took Nip to pull his big frame around the counter and through the shop to the doorway. It would take the man most of the morning to make the two deliveries. Adam wasn't in a big hurry to return home. He could do this favor. "Don't mind a bit, Nip."

"Thank ya much." Nip gave Adam's shoulder a friendly slap on the back that sent him through the doorway and out into the August heat. Nip followed with the two items, his heaving breaths providing further warmth on the back of Adam's neck. He dropped his little bag over the edge of the wagon bed, then took the two deliveries from Nip's big hands.

"Thanks again, boy," Nip said.

"Sure thing. Have a good day, Mr. Tucker."

It would take more time to get Bet and Tick moving again than to simply hoof it. Adam tossed the burlap bag over his shoulder, tucked the roll of screen beneath his arm, and aimed his feet toward the furniture shop.

The small figure stood at the north edge of Tenth Street beside a Baptist church and surveyed the area with practiced nonchalance. Her pa had been in the habit of calling her dim-witted, but her brother David said she was as bright as a new penny.

One thing she knew is that she must be very careful, miss nothing of importance to her plan. But there wasn't much to see as she looked around. Mountain Lake was hardly a town at all compared to where she had been born and raised.

While this town was small, she had to admit the businesses appeared to be well-kept and the houses showed neat yards and recent paint jobs. The people living here apparently took pride in their town. For some reason she couldn't understand, it rankled her a bit.

Meandering on still-bare feet past a pool hall, she headed for the small business district. Across the street, the green wagon and horses she'd seen earlier on the road hunkered down in the shade of a large, gray-sided building with "Tucker's Lumber & Hardware" painted on the side in childish letters. The rather shabby store stood in contrast to the neat park with its mowed grass and tall trees on the next block.

She stepped from the dirt road onto a raised walkway, the boards warm and smooth beneath her feet. A cozy little house sat on the corner of Tenth Street and Fourth Avenue, nestled next to a series of businesses from shoe repair to implement sales to a tall bank building made of stone. Her lower lip pulled between her teeth, her gaze whisked over the signs. *Where was a mercantile?* On the opposite side of the street and down the block, a huge building sported a sign which read "Hiebert & Balzer Store" in fancy painted letters. Hope ignited in her breast.

After a glance right and left, she scurried kitty-corner across Third Avenue and stepped onto another boardwalk running the length of the second block of buildings. She pressed her palm to her rumbling belly as she peeked through the shiny glass window of Hiebert & Balzer's, the words restated in a gold, swirly typeface on the pane. A quick look confirmed it had what she needed. But several wagons waited outside the large store, which meant a number of shoppers would be milling inside. Lots of eyes watching. She held back the impulse to enter the store, do what she'd come to do, and get on her way. Eagerness might lead to carelessness. With a sigh, she moved on.

Scuffing past a drugstore and another general merchandise store which she chose to bypass for the same reasons as the previous, she stopped to scope out the opposite side of the street, scanning the names of the businesses. A hardware store, a tailor shop, a house, another drugstore, and—she let out a little gasp of delight. Between John Schroeder Drug Store and First State Bank stood the Family Mercantile of Mountain Lake.

A narrow, two-story wooden structure with a square, false front painted white and sporting dark green window trim, it took up merely a quarter of the space of the intimidating Hiebert & Balzer Store and was also smaller than A. A. Woodruff's. It displayed the only porch along the length of the boardwalk. Spooled posts decorated with bands of green and yellow held up each corner of the porch roof, giving the mercantile a pleasant, homey appearance. The girl smiled as she examined the shop. *Small. Welcoming to families. Not likely to be filled with people.*

She trotted across the street and leaned against one of four limestone posts, iron rings embedded in their tops, standing in a precise row in front of the bank. One lazy-looking horse hitched to a fancy, two-seater buggy stood dozing in front of the second post, his tail swishing in slow motion.

Relying on the horse to partially hide her from view, the girl licked her dry lips, her thoughts scrambling. South of the mercantile, Tenth Street intersected with railroad tracks angling their way out of town. She curled her arm around the warm limestone post, planning her best course afterward. Straight south through the stockyard—no one would want to follow her there—then west along the railroad tracks until she'd hit the edge of town.

The escape route chosen, she sucked in a big breath for fortification, pushed off the post, and moved purposefully toward the Family Mercantile of Mountain Lake.

Chapter Two

*T*he girl paused briefly outside the scrolled screen door to dampen her dirty palms with her tongue and swipe them roughly against the seat of her equally filthy overalls. She peered at her hands in vexation. Still streaked with dirt. But they'd have to do. One last tug on her hat brim brought it comfortingly low around her ears. She assumed a casual pose, hooking her thumbs in the rear pockets of her britches.

Her boots still swung over one shoulder, thumping her chest and back as she moved. With the other shoulder she bumped the door open. A cowbell hanging above the screen door clanged a noisy greeting, startling her out of her attempt at nonchalance. She regained her composure quickly, though, as the shopkeeper lifted his bald head from measuring flour for a young woman with a shopping basket in hand and a straw bonnet on her head. Looking at the woman's flower-sprigged dress and cheerful bonnet, the girl felt more dowdy and disheveled than ever. The desire to turn tail and run smacked her hard.

"Be with you in a minute, son," the shopkeeper called out. W*hew*! Dirt or not, she was safe for the moment. He was a man small of stature, and he possessed a surprisingly deep voice. Another urge to hightail it out of there pricked hard, but running would look plenty suspicious, so she nodded a silent reply and ambled between two aisles.

The store was as tidy as Gran's pantry at home, the girl noted, and it smelled wonderful. Tangy pickles, malty yeast, and pungent apples combined to create a heady aroma that sent her nostrils twitching, her saliva spurting, and her stomach into spasms of desire. She turned a slow circle, examining, sniffing, enjoying. Canned goods lined up with military precision on homemade pine shelves. Household items stood arranged for easy contemplation and selection. The store epitomized order and cleanliness, as well as a true pride of ownership. Guilt niggled. Could she really steal from this obviously honest merchant? But another sharp pain of emptiness shot through her belly and overrode feelings of remorse.

She shuffled forward, swallowing. A wondrous selection of fabrics and sewing notions beckoned from the northeast corner of the store, stirring a feminine rush of pleasure. But wouldn't she look silly examining the array, all decked out in her overalls and lumpy hat? Besides, she was *hungry*. She moved resolutely to the west side where the canned goods beckoned to her.

The cowbell clanged, announcing the exit of the woman customer, and the shopkeeper began dusting small bottles of medicinal cures lined neatly along a narrow shelf behind the counter. But the girl sensed his watchful eyes following her, measuring her as carefully as he probably measured his dry goods. She tried to appear as if she was checking off a mental list as she made her selections. Bending her arm into a makeshift sling, she loaded herself down with a large tin of Edgemont crackers, two cans of spiced peaches—even though she wasn't sure she'd be able to pry anything in cans open—along with several cans of Van Camps beans. With a burst of extravagance, she added an egg-shaped tin of ham on top of the awkward armful.

While she shopped, she reviewed the simple plan. The mercantile owner would keep an account book for customers to charge their purchases, with balances due at the end of the month. It worked that way at home, but she and Pa were never allowed to charge since Pa couldn't be trusted to pay up. She'd just tell the owner to charge her selections to the Klaassen account, he would do it, the Klaassens would probably never even notice the small discrepancy on their account—from the looks of that fine farmhouse, they sure could afford it—and she'd have food for a couple of days till she hit the next town. It was a good plan, and no one would be the wiser.

Balancing her armload, she leaned back and shuffled her way over to the counter where she dropped it all in a series of resounding thuds. The shopkeeper placed his feather duster beneath the counter, smoothed a pink palm across his equally pink dome, and sent a glance over the accumulated items.

"Is that all?" His tone was pleasant enough.

The girl's eyes settled on the large glass jars displayed prominently on the countertop. Each wide-mouth jar contained a different treat to satisfy the most discerning sweet tooth. From peppermint sticks to sour balls, licorice whips to brightly colored gumdrops and jelly beans, her gaze roved, mouth watering.

The shopkeeper smiled his understanding. He popped the cork on the closest jar and fished out a walnut-sized sugar-coated red gumdrop. He extended it on an open palm almost beneath the girl's nose. Uncertain, she looked up at him, and he bobbed the candy in invitation. "Take it. No charge."

The girl licked her lips in anticipation and reached out for the proffered indulgence. Suddenly a voice in her head snapped, "Never take charity, girlie!" She drew back her hand as if slapped.

The shopkeeper thrust the candy forward. "Go ahead, it's yours."

She reached again, her hand slowly moving toward his. She fought the urge to peek over her shoulder to be sure Pa wasn't watching. Dummy, Pa's not here. She snatched the candy from the man's hand before she could change her mind again. It was settled in a bulky wad inside her mouth before she remembered her manners and muttered around the candy, "F'ank 'oo."

The shopkeeper swished his palms together to disperse the leftover sugar. "Now then, let's tally this up, shall we?"

He produced the stub of a pencil from behind his ear, licked the point, and began figuring on a pad of paper resting near a hinged tin box, which presumably held his cash supply. After scratching out several numbers, he pushed the pad aside and announced the total. He aimed his eyebrows high and peered down at her. "Will that be cash or charge, mi'—I mean, son?"

The girl had chewed down the gumdrop considerably. She swallowed the remaining lump and cleared her throat before managing a low, "Charge, please."

The shopkeeper reached below the counter to bring up a leather-bound book which he plopped on the countertop and opened to the first page. She gazed at the book, her hands clutching the edge of the wooden counter, elbows splayed outward, trying to look calm and matter-of-fact. When he made no move to record her purchase, she glanced up to find him staring at her. Her heart skipped a beat.

He cocked his head. "Account name?"

Mentally kicking herself for being so dense, she drew herself upright. "Klaassen." She blew out a breath and dropped her gaze back to the book. His hands didn't move. She looked up again. The man's stare was accompanied by a frown that brought his bushy eyebrows downward and created a series of deep furrows across his pink forehead. "Klaassen, did you say?" His voice came out low and rather steely.

She gulped, her pretend bravado fading fast.

She lowered her hands to her sides. "Y-yessir."

He leaned forward, his gaze narrowing. "*Simon* Klaassen?"

She couldn't be certain it was Simon Klaassen's house she'd seen, but she felt agreeing was the safest bet. So she nodded, her heart pounding in her throat.

The man snapped the book shut, and for a fleeting moment the girl wondered if Mr. Klaassen hadn't paid his account regularly. The shopkeeper's eyes pinned her in place as effectively as a nail holds a shingle. "And just which of the Klaassen boys are you?"

She felt like she had a hairball stuck in her craw, but she choked out a reply. "Uh . . . S-Sam."

The man lowered his chin and scowled at her through the curly hairs of his eyebrows as he slowly rounded the counter. The girl backed up a step as he neared. Her muscles tensed, poised to run.

"Sam . . . hmmm." He crossed his arms. His forehead puckered so tightly it looked painful. "Funny. My brother Simon has five sons, but I don't recollect a one of them's named Sam."

His brother. The shopkeeper was kin *to those Klaassens*!

The girl's chest clenched in panic, and as the man reached for her, she reacted instinctively. She kicked him as hard as she could in the shin, which no doubt hurt her bare toes as much as it did his leg, grabbed up the tin of crackers, and careened out the screen door, sending the cowbell clanging angrily behind her. Risking a glance back over her shoulder at the no-doubt furious shopkeeper, she missed seeing the tall, straw-hat-topped young man stepping up on the planked walkway. She ran full-tilt into his solid chest. He lost a roll of screen he was carrying, and her tin of crackers fell to the boardwalk with a clunk.

He caught her by the shoulders, chuckling. "Whoa there, what's your hurry?"

Frantic, she pushed on his chest with both hands. The shove off-balanced him, dislodged his hat, and nearly threw him on his backside. His hands flew from her shoulders, and she leaped from the boardwalk. Her original plan in tatters, panic racing through her veins, she ran a zigzagged pattern up the center of the dusty main street of town.

Chapter Three

*A*dam shook his head, watching the kid go, and leaned down to scoop up his hat and the roll of screen lodged against the side of the building. The cowbell above his uncle's shop door clanged, and his uncle stood in the doorway, shaking his finger and pointing after the fleeing youth.

"Get 'im! Catch 'im! A thief!"

"Uncle Hiram, what—?"

But after a quick glance at his uncle's expression, Adam thrust the roll of screen into his uncle's midsection and took off down the street. The thief had gotten a good head start, but Adam's stride was twice the length of the fleeing figure, and his feet were protected by sturdy work boots. It wasn't hard to overtake him. Adam reached out a long arm and caught an overall strap, swinging the lad around.

The stubborn kid spun in circles, trying to free himself. Suddenly he swung his boots by the laces. The heels smacked Adam hard on the shoulder and bounced off the side of his head. He released his hold, his ear ringing from the blow, and stumbled sideways a few steps. Before he could regain his balance, the boy charged at him, burying his head in Adam's stomach.

The motion carried them both several feet back before Adam fell, snatching an overall strap once more as he went. He landed flat on his back with the kid sprawled across his chest. Now instinct took over, and with a simple maneuver Adam rolled over, pinning the scrappy youngster neatly beneath him. He panted with exertion from the brief chase and subsequent scuffle, but he managed to hold the boy, who bucked and bellowed, by the shoulders against the ground.

"Get off me, you stupid honyocker!"

Adam didn't know whether to chuckle or give the kid a sharp clop for using the insulting label for farmers. "Not till you promise to behave yourself." He sat a little harder on the boy's stomach, and the wild kicking calmed. But the youth's pale, frightened face stirred Adam's sympathy. He said in a soothing tone, "That's better. Now, if you'll be still, I'll—"

Adam stopped and stared, astonished. His assailant's battered hat flipped off, revealing a mane of tangled auburn curls. Eyes as blue as cornflowers stared back at him. Slender arms flailed to reach the hat, but Adam still held the boy's—the girl's—shoulders against the ground, and she couldn't reach it.

"Sure enough, it's a girl." Uncle Hiram's voice blasted out from behind Adam. "I had an inkling something like that might be going on."

Adam heard an amused guffaw, and he looked beyond his uncle at spectators—overall-clad men, women in go-to-town dresses and bonnets, and a cluster of snickering youngsters with cane poles propped on their shoulders—gathering on the boardwalk. Even the banker stood in his doorway, watching with an amused look on his mustached face.

Adam leaped up, never having been as embarrassed as he was at that moment. Why, he'd never tackled a girl before. Not even his sisters. And he'd done this in the middle of main street while townspeople lined the boardwalks. Heat rose from his neck to his hairline.

The girl rolled over and pushed herself to her feet, and Hiram grabbed an overall strap. She tried once to pull away, but he gave her a firm shake. "You're coming with me, missy." He began herding her back toward his store.

Shame faced with the public humiliation, Adam grabbed up the ugly brown hat and followed. Uncle Hiram's feet sent up angry puffs of dust with each step. The girl walked stiffly with her chin held at a defiant angle, but she seemed to have lost her fire. Back in the store, Hiram gave her a shove toward the apple barrel. "You sit right there, young lady."

She did so without a fuss and held her knees together with her palms pressed between them, back ramrod straight and head tipped downward. Adam held out her hat, but she didn't even glance up, simply snatching it with a dirty hand and throwing it to the floor by her feet.

Uncle Hiram paced the floor, his bald head glowing bright red. Adam had never seen him so upset. Adam adopted a calm voice. "Uncle Hiram, what's she done?"

"Done?" He whirled toward Adam, his arm gesturing vigorously toward the girl. "What's she *done*? Why, she tried to make out with half the store and put it on your father's account, no less. Stood right there at my counter and claimed to be Sam Klaassen. That's what she's done."

Adam raised an eyebrow and looked over the girl, sitting stiff as a board and poker faced as a judge, not even flinching. If she was scared or nervous, she hid it well.

"I knew something was amiss the minute I laid eyes on him—her." Uncle Hiram aimed himself for the door. "I'm going for Sheriff Barnes. I can't believe how she tried to hornswoggle me, and after I'd given her something. For free." Over his shoulder he said, "Adam, you stay here and see she stays put." At the girl he waggled a finger. "Don't you move an inch, missy, you hear?"

If the girl heard, she gave no indication of it. She didn't even blink. Hiram snorted and shoved his way out, sending the cowbell into frantic clamor once more. Adam reached up and caught it, stilling the sound. He stayed by the doorway, arms crossed over his chest, and watched the girl as Hiram stomped away. Adam speculated that his uncle didn't really want to file formal charges but wanted to scare the young thief—wanted her to sweat a bit. The girl sat still, staring at her hands in her lap, a sullen expression on her face. If Adam hadn't known better, he might have thought she was carved of stone. He'd never seen anyone who could sit without even a muscle twitching.

After a few more tense minutes, the silence began to grate on Adam's nerves. He cleared his throat, and the girl's jaw tightened, but she didn't look up. Adam dropped his arms and sauntered across the floor, seating himself on a keg nearby. She shifted slightly to increase the gap between them. Adam swallowed a grin. *Sure is a belligerent little thing.*

"What's your name?" He used his friendliest voice, but she gave no response. "Who're your folks?"

The girl shook back her hair, aimed her gaze to the side, and set her lips in an even more grim line.

Adam tried another tack. "You do realize stealing is a crime, don't you?"

The girl angled her face to give him a narrow-eyed look that demanded his silence. Their eyes locked—Adam's amused, hers stony—and both seemed stubborn enough to hold that gaze for an eternity.

Uncle Hiram shoved his way back into the store, and Adam stood to meet his uncle halfway across the floor. The girl went back into her head-down pose.

"What'd the sheriff say?"

Uncle Hiram threw his arms around in agitation. "Wasn't even there. Old Hilarius Schwartz's cow wandered away again, and Sheriff was out helping hunt her down. Honestly, if Hilarius would put a bell on that animal, it would make for a lot less fussin' and bother."

Adam hid his smile. Uncle Hiram had to be mighty upset to complain about ninety-year-old Mr. Schwartz and his beloved bovine. Everyone knew Rosalee was Hilarius's best friend, and Hiram himself had helped bring the wandering cow back in the past. Whenever the cow took a mind to meander, finding her was a challenge without the telltale clang of a bell to guide the posse. Hilarius believed a cowbell would make Rosalee nervous and refused to hang one around her neck. Any other day, Hiram would have laughed it all off. But not today.

Adam leaned against the counter, watching his uncle pace. "So what are you going to do with her?" He kept his voice just above a whisper.

Hiram stopped pacing to fire an angry glare at the still-silent girl. "I guess just send her home." He marched across the room to stand in front of her, hands on his hips. "Okay, young lady, what's your name?"

The girl didn't give him any more attention than she had paid Adam.

"You've got a name besides 'Sam Klaassen,'" Uncle Hiram spat. "So what is it?"

When the girl did not so much as move a muscle, Hiram let out a mighty snort and shook his head at Adam. "I guess I'll just have to keep her here till Hank comes back, then hand her over to him. Maybe a night in the hoosegow will loosen up that tongue."

"Jail?" Adam straightened quickly. "Do you really think that's necessary?"

"The last I knew, stealing was still a crime." His uncle's eyes narrowed. "Besides, there's also the matter of assault, and—"

"Assault?"

Uncle Hiram glared at Adam, his expression daring his nephew to argue. "Yes, assault. She kicked me hard enough in the shin to raise a welt, not to mention how she barreled into you."

Heat filled Adam's face. "Well, I'd as soon forget—"

"Besides," Hiram continued, "you know as well as I do there'd be nobody at the jail except old Fitz sleeping off his weekday drunk. She'd be out of harm's way until her family could come and get her." He shot the girl a meaningful look. "Assuming, of course, we can figure out who she is."

Adam leaned in close to his uncle and spoke softly, but loud enough for the girl to hear if she wanted to. "Uncle Hiram, I'm not sure jail is the answer here."

"What then?" Hiram lowered his voice to match Adam's.

"Look at her." Adam waited until his uncle's face turned toward the scrawny girl so bent on ignoring them. "She's just a kid, probably no older than Arn." His fourteen-year-old brother had always been Uncle Hiram's favorite. "And look how thin she is. Stealing isn't right, but doesn't she look hungry? Seems to me what she needs is a bath, a good meal, and a warm bed, in that order."

The lines around Uncle Hiram's eyes softened.

Adam plunged on. "Since she tried to charge the food on Pa's tab, maybe I ought to go ahead and take responsibility."

"I'll take her home, let Mother see to her needs, and you can get hold of Sheriff Barnes and have him get word to her family. I reckon her own pa will have a dose of medicine waiting for her when he hears of her mischief, so let's let him handle it."

A slight movement captured Adam's attention, and he glanced over at the girl. Her face had gone white, and she clenched her fists in tight balls. Suspecting she might bolt, Adam shifted his body to block the door.

"What do you think, Uncle Hiram? Should I take her home?"

Hiram shrugged and shook his head. "All right, Adam. I'll walk over to the post office and leave a message for the sheriff that we've got a runaway on our hands. I imagine he'll come to your place and get her name out of her." He pointed a finger at his nephew. "But you watch her. Don't let her rob you blind."

Adam crossed his finger across his chest, tongue in cheek.

Uncle Hiram snorted. "You and your strays." He shook his head again, but his eyes now had a twinkle in them. "Never could stand to let so much as an abandoned kitten starve in an alleyway, could you?"

Adam lifted his shoulders and quoted, " 'Whatsoever you do for the least of these . . .' " He let the words drift away.

Hiram gestured toward the girl. "Get her out of here before I change my mind." He headed to the counter and began to gather up a variety of cans scattered across the wooden top.

"Ain't going."

The low voice from the thus silent girl startled both men.

She lifted her head and fixed Adam with an icy glare. "I'm no stray."

So she had been listening. Adam examined the stubborn jut of her chin. She tried to look tough, but with all that wild hair falling around her face, she just looked ridiculous. And vulnerable.

Uncle Hiram took a step in her direction. "Listen here, young lady, I don't recall you being given any choice in the matter."

The girl went back to folded arms across her chest. "Ain't going."

Uncle Hiram opened his mouth, but Adam held up a hand and sent the girl a steady look. "You can come home with me to a good meal and a warm bed. . . ." He paused for effect. "Or you can spend the night in the city jail. Actually, it's just the cellar under the post office, so it's not so bad except for the mice and spiders. And Fitz is harmless. Just snores and spits a lot."

The girl winced at the mention of spiders, but then she shook her hair back and thrust out her chin. "I don't cotton to no charity."

She had spunk—Adam would give her that.

"You sassy, ungrateful little wretch!" Uncle Hiram threw his arms wide. "You'll try to steal me blind, but you won't take what's offered? Why, I ought to—"

Adam put a restraining hand on his uncle's arm. "Home with me, or the jail. It's your choice. What'll it be?"

Her chin quivered, and for a moment Adam thought she might cry, but a fierce pride must have kept the tears at bay. She sat in silence for several long seconds before heaving a mighty sigh. "All right. I reckon I'll come with you." She stood and bounced a glare between Uncle Hiram and Adam. "But I'm leaving at first light tomorrow. And all I want is the meal and bed—no bath."

he ride to the farm from Mountain View was totally silent. Adam had tried to help the girl up on the buckboard seat beside him, but she had shrugged him off and climbed over the sides into the back. Once home, Adam handed a stiff, sullen girl over to his mother's capable hands. Ma's eyes softened with genuine care as she looked at the skinny, filthy waif before her, and pride swelled in Adam's chest at his mother's innate compassion for those in need.

"I don't know her name," he admitted.

"That's all right." Ma placed her hand on the girl's flannel-covered arm, and she jerked away as if struck. Ma's brows came together in momentary concern, then smoothed out. She spoke gently to her new guest. "We can get acquainted when you're cleaned up. Come with me, and we'll get a bath drawn for you right away." She placed an arm around the girl's stiff shoulders to guide her.

Adam watched the pair enter the house, one smiling and one scowling in what was an already familiar look of defiance. Turning away with a shake of his head, he sought out his father. He found Pa in the tool shack where he was braiding several thin strands of leather together to repair a broken harness.

Adam leaned against the door frame. "Hey, Pa. I'm back."

Simon Klaassen looked up and shot his son a lopsided grin. "I thought maybe you'd decided to spend the night with Nip." His comment was as close as he would come to commenting on Adam's late return.

Adam chuckled. "Not this time. But I did bring someone to spend the night here."

Pa grinned. "Nip?"

Adam gave an amused snort. "No, not him." Briefly he explained his encounter with the young lady he'd left at the house, being careful to leave out the part about tackling her in the street. Just thinking of it made the blood rush to his face—the fewer who knew, the better. Although with half the town watching the incident . . .

"You did the right thing, son," Pa said at the end of Adam's report. He released a throaty chuckle. "I sure would've liked to have seen Hiram's face when he knew his thief was a girl."

Adam smiled in spite of his own embarrassment at the revelation, recalling his uncle's expression. "I left her at the house with Mother. She had sworn off a bath, but, knowing Ma, I expect she'll be convinced of the benefits one way or another."

"Reckon so." Pa raised one eyebrow. "Now, about the chicken coop . . ."

"First thing in the morning, sir," Adam promised with another chuckle and a crisp military salute. He headed back to the wagon to unhitch the horses and give them their supper and a good brushing.

As he loosened the animals from their riggings, he saw his younger brother and sister, Teddy and Becky, filling buckets at the iron pump. The youngest Klaassen, Sarah, waited by the back door, ready to open it for their return. He grinned to himself as he led the horses to the barn. It looked as if there'd be a clean young lady at the supper table after all. His mother was gentle and strong, all at the same time.

He came in from putting up the horses and crossed straight to the wash basin tucked below the stairs next to the pantry. He dropped his suspenders from his shoulders and let them dangle at his knees. After pushing his shirtsleeves well above his elbows, he leaned over the basin to splash water on his face once, then again. He lathered his hands with his mother's homemade lavender-scented soap, scrubbed his face, washed clear to his forearms, then rinsed. Only when he had dried himself with the rough towel hanging conveniently on a nail hammered into the pantry doorjamb did he realize he was being watched. As he pulled his suspenders back in place, he looked over his shoulder to find himself under the careful scrutiny of a young girl.

She sat on a chair in the corner of the kitchen. A light spattering of freckles danced across her cheeks and the bridge of her nose. Her hair, damp, hung in shining curls well below her shoulders. In the yellow lamplight of the kitchen it held a reddish cast. Had it not been for the unwavering stare from her unusual eyes of cornflower blue, he might not have realized it was the same girl he'd tussled with in the street only a short hour or so ago.

Gone were the grimy overalls and the man's hat. In their place she wore a lightweight calico dress that Adam recognized as having belonged to his sister Liz. The transformation amazed him. She looked small and vulnerable . . . and painfully young. Adam felt a swell of sympathy. He sent her a smiling nod, but she responded by turning her head toward the commotion in the kitchen. And there was quite a commotion.

At mealtime, Laura Klaassen was fond of saying, the children melted out of the wallpaper. It must have appeared that way to the Klaassen's dinner guest. She tucked her bare feet under the straight-backed chair on which she perched, left foot over right. Occasionally she rubbed her left foot up and down the top of her right one in apparent nervousness. The only other movement she made was the widening of her eyes as the number of people in the kitchen multiplied with the slam of the back door or a clatter of feet on the stairs.

As for the Klaassen children, they eyed their guest with friendly interest, some smiling and others speaking a polite greeting. The girl remained still and silent on the chair, watching with wariness the bustle of activity. Each Klaassen had a job to do, and they accomplished the tasks amongst teasing comments and much laughter. Seeing to his own responsibilities, Adam caught himself wondering what thoughts lurked behind the girl's watchful gaze.

Pa entered the house, and Sarah clattered her handful of silverware onto the tabletop and raced to him. Pa swung her into his arms, making her squeal. She rode his hip as he crossed the floor to deliver a kiss on Ma's upturned cheek. Adam had witnessed this ritual for as long as he could remember, but tonight he viewed it through fresh eyes. Although the girl angled her face toward the corner, he noted her eyes shifting to take in every bit of the bustling scene. And he was certain he glimpsed jealousy pinching her lips into a scowl.

Pa lowered Sarah to the floor and whispered something in her ear. The child scampered off with a cheerful giggle, and Pa moved to take his turn at the washbasin.

Adam crossed the kitchen and lifted the lid on a heavy black skillet resting on the stove.

"Here, now, no sampling." His mother took the wooden spoon he'd picked up for that purpose and replaced the lid on the pot. When he made as if to reach around her, she gave his wrist a playful pat. "You can wait a few more minutes."

Adam rolled his eyes, feigning frustration. Then he grinned and planted a kiss on his mother's cheek. It never ceased to amaze him that his tiny mother had brought ten children into the world and still had the energy to keep up with all of them. He respected his father, he loved his sisters and brothers, but he adored his mother. It was on her lap that he'd snuggled to hear his first Bible story, and it was beside her he'd knelt in the chicken coop—of all places—when he was only five years old to ask Jesus into his heart. Yes, his mother was special.

Pa joined the pair at the stove and reached past Ma to sneak one of the pickled eggs she'd arranged on an oval platter. Adam noticed Ma didn't slap Pa's hands.

"So what's the story on our little beggar?" Pa asked quietly behind Ma's ear.

Ma shot the girl a quick look. Adam listened in when Ma replied. "She says her name is Frances Welch. She claims she's nineteen years old"—Pa's eyebrows raised to his hairline and Ma nodded in understanding—"and on her own."

Adam repeated what he'd shared earlier with his father about the attempted grocery theft.

Ma shook her head sadly. "Poor thing. She must have been awfully hungry to try something like that."

They all looked over to observe the girl. Little Sarah animatedly entertained their guest with a picture book. Frances Welch wore the closest thing to a smile as one can get without actually smiling.

Pa exchanged a look of indulgence with his wife, then brought his palms together in a brisk clap. "Come, family. Let's eat."

With much foot stomping and careful shoves, the siblings slid into place on long benches that lined both sides of the plank table that took up much of the center of the kitchen. Ma carried the platter of pickled eggs to one end of the table, and Si moved to the opposite end. Ma set down the platter and held out a hand to the girl who remained in the corner.

Her shoulders hunched in a self-conscious gesture, the girl rose and crossed to Ma. Ma slipped her arm around the girl's shoulders and sent a beaming smile down the length of the table.

"Children, this is Frances Welch. She is going to be staying with us for a few days."

The girl shot Ma a startled look. Her jaw dropped open, but before she could speak Ma went on.

"You won't be able to remember all these names right at first, but . . ." She introduced each member of the family in turn. "This is our youngest, Sarah." Sarah beamed a bright toothless smile. "Then there's Teddy, Becky, and Arn." Teddy, nine years old and scared of girls, ducked his head and blushed when his name was mentioned. Becky, eleven years old and fearless, nudged him and snickered. Arn's freckles seemed to glow like copper pennies in his friendly face.

"On the end is Mr. Klaassen," Ma continued. "You met Adam in town"—Adam waved a hand in casual response—"then there's Frank, and Josie."

Frank bobbed his chin, and Josie offered a soft smile which Frances did not return.

Ma finished, "We have two more children, Liz and Daniel, but they're married and living on their own now. You might meet them later."

The girl cast a doubtful look in Ma's direction.

Ma gestured to the spot on the bench next to Josie. "You slide in here next to Josie now."

Josie smiled and patted the seat next to her. The girl's muscles tensed, and Adam braced his hands on the bench, ready to bounce up and take pursuit if she chose escape. But after a moment's hesitation, her shoulders wilted and she slid into the bench. Adam released a sigh of relief, and his father clasped his hands in front of him.

⁓◌

Miss Samantha O'Brien, masquerading as Frances Welch, watched beneath eyebrows drawn into a frown as everyone around the table followed the father's example. They all folded their hands in front of them, then bowed heads in unison. All but Samantha.

While the Klaassen family listened to the head of the household deliver thanks for the evening meal, the girl silently filled her pockets with two pickled eggs, a funny little double-decker roll, and a chunky piece of sausage, all the while carefully observing the bowed heads to be sure she wasn't caught.

At the other end of the table, Mr. Klaassen concluded his prayer with a reverent "Amen" that all family members, large and small, echoed. Then bowls and platters of food started around the table, everyone spooning healthy servings onto the well-used Blue Willow plates.

Samantha's empty stomach growled in anticipation as she helped herself to crisply fried potatoes, garden-fresh tomatoes and green beans, puffy browned rolls—funny-looking buns with a top that was smaller than the bottom—sausage links, and a host of relishes. She thickly spread the buns with butter and sweet-smelling preserves. It took every bit of self-control she possessed to avoid sneaking bites between the passing bowls.

At last each plate held all it could hold, and the eating commenced. Samantha attacked her plate with the single-minded purpose of filling herself to the limit. Her nose hovered mere inches above her plate, the fork moving steadily between plate and mouth. Conversation buzzed around her, accompanied by the clink of silver utensils against china plates, but she ignored it all and didn't lift her head until every bite was gone and she'd sopped up the remnants of grease from the sausage and potatoes with a last one of those funny-looking but delicious two-level rolls.

When she finished, Samantha sat up and wiped her mouth with the cloth napkin resting beside her plate. She suffered a moment of embarrassment when she realized none of the others were even close to finishing, but no one seemed to take notice.

Mrs. Klaassen turned toward Samantha. Her smile brought out gentle lines around her eyes and mouth. "Frances, would you care for anything else?"

Samantha offered a silent shake of her head.

"Would you like to be excused? Maybe look around a bit?"

Without replying, Samantha slipped off the bench and headed for the back door.

"Frances?"

She froze, her hand curled around the porcelain doorknob, at the sound of Adam's voice.

"Don't wander too far away. It'll be dark soon."

Resentment prickled. *What makes him think he's my keeper?* She sent as withering a glance as she could muster over her shoulder. "Seein' as how your ma took my shoes, don't know how I can go far. So don't be frettin' over me." She witnessed expressions of shock and dismay coloring the faces around the table. She expected anger to flicker over Adam's, but only a slight amusement lingered there.

She swung around and marched out the door, though the boots sure would have helped make her point more firmly.

amantha located the porch swing by accident, but once she was settled in the shadowy corner set off by lilac bushes she felt more secure than she had for a long time. She needed a quiet spot to think—not only about her plans to move on, but also about the funny feeling inside.

She furrowed her brow, perplexed and unsettled, pressing her arms across her midsection, and tried her best to figure out the strange feeling. Not the fearful churning produced by her father's drunken rages. Not hunger pangs, for sure. She'd not only eaten a plateful of food in the house, she'd already consumed everything stashed in her pockets. Had she made herself sick by eating too much? But no, it wasn't a sick feeling, either. More a hollowness—an emptiness that eating couldn't fill.

She'd watched the family inside the house preparing for their supper, working side by side with smiles and laughter. She'd seen their genuine enjoyment of being together, and it touched something deep inside of her. When the father swung his little girl high in his arms for a hug, she had wondered what it felt like to be lifted high in a father's strong, capable arms and held there. Even the praying part had stirred a reaction, a yearning. All those heads bowed together, sharing something they all believed and respected . . . She started the swing in motion with one bare foot, restless, wanting to escape. But how could she escape these feelings? Wouldn't they go with her?

When she was riding with Adam in the wagon—after deciding it would be easier to slip away from a bunch of honyockers than from a lawman—she'd concocted the name Frances

Welch. If they didn't know her name, they couldn't send her home. That mother—Laura—had accepted her words as fact without a question. It should have pleased her, knowing she'd fooled them. But instead it left her with a scorching remorse. They were obviously good people, and they deserved better than a thief and a liar in their midst.

And that's what she was—nothing but a sneaky, lying criminal. Samantha hugged herself fiercely, anger binding her in knots. A bunch of farmers shouldn't have such an effect on her.

But her thoughts pressed onward in spite of her attempts to put them aside. Samantha remembered a time when she'd been loved, when she'd been taught to kneel beside her bed and recite her "God blesses" at the close of a day. There was a time when grace had been spoken before meals, too, but it was a long time ago. When Gran was alive. Even now, after more than ten years, the lonely ache of Gran's death was still there.

Samantha wrapped her arms more tightly across her tummy and spoke softly into the slight breeze whispering through the thick leaves of the huge bushes. "Oh, Gran, I miss you so much. Why'd you have to go? Why'd you have to leave me? And David . . . gone, too. Everybody I've loved, gone. Why? Why . . . ?"

No answer came. Not that she expected one. She'd asked the questions before. Her father had caught her talking to the wind one day and had called her foolish. *"Real smart,"* he had sneered, *"yappin' at the breeze. All it does is grab your words and carry 'em away."* And he'd made her come in the house. Even so, foolish or not, she still talked to the wind. It was comforting somehow, talking to something more powerful than herself. Only she was careful about staying far away from her father when she did it.

Lifting her face to the graying sky, she spoke proudly. "It's not foolish, Gran. 'Cause maybe, just maybe, someday those words will be swept up to heaven and you'll hear me. And you'll send me somebody who will listen when I talk, like you used to, and maybe even care about what I say. And then I'll feel good again. Can you do that, Gran?"

She paused, face turned to capture the faint breeze, breathing in the sweet scents of nature and the leftover aromas from supper. Eyes lifted heavenward, she held her breath as her heart begged for a response. Then she heard a twig snap and went cold all over.

She clutched the swing seat, her feet planted and ready for flight. "Who's there?"

"Just me—Adam." He stepped up on the porch, stopping a few feet away from her and leaning against the railing that separated the slender posts. He gave her a brief glance over his shoulder. "Nice night, isn't it?"

She looked at him sideways, her heart pounding. Had he heard her? She searched his face, looking for signs of the amusement she'd glimpsed earlier. If he laughed at her, she'd tackle him again. And she'd come out the winner this time. No humor sparked in his eyes, and gradually her racing pulse calmed. She sank back into the seat, making the chains squeak. "Yeah. It's nice enough."

He turned, face up to the sky where the first stars were beginning to appear. He seemed completely at ease with himself. Almost unaware of her presence. Apparently he hadn't heard her babbling. This time. But she'd have to be careful until she left. There were too many pairs of ears around this place.

Adam asked, "Are you tired? Mother sent me out to find you and offer a bed."

Samantha fought back a yawn at the idea of bed—a real place to sleep after all those nights in barns, sheds, and even a mossy place in the woods. "I guess." Then she bolted upright.

"But just for one night. What your ma said at supper, 'bout me being here a few days? That's not right. I'll be on my way tomorrow."

"Well, I haven't got a problem with that, but I imagine the sheriff will want to talk to you first." Adam shifted his weight on the railing and crossed his arms. After a while he turned his head to look directly at her. "I tell you what, come on in now and let Mother show you your place for the night, then we can worry about arranging your travel plans in the morning."

Samantha stared outward, trying to decide how to respond. At last she sighed and pushed to her feet. "All right. I'll talk to your sheriff. But after that, I'm leaving." She pressed her lips together, thrust out her jaw, and glared at Adam to emphasize her words.

Adam raised his hands, palms up, and she marched past him and headed for the back door. She heard a soft snort behind her, but she decided to ignore it.

⌒◌

Laura Klaassen tucked the younger children into bed, checked on each of the older ones—their guest lay stiffly next to Josie in her big feather bed—then paused at the head of the stairs to call her customary blessing brought over from the Old Country, "*Schlop Die gesunt,*" before returning to the kitchen.

Adam leaned in the kitchen doorway, but he shifted to let her pass, nodding a silent communication as his head tilted toward the kitchen. She turned the corner and found the swarthy sheriff seated at the plank table with Simon, enjoying a cup of coffee. Laura smiled and crossed to the man, holding out her hand.

"Good evening, Sheriff. I imagine Hiram sent you out?"

Sheriff Barnes chuckled. "He sure did. He's got a head full of steam, too. Si and Adam here filled me in on what you folks know about the girl." He shook his head, his lips pursing. "Didn't take 'em long. You don't seem to have been able to find out much."

Laura sighed in acknowledgment of the sheriff's comment. She sensed there was a story hidden beneath the girl's sullen exterior, but it would take a great deal of time to extract it. The young woman carried a stiff shield of defensiveness. "Would you like a piece of pie to go with your coffee? I have a big slice of rhubarb in the icebox."

The sheriff declined with a humorous pat on his extended belly, so Laura poured herself a cup of coffee and sat down with the men. Si slipped his arm around her, connecting them. She always found security in her husband's presence.

"Our young guest feels compelled to leave first thing in the morning," Laura informed the sheriff, one hand curled around her coffee mug and the other reaching up to grasp Si's draped over her shoulder. "Although I think she's very good at hiding her feelings, she still seems frightened of something." She turned to her husband, worried. "You don't think she's running from the law, do you?"

Si squeezed Laura's shoulder. "I realize she was trying to steal from Hiram," he said, "but she hardly seems old enough to have gotten into too much trouble yet." He quirked his lips into a grin. "She might have told you she's nineteen, but I have my doubts."

Sheriff Barnes stroked his bushy mustache thoughtfully with a forefinger. "My guess is she's a runaway—wants to be on her own. I suspect a mighty big hunger led her to attempt the food robbery. She didn't threaten Hiram in any way." He grinned. "Although she did give him a pretty good bruise on the shin. And barefoot too. She's probably got a very worried mama sitting at home, waiting for her return."

When Laura and Simon exchanged glances, Adam caught her eye. Concern pinched her son's brow, and Laura's heart turned over. Of all her children, Adam possessed the biggest dose of compassion. He already cared about Frances Welch's well-being. And he would be most bothered if they were unable to help the girl.

She turned to the sheriff again. "What do we do in the morning when she tries to leave?"

Sheriff Barnes snorted. "Whatever her reasons for being here, her family will have to be contacted. Despite her claims to the contrary, it's obvious she isn't old enough to be on her own. She'll have to be sent home."

Behind the sheriff, Laura could see Adam's flinch.

The sheriff continued, "If we find she doesn't have a family . . . Well, we'll cross that bridge if we come to it. To keep her here, threaten her with criminal prosecution for attempted theft. For good measure, throw in assault and battery for that kick Hiram got. I'll do some checking—her family will have gone to the authorities about their missing daughter, so someone will know something."

The sheriff stood to leave. He thanked Laura for the coffee, took a big breath that expanded his middle, then rolled back on his heels and gave Si and Laura a stern look. "Si, Laura, you're good people. You mean well, and I know I'm leaving that girl in good hands. But I feel I should offer a word of warning. Be *careful*. No telling where she comes from or what she's learned. I'd hate to see you taken in by a little con artist. Or worse."

"We'll be careful, Hank." Si rose and shook the sheriff's hand. "Thanks for coming out."

"Just doin' my job." Sheriff Barnes grinned, plopped his hat back on his head, and left.

Laura lifted her cup for another sip as Si locked the door behind their visitor. When Si returned to the table, Adam moved forward and slid into the space the sheriff had vacated. "Pa, Ma, I know what Frances did was wrong, but deep down, I don't think she's *bad*."

Laura searched her son's face. Adam met her gaze, his cheeks flooding with color. She stretched out her hand and placed it over her son's wrist. "What are you thinking, Adam?"

Adam drew a deep breath. "I think she's scared, and I think she was really hungry and desperate. I don't think stealing is something she does as a habit." He paused, lowering his head. "When . . . when I went out after supper to find her, I . . . I heard her talking."

Laura offered a gentle squeeze, encouraging Adam to continue.

He lifted his face. True concern shimmered in his gold-flecked brown eyes. "At first I thought she might be talking to someone else—maybe a partner in crime, so to speak, but then I understood what she said." His brow furrowed. "I won't repeat it. I think it's private. But after hearing it, I just know she isn't bad. She's . . . *sad*. And very lonely."

Adam heaved a sigh, slipping his hand away from Laura's touch. "I don't know how long she'll be here, but I think what she needs from us is someone to be her friend, her listener." He flicked a glance at Si, then turned back to Laura. "I intend to be her friend, Ma. And maybe, with someone around who cares, we'll see a change for the better in her life."

Laura offered her son a smile she hoped communicated her approval of his tender heart. "I think you're right, Adam. I think beneath that defensive frown is a hurting little girl in need of a friend." And Laura knew exactly what Friend would offer the very best help to their small guest.

Adam rose. "Well, I guess I'll turn in. I've got a chicken coop to work on tomorrow in addition to my other chores. 'Night, Ma, Pa." He gave his mother a kiss on the cheek and squeezed his father's shoulder as he headed for the stairs.

Si watched Adam go, then looked again into Laura's face. His brow etched into lines of worry. "You don't think he's smitten with the girl, do you?"

Laura laughed softly, rising and carrying their coffee cups to the sink. "Si, you know as well as I do, Adam has always been our champion of the underdog. He sees a person in need, and he can't stop himself from reaching out. He isn't smitten. But he does care." She smiled over her shoulder. "We raised him right."

Si nodded, but she noted his forehead remained creased.

Laura turned to the sink and began washing the cups. Her thoughts turned inward, Adam's concerned face playing in her mind's eye. Yes, her son had a gift for compassion. *Which means he could be easily hurt, Lord.*

Laura stacked the clean cups on their shelf while her silent prayers whispered through her heart. *Let us minister to this stranger in our midst, Father, but guard our hearts from stepping beyond Your will. For her. For our family.*

Chapter Six

*S*amantha slowly drifted awake to the soft patter of raindrops against cedar shingles. She stretched beneath the warm covering, eyes closed, savoring the comfortable feather bed and sweet-smelling sheets. She brought her fists up and rubbed her eyes, yawning as she did so, then opened her eyes slowly to squint around the dusky room.

She jerked upward and leaned back on her elbows, disoriented. Remembering, she fell against the thick pillow while it all came tumbling back. Her long sigh captured all the swirl of emotions she was feeling.

She pushed back the colorful patchwork quilt and padded on bare feet to the window. She drew the green gingham curtains aside and peered out at the late-summer rain and groaned her frustration.

"Oh. You're up."

The little voice from behind startled her, and she quickly spun around.

"I'm thorry." The smallest Klaassen peered up at Samantha with large blue eyes. "I didn't mean ta thcare you."

"Y-you didn't," Samantha lied, entranced in spite of herself by the child's china-doll features and endearing lisp. "I just didn't hear you come in, that's all."

Sarah laughed, a tinkling sound that reminded Samantha of sleigh bells. "I can be quiet ath a cat when I want. Frank thinkth I try to be thneaky, but I don't. I'm jutht not big enough to make a lot of noithe yet."

With effort, Samantha stifled a chuckle. The child was animated and lively. Completely irresistible.

"Sarah Louise . . ." Mrs. Klaassen stepped through the doorway and gave the little girl a stern look. "Did you wake up poor Frances? She needs her sleep—."

"She wath awake already," Sarah explained quickly as she wrapped her arms around her mother's waist and turned an innocent face upward. "I jutht came in to talk to her."

The woman's eyes crinkled over a smile. "Well, I can't say I'm surprised, my little chatterbox." Mrs. Klaassen lifted her head to smile at Samantha. She said to Sarah, "Why don't you go downstairs and tell Josie that Frances is awake and will be needing some breakfast, hmm?"

Sarah skipped to the door, then paused to wave to Samantha. "Thee you later, Frantheth." She disappeared around the corner.

Samantha fixed her face in a frown and took a step forward. "Thanks for the bed an' all, but I don't have time for any breakfast. I need to get my hands on my own set of clothes. Then I'll be on my way."

Mrs. Klaassen's brows rose. "On your way? But, my dear, it's raining. You surely don't expect us to allow you to run off in the rain, do you?" She moved into the room and scooped up the dress Samantha had worn after her bath yesterday afternoon. "No, you'll stay until the weather clears," she said, her tone matter of fact. "Why, you'd catch your death out there."

The woman pressed the dress into Samantha's unresisting hands. "I doubt this got soiled at supper last night, so just slip it back on after you wash up. Your other clothes are in need of washing, and we do the wash on Friday. By then the rain will have let up, and you'll be able to be on your way. Oh, and I brought you a pair of shoes—too small for Josie and too big for Becky." She set them down by Samantha's feet and headed toward the doorway, gesturing toward the washstand with its full pitcher of water. "Wash the sleep from your eyes, my dear, dress, and come on down. You know where the necessary is. One egg or two?"

Samantha's mouth dropped.

Mrs. Klaassen paused in the doorway, her expectant face aimed in Samantha's direction.

Samantha gulped. "Uh, one'll be fine."

"Very well." Laura smiled. "Now don't dally. The water's still warm for you." She left, closing the door firmly behind her.

Samantha plunked her hands on her hips and glared at the door, then at the dress and shoes. That woman sure took a lot for granted! After a moment's worth of stewing, she sighed, shrugged her shoulders in defeat, and moved to the washstand.

Samantha finished her breakfast—two eggs along with three more of the rolls she'd enjoyed at supper the night before. Becky called them *zwieback*, which she said meant "two buns." Samantha had never heard of such a thing, but the bread had a soft texture and delicate flavor that pleased her taste buds. She drank two cups of coffee and a big glass of milk, then moved over to the sink to wash her dishes. And the entire process took only thirty minutes. The day ahead stretched out endlessly before her. Samantha's stomach jumped with nervousness and questions. How would she fill the long hours? What was going to happen to her?

Sarah and Becky tried to engage her in conversation. Samantha's short responses stilled their questions. They brought out puzzles and asked Samantha to help them put the pieces together, but she shook her head. After an hour of being re-buffed, the pair scampered up to the attic to play with their rag dolls. Samantha sighed with relief at their departure. Time with people led to attachments. She had no desire to form anything of that sort here.

The men, from Mr. Klaassen on down to Teddy, must have been outside somewhere. There wasn't a male in the house, at least. That suited her fine too. Samantha wasn't much on the company of males—whatever their ages. In her experience, men were demanding and temperamental—not the type of company one sought out for any length of time. Samantha's experience with females wasn't much better. Where she came from, girls her age were catty and condescending, seeming to take great pleasure in making one feel foolish and gauche.

Trust in humankind had definitely not had any chance for development in Samantha. She basically had been on her own since she was six years old, and she didn't see that changing in the near future. Nor did she see any need for it to change. *I'm doing fine*, she told herself firmly as she wandered hesitantly into the parlor.

She moved carefully to the middle of the room and looked around. The plain whitewashed walls, lacy curtains, and fine furnishings looked so beautiful and welcoming. She thought about the three-room cracker-box of a house that she called home back in Wisconsin. The Klaassen's home was as clean as rain-washed flowers. The room smelled good, too—herbal and fresh. A little snooping uncovered a tiny mesh bag filled with dried flowers hanging on the wall near the corner woodstove. She sniffed the contents of the bag, absorbing the delicious aroma, then tucked the bag into the pocket of her dress to carry the good smell around with her. But after a moment, she returned it to its place on the wall. It might only be a tiny bag of dried petals, but it wasn't hers.

She seated herself on the edge of the camelback sofa, taking care not to touch the highly polished wood-trimmed armrest to avoid smudging its surface. She rubbed her hands over the dark-brown upholstery, noting that it was smooth when she moved her hand one way, rough when she slid it back. She gazed at the window, where rain continued to fall. Her thoughts ran faster than the raindrops racing down the long, narrow panes.

Despite her uncertainties about it all last night, she felt pretty clever now, having come up with a false identity. If she was stuck here, being known as Frances Welch would make it nigh on impossible for them to trace her back to Pa. A small-town sheriff wouldn't be terribly bright, she was sure, so no doubt he'd only look into the name she'd told them, not her description.

She gave a little sniff, imagining how Pa would have described her when alerting the authorities that she'd run off again. *"Jest a sawed-off runt, spindly, with a long ol' rat's nest o' red hair on 'er head . . . an' dumber'n a rock, that'd be my girl,"* she'd heard Pa say about her to one of his cronies. At the time she'd trembled with rage and had wished him dead for the hundredth time.

Pa was right about one thing. She wasn't so awful big. But dumb? Not hardly. She'd managed to get away, and he hadn't found her, not yet. She fully intended to stay away this time. Never, never would she go back to that house and her drunk of a father.

Anxiety twisted its way through her chest like an undergrowth of creeping charley. If only the rain would stop so she could get moving! The longer she stayed in one spot, the more likely it was that somehow, someway, Pa would catch up to her. He seemed to possess some sort of sixth sense peculiar to drinking men; he always found her. And she was determined to escape the prison that had been home, just as Davey had escaped.

As always, thoughts of her brother brought a lump to her throat. She swallowed hard, trying to force it down. That deep longing also made the tears come, and Samantha didn't cry—not anymore. Tears were for weaklings, and Samantha was no weakling. She'd kept any weeping at bay since she was six years old, and she wasn't about to let down her guard now. She was going to prove to Pa and to anyone else who cared to look on that she was strong enough to stand on her own, just like Davey was. He had proved it when he'd run off almost seven years ago. He'd promised to come back for her, but she figured that once he'd gotten settled, he'd decided it was easier not to have to worry about a kid sister. She had waited and watched for him, but he hadn't come back. And after all this time, Samantha had determined she couldn't rest her hopes on Davey; she'd have to depend on herself.

From the kitchen came the murmur of voices. Josie and her mother must have finished their upstairs housekeeping chores, for she had heard them come down the stairs, chuckling together at something or other. From their voices and the occasional burst of laughter, Samantha could tell their conversation was lighthearted. She felt a pang of desire to join them, to feel just once what it was like to be part of a family such as this one. But she quickly squelched the yearning. *Not for the likes of me*, she told herself as she stood up.

She marched over to the kitchen doorway and interrupted. "Can I go out and sit on the porch swing?" If she was outside, she wouldn't be tempted to pretend she belonged.

"Certainly, Frances." Mrs. Klaassen offered one of her a crinkling smiles. "I enjoy that swing too. Perhaps I'll join you when Josie and I have finished mixing the bread dough."

Samantha shrugged. "Suit yourself." She slipped out through the parlor door which led directly to the swing area of the large, covered porch. She sat in the center of the swing and pushed her feet against the wooden porch floor, setting the creaking swing in motion. The scent of rain filled her nostrils and suddenly, unbidden, a memory surfaced, no doubt aided by the quiet patter of rain and the fresh smell.

She was a little girl again, standing in the rain at a gravesite, holding a large cluster of wildflowers beneath her chin, listening to the droning voice of a minister give the words of the final farewell. Samantha squeezed her eyes tight, trying to shut down the replay in her mind, but behind her closed lids she could see clearly the plain pine box which held the body of her dear Gran. She could see her pa, too, standing sullenly beside her, chin thrust out, hands behind his back, his hat firmly on his head to shield himself from the falling rain. And Davey was there too, hat in hand, his tears mixing with the raindrops that ran in rivulets down his thin cheeks.

She stood abruptly, sending the swing banging against the wall, and moved to the porch railing. She dug her fingers into the painted wood as pain and fury mingled in her chest. Had Pa been sad that day? Had he cried on the inside only, as she had, afraid that if the tears began they would never end? Gran was his own grandmother. Did he miss her at all? Somehow, Samantha doubted it. Someone as self-centered as Burt O'Brien had thoughts for no one but himself.

In all likelihood, any of Pa's contemplations that day had been on who would do the cooking and cleaning with Gran gone. How he'd ranted that night, complaining about the scanty meal six-year-old Samantha had done her best to put together for them. David had eaten silently, not a word of complaint, but Pa . . . but then Pa always bellyached about everything.

Samantha scowled, despair filling her once more as she remembered helping Davey pack. He whispered in the dark so Pa wouldn't hear. *"Soon as I'm settled, Sammy, I'll send for ya. Just wait for me, okay, Sammy?"* And Samantha, trusting, had waited. Waited seven long years. Years of Pa's drunken rages, years of lying awake in the dark, thinking, *This is the night Davey'll be comin'.* Well, she wasn't waiting anymore.

She pushed herself away from the porch railing and stood as straight as she could, arms folded across her chest. From now on, Samantha O'Brien was responsible for Samantha O'Brien, and the fewer people she trusted, the better.

Across the wide yard, young Teddy caught her attention as he splashed through a mud puddle, a huge grin splitting his face. The boy was soaked, his pants muddy to the knees. Samantha stiffened, imagining the trouble he'd be in when his pa caught him fooling around so. Mr. Klaassen stepped into the doorway of the barn, and she held her breath.

Although Samantha couldn't make out Mr. Klaassen's features from this distance since he stood in the shadow in the barn doorway, his stance seemed relaxed, not angry. Feet planted wide, torso leaning back, hands resting loosely in his overall pockets. Then, much to her surprise, he bent down and yanked off his boots and socks. With a gallop he crossed the ground to join his son. The man and boy hooted with laughter together as they splashed around in the muddy water. "Feels good on my hot feet, Teddy boy! Great idea . . ."

And something thick and stifling rose within Samantha. She turned away only to catch a glimpse of Laura's laughing face in the parlor window, watching their antics with obvious pleasure. She spun away, her heart pounding.

As a child, if Samantha had come home dirty, she got a good licking for soiling her clothes. She had learned early to sidestep mud puddles and to hold her skirt high to avoid being splashed by others sloshing through them. But here was a grown man, playing like a child, and his wife laughing about it.

Samantha stared from Si to Teddy to Laura, then back again. Had she ever witnessed such strange behavior? *What's wrong with these people*? She turned her face to the rain and sent a silent wish for sunshine so she could be on her way before she was totally undone by this family and their cheerful manner of living.

Chapter Seven

*T*he rain lasted three of the longest days of Samantha's not-so-long life. During that time she watched and listened, expending a great deal of energy trying to look as if she *wasn't* watching and listening. By the end of the third day in the Klaassen household, Samantha convinced herself there had to be something seriously wrong with the whole family.

For one thing, Mr. Klaassen didn't go into town to be with the men and didn't seem to require whiskey to keep him happy. Samantha couldn't get over how hard he worked. Had she ever seen such an industrious man? Yet he was lighthearted, too. She'd seen it the day he'd pranced in the mud puddle with their youngest son, Teddy.

The children all minded him, but Samantha never once heard him raise his voice, and certainly never saw him raise his hand to any of them. Samantha couldn't figure out for the life of her how he and Laura Klaassen managed to keep everybody doing what they were supposed to be doing. Oh, she'd seen an occasional friendly tussle between Arn and Ted turn into something else, with their father or mother having to intervene—making them stop and shake hands. But any argument that might look like it was getting out of hand was nipped in the bud.

And Mrs. Klaassen was even more of a puzzle. Her face always held a hint of a smile. More in her eyes than on her lips. Samantha thought people who grinned all the time seemed feeble-minded, but she'd never be able to accuse Mrs.

Klaassen of lacking intelligence. The woman had tons of work to do, too—chickens to look after, wash for her large family as well as meals three times a day and all the baking that went with it, a garden to care for, a house to keep clean. . . . The tasks seemed overwhelming to Samantha, who was accustomed to a very small home and very few people around to look after. Yet Mrs. Klaassen never complained. She smiled and teased her way through the days, completing her tasks in a cheerful manner. One afternoon Samantha had even found the woman sitting in a rocker in the parlor with a book in her lap! Of course there was Josie to help, but still. . . .

Samantha had always been a hard worker herself—more by necessity than design—but she couldn't claim to be cheerful about it. At home, she'd no more than get things straightened around when Pa, alone or with some of his cronies, would come through with dirty feet and lips full of snuff and muck things up again. With so many Klaassens coming and going, every day contained its share of messes. How could Mrs. Klaassen maintain a happy attitude with so much to do?

And what about the Klaassen kids? Consider Frank, nearly as big as a barn himself, still living at home and minding his Pa. Samantha figured once kids grew to be big enough to take care of themselves, out they'd go in a flash. But Frank—and Adam, too—were more men than boys, still following their father's lead and seeming to not mind it a bit.

Josie, and Becky, too, had lots to do, helping their mother keep things in order. Arn was always out with the men— every time Samantha looked at him he'd go red in the face, which made his freckles glow—and didn't seem to mind the work either.

Teddy and Sarah didn't have as many responsibilities as the others, being the youngest, but they had their own chores.

Only once had Samantha seen any of them shirk their duties, and that was Sarah, whom Samantha had decided was just a wee bit spoiled. But she was sure the family couldn't help themselves—even Samantha found her own heartstrings pulled by the loving little "Tharah."

When those occasional scuffles between siblings arose, they ended quickly with apologies and forgiveness. And at times with no interference at all from the Klaassen parents. Apparently the family didn't know about carrying grudges. Yes, something was definitely not right here.

But if this was "not right," it wasn't exactly wrong, either. It sure wasn't normal—not from Samantha's standpoint—but it was . . . well, peaceful, a feeling Samantha hadn't known heretofore. And she wondered if, when she left, she'd be able to find it somewhere else on her own.

~⊙

Adam spent time in deep thought during the rainy days that kept him and the other Klaassen men holed up in the barn. There was always busy work to fill their days, but they wished they could be in the fields. The vow he had made to himself to be a friend to Frances Welch turned out to be a pie-crust promise—easier made than kept. The girl eluded him at every turn. Any attempt at conversation was met with an even stare that seemed to look through or past a person. If any response came at all, it was in monosyllables at best.

Adam scrubbed at the old paint on the hay wagon, thinking of the way Frances's big eyes watched all of them. Usually you could look into someone's eyes and tell what that person was thinking, but not this Frances. She could hold a blank face better than anyone he'd ever met. Often he'd covertly watch her watch them and wish he knew what she was thinking. It was obvious she was uncomfortable—she was restless, almost like a caged animal, pacing from place to place in the house and avoiding all of them whenever possible. Had she been mistreated at some point in her life? She was so distrustful of everyone, particularly older male family members. He'd also noticed that whenever his mother tried to touch her—Ma was a very demonstrative person, and touching and hugs came naturally to her—she would pull away.

His hands stilled momentarily as he tried to pinpoint what it was that made her so different. Then it came to him. There were no emotions. She didn't smile, didn't laugh, didn't cry. . . . Her face wore a mask of indifference to everyone and everything around her. What kind of life had she led that would bring about such a closed, empty shell of a person? Such an impenetrable barrier she'd built around herself. But why? Whatever the answer was, he was sure he wouldn't hear it from Frances's lips.

He set to work again as his thoughts tumbled onward. He hadn't known such close-mouthed females existed. All the ones around this house were chattering all the time. Had the situation been less serious, he might've had some fun with that little characteristic of hers. The only person able to put her at ease was Sarah. The six-year-old, with her bright smile and endless babble about this and that, seemed to be winning Frances over from sheer innocence.

Adam frowned, his hands slowing. There had to be a way to gain Frances's trust and let her know that someone cared about her. Especially the One he'd come to know when he was a very small boy out in the chicken coop. If only he could tell Frances about the loving God in whom Adam and his family placed their trust, she would have a permanent friend—a "listener," as she had put it that night he'd heard her on the swing—to be with her no matter where she went.

Adam ceased his scraping and paused to look out the open barn door. Becky and Josie bent over the washtubs, scrubbing bedsheets. He sighed. With all of them busy with chores, there wasn't much time to talk to Frances about God's unwavering love for her. But even if they didn't find time to speak of God, they could show Frances through their actions the importance He held in their lives. Everyone down to Sarah could help with that.

Adam returned to his task, determined to somehow break through the barrier his family's guest had built around herself. He decided to talk it over with his pa as soon as he could find him.

Arn came bursting into the barn. "Pa says come quick and help. Hilarius's Rosalee is loose again."

Adam dropped his scrub brush over the edge of the wagon. "I'm a-comin', Arn." He would watch for a chance to talk with Pa.

"Frantheth, gueth what?"

Samantha stood at the parlor window, inwardly rejoicing that the rain was letting up. Freedom was near! She shifted her gaze to Sarah, who peered up at her with those blue, blue eyes that always seemed to catch Samantha off guard with their depth and expressiveness. "What it is, Sarah?"

"Day after tomorrow is Thunday, and Liz an' Jake are going to come here for dinner. Mama'th gonna make a thcripture cake, too. Won't that be good?"

Samantha nodded dumbly, wondering what in the world a "thcripture cake" was. By now she knew what Scriptures were, that's for sure. After three days of being stuck in this house with the Klaassens, she'd been introduced to a fair amount of it. Mrs. Klaassen had a verse for every occasion, and her children often winked at one another when their mother got to quoting. Plus the day got started with everyone sitting around the table, listening to Mr. Klaassen read a little something from the Bible then all holding hands for the prayer. Samantha had been invited to join them, but she'd felt foolish sitting there holding hands with Becky and Josie, so after the first time, she'd stayed out of the kitchen till all that stuff was done. Though she'd caught herself listening to a story that had somehow gotten her attention from her perch in the parlor, something about Jesus and His "disciples"—whatever they were—on a little boat in a storm. Her imagination had captured that image in her mind, and it stayed with her through the rest of the day.

Sarah now caught Samantha's hand and drew her into the kitchen. "An Liz ith going to have a baby, too," the little girl was saying. "It'll be jutht a while now an' that baby'll be here. I'm gonna be an aunt again."

Samantha's eyes grew wide. "You're an—an *ahnt*?" She pronounced the word the same way Sarah had. "But you're just a little kid."

Sarah laughed. "I'm little, but Liz ithn't. She'th real big an' fat now." She held out her arms in front of her tummy to illustrate. She pushed Samantha onto the nearest kitchen bench, then straddled the wide plank seat and swung her feet as she continued. "After Liz hath her baby, there'll be three babieth in the family. My brother Daniel got married to Rothe, and they have two babieth already—Chrithtina and Katrina. They're real cute. They live way away in Minneapolith, but Liz an' Jake live in Mountain Lake. Not far. I'll get to thee Liz an' Jake'th baby a lot more than Chrithtina and Katrina, for sure."

Sarah finally stopped talking long enough for Samantha to absorb it all. If Sarah was an aunt already, then Mrs. Klaassen was a grandmother. Samantha turned her gaze to watch the woman at the dry sink, rolling out dough to cut noodles. She looked nothing like the grandmother Samantha remembered. Mrs. Klaassen was tiny—eleven-year-old Becky was only a little bit shorter than her mother—and the coil of her nut-brown hair sported fewer than a dozen white hairs. Her brown eyes sparkled with vitality. She looked far too young to be a grandmother.

Mrs. Klaassen looked over at Sarah, eyebrows pulled down a bit. "Sarah, aren't you supposed to be helping Josie and Becky with the wash? If everything is to be dry by evening, they'll need your help."

Sarah gave her mother a pleading look. "I wanna thtay here and talk to Frantheth. It'th hot outthide. Why do I have to hang wash?"

"Because when everyone does his or her share, the work gets done much faster." Mrs. Klaassen's tone brooked no nonsense. "Now scoot along with you."

Sarah's lips pulled down for a moment, then she sighed and swung her leg over the bench. As she stood, she looked at Samantha, hope dancing in her wide eyes. "Want to come, too?"

Samantha hesitated.

Mrs. Klaassen sent a smile across the kitchen. "Go ahead, both of you. Just don't let Sarah try to talk you into doing her share of the hanging."

"Come." Sarah captured Samantha's hand and pulled her out the back door.

Samantha hop-skipped after Sarah, who refused to relinquish her hand until they had reached the other two girls. They were wringing out the wet wash and hanging it over the lines to dry. Becky turned, spotted Sarah, and made a sour face.

"Where have you been? We're practically done."

"Now, Becky," Josie said, "you weren't much better about your chores when you were Sarah's age." Becky opened her mouth in protest, but Josie shook her head. "Let's not spend time fussing, or we'll be out here all afternoon."

Sarah stuck out her tongue at Becky, grinned at Josie, then giggled and ran to the basket. She wrestled out a towel and twisted it, but her small hands proved inept at wringing out the water.

Samantha moved over to help. She showed Sarah how to hold tightly to one end of the towel while Samantha twisted it. As she hung the heavy towel on the line next to similar items, she noticed her own overalls and flannel shirt hanging amongst the men's things closer to the barn. Her heart did a happy flip-flop. With her clothes clean and dry, she could be on her way. Maybe even by this evening.

Josie started singing a nonsense song about little children eating oatmeal, and Becky joined in. Sarah lisped her way on the words she could remember, just singing "La, la, la" in place of the ones she couldn't. Samantha listened to it all while moving between the baskets of wet laundry and the clotheslines, her hands busy and her heart lighter than it had been for quite a while.

Before she knew it, the baskets were empty and three long lines of wet clothing, sheets, and towels flapped in the warm, end-of-summer breeze.

Becky stood back, hands on her hips, and surveyed the rows of clean items with satisfaction. "Sure feels good to have that done."

"Sure does." Josie stacked the empty baskets together and scooped them up. "It'll be nice to sleep on those sun-dried sheets tonight, too."

Sarah skipped along beside her older sister as the four girls headed toward the house. "I love the thmell of fresh sheetth."

Josie reached out a hand to rustle Sarah's soft blonde curls. "Me, too, *liebchen*."

Samantha had heard Mr. and Mrs. Klaassen use the nickname when addressing Sarah. She wondered what it meant, and she started to ask Josie. But a shout stopped her words.

"Hey! Girls!"

All four twirled to see Arn coming from behind the barn at a trot. He panted to a stop in front of them, his face beet red. "Guess what we found?"

Becky huffed, impatience crinkling her nose. "Just tell us."

A huge grin split Arn's freckled face. "Mushrooms! Pa says if we get 'em picked now, Ma'll have time to fix 'em with our gravy. Want to help?"

The younger two girls squealed and dashed to Arn's side. Samantha shrugged and moved a step toward the boy.

Josie said, "Let me put these baskets on the back porch and check with Mother to make sure she's done with us for now."

Arn gave a teasing snort. "Well, hurry up, grandma!"

Josie made a face at him and hurried to the back door.

Becky pulled at Samantha's hand. "Have you ever hunted mushrooms, Frances?"

Samantha tugged her hand free of Becky's grasp. These were the touchiest people she'd ever met. "No. I never ate one neither."

Arn, Becky, and Sarah stared in amazement. Becky shook her head, her brown braids flopping. "You've never eaten a mushroom? Didn't they have 'em where you used to live?"

For reasons she couldn't explain, Samantha experienced a rush of irritation. She answered sharply. "I don't know. I never asked."

Becky ducked her head, her cheeks splashed with pink. Samantha considered apologizing for her brusque tone, but Josie raced out the back door, letting it slam behind her.

"We can go as long as we're back in time to make the beds before supper. Come on."

"Great!" Arn's voice cracked on the single word. He was at the awkward age between boyhood and manhood, and his voice tended to run the scales like an inept piano tuner.

His sisters giggled and poked at him as they dashed off at a pace that wasn't sensible considering the August heat. Samantha followed automatically, curiosity about mushrooms propelling her along behind the others. Between these mushrooms and the promised "scripture" cake—whatever that was—meals around here were getting to be quite an adventure.

The girls followed Arn past the grazing area behind the barn clear out to the stand of maples, apple, and mulberry trees that bordered the Klaassen property. Sarah shivered and reached to grab Samantha's hand. "Oooh! We're goin' in the woodth!"

Becky rolled her eyes. "This isn't the *woods*, silly."

"I can call it the woodth if I want to," Sarah argued.

Josie slowed her pace to fall in with Samantha and Sarah. "Woods or not, isn't it a pleasant place to be? I love to come out to the trees. Especially in the spring and summer. It's so nice and cool, and the breeze stirs the scents of ripened fruit, damp earth, and decaying leaves—."

"Stop talking like a teacher, Josie." Becky shot a wrinkle-nosed look over her shoulder.

Josie laughed. "But I want to be one! Why shouldn't I practice?" She aimed a quick smile at Samantha. "I also like all the wildflowers that grow here in the protection of the trees. God did an amazing job, making the world so beautiful."

Samantha considered Josie's comment. Caught up in mere survival from day to day, she'd never taken the time to examine the world's beauty. But now she looked around at the delicate white angel's breath and chubby lavender bluebells. Fallen mulberries lay like a purple and magenta carpet beneath her feet. She felt her heart expanding inside her chest. Loveliness did exist here. But was it to be found in other places too?

Arn came to a halt, his head swinging back and forth. Then he yelped, "This is the spot." He dashed ahead to a row of spine-covered bushes, one of which sported a red bandanna tied to a spindly branch. He pushed aside the branches so the girls could pass. "Look out for prickles. The mushrooms are under the trees there."

As she came through the bushes, Samantha stopped short at the sight of Adam on his knees, plucking squatty, round-topped plants from the soft ground and dropping them into a burlap sack.

Sarah ran to him, obviously delighted. "Adam, how come you're not in the fieldth?"

Adam poked a finger into her round middle, making her laugh. "Because the 'fieldths,' as you say, are too wet to be worked. We'll get out there Monday if the sun holds through the weekend. So today I hunt mushrooms."

Samantha swallowed a rush of apprehension. Being with the girls and even Arn was one thing, but being in the vicinity of Adam was another. He was as tall as her father—a boyish face but he looked big enough to be a man. Every time she found herself within Adam's range, she remembered the humiliation of him sitting on her, holding her down, in the middle of the street.

Of course, he'd done nothing remotely close to that to her since. He'd been kind and considerate. But his kindness only added to her shame as she recalled calling him "a honyocker." She wasn't exactly sure of the meaning, but she knew the term to be uncomplimentary. Adam hadn't deserved to be called that awful name, and she wished she had the nerve to apologize. But to apologize, she would have to engage him in conversation, and that was far more difficult than bearing her guilt.

She now turned her flustered gaze away from him and became overly interested in a dry piece of skin on the cuticle of her left thumb.

Adam grinned around at his family. "Pick away. That rain probably brought them out. There must be a hundred."

Josie and Becky knelt and began picking the smooth, brown-capped mushrooms. Sarah danced around excitedly, stubbing her toe at one point and howling in indignation. Adam spared a moment to give her a consoling hug, then went back to collecting. Samantha, thinking the mushrooms looked like ugly toadstools, sat off to the side and watched.

Arn squatted close to her, apparently feeling his job had been to fetch more pickers, not pick the mushrooms himself. "Ma will cook those in butter, then mix 'em in with some gravy to pour over potatoes or cornbread stuffing." Arn's cheeks blotched pink, and he whisked a sideways glance at Samantha. "They're really good."

Samantha hadn't spent any time near Arn. He seemed gangly and awkward to her with his long limbs that hadn't yet filled out and a wide face full of freckles. If she was going to choose the company of any of the Klaassen males, she'd probably pick Teddy since he was small and unassuming—and if she had to, she could beat him up. But Arn sat looking at her expectantly, as if a reply would be a gift. So she gathered her courage and ventured to ask, "Do you eat them a lot?"

Arn shook his head, making his cowlick bounce above his forehead. "No, they're pretty hard to spot. We look at 'em as pretty much of a treat."

That explained why they'd all come running. "How'd you find them this time?"

Arn chuckled low in his throat. "I didn't. It was Rosalee."

Josie quickly looked over at them. "Rosalee?"

"Yep." Arn turned to Samantha. "Hilarius Schwartz is our nearest neighbor, and Rosalee is his old milk cow." He shifted to address his siblings. "She wandered clear over here this morning, and Pa asked me to herd her back before Hilarius called out the sheriff. When I was taking her home, I spotted the mushrooms."

Becky wiped at a trail of sweat running from her temple. "Maybe we should take a few to Hilarius as a thank you. Or maybe Rosalee too."

Josie and Arn exchanged glances. They chorused, "Or maybe not." All of the Klaassens laughed together.

Josie said, "We'll think of another way to thank them," and this brought another shared chuckle.

Samantha watched Adam tie a knot in the top of the burlap sack, now full of the funny-looking plants, and toss it over his shoulder. Those mushrooms must be pretty special. The Klaassens had decided they wanted to keep the mushrooms all to themselves.

As she followed the others back to the farm, trailing well behind Adam, she decided maybe she'd stick around just one more night. She could start out fresh after a good night's rest. Besides, she had a sudden hankering to sample some of those mushrooms.

Chapter Eight

*T*he mushrooms proved to be sumptuous fare indeed. By the end of the meal, Samantha's stomach was aching. They'd feasted on fried pork, stewed tomatoes, fresh ears of corn, and cornbread stuffing which they doused with the delicious brown mushroom gravy. Samantha could hardly believe that the Klaassens had produced every last bit of food on the table themselves.

She had discovered they raised and butchered their own hogs and chickens, kept a massive garden, canning enough vegetables to last the winter, had their own wheat ground into flour, and cared for three cows that provided milk and butter for their own needs as well as for Simon's brother Hiram and his wife in town. All this, plus raising a money crop of corn along with the wheat. And of course the work of keeping up a house—one with a couple of additions jutting out as their family grew—and caring for horses besides. If she hadn't seen with her own eyes how much Mr. and Mrs. Klaassen genuinely loved their children, she'd suspect they'd had a big family just for the help in keeping the farm running smoothly.

After supper Samantha joined the female family members in clearing the dishes and preparing for the washing up. The idea of accepting charity still stuck in her craw, so helping out with the chores, she figured, took care of their providing her with meals. Besides, it helped pass the time.

Before the meal Arn had brought in a big kettle of water to heat, so hot water was all ready for the task. "Josie, you and Becky bring in the wash from the lines," Mrs. Klaassen told the two. "Since the sheets weren't dry before supper, you two now can get the beds made while Frances, Sarah, and I do the dishes."

Josie dropped the dishrag in the sink and moved toward the door. "Sure. I'd rather make beds and fold laundry than wash dishes any day." She and Becky headed outside.

Sarah cast a hopeful look in her mother's direction. "Can I make bedth, too, Mama?"

Mrs. Klaassen smiled at the cherub. "Why, certainly, *lieb-chen*." She tapped the end of Sarah's nose with a finger. "You can make your own bed *after* the dishes are done."

Sarah stuck out her lip in a pout, but when no one paid any attention to her, she trotted over to the dry sink and began stacking dirty plates together.

Mrs. Klaassen scraped bits off a bar of lye soap into the enamel wash pan and swished her hand through the water to make some suds. She turned her head toward Samantha. "What are your plans now, dear?"

Samantha blinked. "Well, ma'am, I reckon since my clothes are clean again, I'll just be on my way. I reckon I've eaten up enough of your food by now."

Mrs. Klaassen set the bar of soap aside. "Oh, no, that's not what I'm worried about at all. I'm thinking about you, dear, and how you'll manage. I'm assuming you don't have a definite destination in mind?"

Samantha bit down on her lower lip. Sometimes when Laura talked, she sounded like a fancy lady, and the words didn't match the picture of a farmer's wife. She couldn't decide how to respond.

Mrs. Klaassen's face softened. "Have you thought about where you'll settle?"

Samantha's cheeks heated. "No, ma'am. Not exactly yet."

Lifting the steaming kettle from the stove, Mrs. Klaassen sloshed more water into the waiting wash pan. "I've been thinking. You'll need money for the journey, and money to pay for lodging once you've decided where to stay. I can imagine you're a little low on cash. Am I right?" She sent a sideways look at Samantha, her eyebrows high.

The heat in Samantha's face increased. She offered a hesitant nod.

"It seems to me that before you leave, you will need some money."

Suspicion rose in Samantha's mind. She backed up two steps. "I know I've been eating an' sleeping here, but I won't take money from you too. Don't ask me to do that, ma'am, because I won't."

Mrs. Klaassen reached for a dishtowel and dried her hands. Then she caught Samantha by the shoulders and looked her straight in the eyes. "Frances, I wouldn't shame you by offering you money."

Samantha stiffened beneath the woman's hands, but Mrs. Klaassen held firmly.

"I was going to offer you a chance to *earn* some traveling money."

Samantha gulped. "Earn it?"

Mrs. Klaassen turned back to the wash pan. After instructing Sarah to be careful with the glasses, she said, "You see, as Sarah told you, our daughter Liz is expecting her first child. Now, I would dearly love to go and spend a few days with her after the baby is born. But this is such a busy time of year I can't afford to be gone. Too many vegetables are awaiting canning, and school will start soon so I must get clothes ready for the children. Then there's all the work that goes with harvest. . . . There are too many needs here to be met for me to be somewhere else right now."

Samantha lifted the glasses Sarah had dried and stacked them in their places on the cupboard shelves. "Can't—can't Josie stay with Liz?"

"She could, if she weren't going to be in school." Mrs. Klaassen pulled a soapy plate from the pan and set it aside. "This will be Josie's last year of schooling, and then she'd like to test for a teaching certificate. It's important for her not to miss any of the school year if she plans to teach. Besides, I depend on Josie for help with canning and sewing. She can't be spared either. I'm thinking Liz could use your very capable hands, Frances."

Samantha couldn't help a quick glance at her hands. She'd never thought of herself in the same sentence with a fancy word like *capable*. She moved on about her task, thinking. She paused in front of the possum-belly cabinet that housed the larger bowls, chewing on the inside of her lip. It would be nice to have some traveling money, to be able to buy food instead of steal it. But by taking the job, she'd be stuck here in Mountain Lake for a while longer—maybe a *long* while longer.

Samantha turned back to Laura. "I'd like to dwell on it some, if I could. Maybe meet Liz and see how we'd get on and such . . ."

Mrs. Klaassen reached out a damp hand to Samantha's cheek. "That sounds very sensible, a practical approach to your decision. You sleep on it, and I'll pray about it. The Lord will let you know the best thing to do."

The older two girls trooped through the back door, full baskets in hand. Mrs. Klaassen reached toward Sarah, trailing behind. "Come along now, *liebchen*. We'll make your bed."

Samantha watched the mother and daughters turn the corner of the stairs. Her cheek still tingled from the whisper-touch of Laura's hand. There hadn't been time to back up and avoid it, and emotion built in her chest at the longing the touch inspired. She put the last of the dishes in the cupboard and headed out to her favorite spot—the porch swing behind the lilac bushes—to give this job idea some serious thought.

⁓෨

Saturday began with an announcement from Si that they'd all pitch in to get usual chores done as quickly as possible, then everyone out to the fields to make up time for the days they'd lost to rain. Rather than whining, the children all brightened and flew around getting things in order. Mrs. Klaassen supervised the preparation of a picnic lunch, and finally they climbed into the green-sided wagon for the trip out to work on the harvest.

Samantha stuck close to Josie, following her lead on what needed to be done and how to do it—mostly gathering wheat stalks for the boys to fasten into bundles and stack for drying. She was as glad as anyone when it was time to stop for their lunch.

By the time the little team of harvesters had returned to the farmhouse and eaten a quick meal of leftovers, Samantha could hardly climb the stairs, she was so tired. She discovered, though, that Saturday night was bath night in preparation for Sunday, so she reluctantly joined in the ritual. Actually, it felt kind of good to be clean from head to toe once again.

The next morning, Samantha awoke to a whirlwind of activity. Everyone flew around, readying themselves for church. The night before, Mrs. Klaassen had given everyone's shoes a going-over with a cold biscuit so they'd be shiny for the service. Talking all the while, she'd also found a fresh, clean "dress of Liz's that doesn't fit her anymore and would fit you just perfectly, Frances. . . ." and she couldn't get a word in edgewise about not accepting any more "charity."

Now Sarah was in a tizzy because she couldn't find her good hair ribbons, and Teddy had pulled a button from his pants. There was some discussion about whether a button could be reattached on the Lord's Day, but they soon decided "yes" when Adam reminded them of the scripture about a cow being pulled out of a hole on the Sabbath, ". . . and we sure wouldn't want his britches to fall down in church," Adam finished to gales of laughter.

"Josie, grab a needle and thread and help Teddy with his button." Mrs. Klaassen swept a wet rag over the crumb-spattered table top. "Sarah, stop sniffling and go look under your bed. That's where we found your ribbons the last time. All right, Teddy, no need to remove your trousers, just hold still. Josie won't stick you." Samantha would have yanked out her hair in frustration had she been in charge, but Mrs. Klaassen seemed to take it all in stride.

Samantha had found a pair of black lace-up shoes to wear over borrowed stockings at the end of the bed that morning. Josie offered to braid her hair, but since her hair was clean and extra curly, Samantha simply brushed the front of it back from her face and tied the rest of it with a ribbon loaned by Becky. She felt fresh and ready to face the day. Of course, if she'd had a choice, she'd be wearing her own overalls and shirt and wouldn't be going to church at all. But everyone seemed to expect it of her, and she decided it was best to go along with the tide rather than create more conflict for Mrs. Klaassen.

After a cold breakfast of biscuits and jam, everyone climbed into the back of the clean hay wagon and settled in amongst the piles of straw Adam had thrown in for the occasion. The Klaassens sang all the way to church, rivaling the goldfinches that sang from the fence lines as they rattled by. Everywhere Samantha looked, fields of golden wheat stretched toward the horizon. The wind passed across the prickly tops of the shafts, creating a soothing waving motion she found pleasing.

Josie had told Samantha that with harvest here, all the men in the community pitched in to help in their neighbors' fields. According to Josie, this was an exciting time for the community, and when it was complete, there would be a big party at the schoolhouse to celebrate. Josie seemed to assume that Samantha would still be here by then, but Samantha wasn't so sure. *All depends on how well Liz and me get along*, she told herself.

At the south edge of town, they drove up to a simple white clapboard building with a door on each side of the front. Mr. Klaassen drew the wagon alongside many others lined up in the grassy area at the side of the building. It seemed as if the whole town turned out for services.

Samantha wasn't much of a churchgoer. As a small child she had gone with her gran, but Pa hadn't shown any interest in taking her or David after Gran died, so Samantha had stayed home. Everyone here looked as spit-shined as the Klaassens, and Samantha surmised they'd all turned out in their best clothes. Ladies wore straw bonnets with little flowers, and most men had on black coats over their white shirts even though the late August heat was stifling. Men and women were separating as they walked toward the building, the men entering the door on the right, the women and young children on the left. Samantha turned to Josie to ask about the practice, but the bell in the tower began ringing loudly, making conversation impossible.

Adam helped Sarah and Becky over the edge of the wagon, then reached a hand to Samantha, but she braced herself on the edge and leaped out without his assistance. The dreadful memory of their Main Street tussle filled her mind, and she couldn't meet Adam's gaze. Would any of these churchgoers recognize her as the same girl who'd been rolling in the dirt with Adam just a few days ago?

The Klaassen family took up quite a bit of space as they entered from the assigned doors and met in the aisles. The two parents ushered their offspring toward what must have been familiar benches. Samantha followed blindly, eager to find an inconspicuous spot to sit. Hovering between Josie and Becky, Samantha watched Laura move into the center aisle to greet with a hug a pretty young woman. As the pair pulled apart, she realized the young woman had Laura's soft brown eyes and long, thin nose—plus a popping belly. This must be Liz, and the good-looking tall man her husband, Jake. Samantha examined them through squinted eyes. They were a nice-looking couple, and they held hands even in the church. Embarrassed, Samantha turned away.

"Let's sit," Becky said, pushing Samantha with her elbow.

She plopped herself onto a backless bench between Sarah and Becky, with Laura, Josie, and Liz taking up the rest of the bench to Sarah's left. Samantha peeked back over her shoulder and realized with a start that the whole left section of the church was filled with women, and the right was all men. What an odd setup. But there wasn't time for further wondering, for things were starting.

She did her best to pay attention, but Sarah and Becky kept leaning across her lap to whisper. Each time Laura would look over and frown. The unpadded benches were not comfortable, and she was relieved when they stood up for hymn singing. She couldn't join in the songs, however, because they sang in some foreign language—German, she surmised, from having heard Mr. and Mrs. Klaassen converse in similar words at their home. So she stood silently, listening to the others.

Mrs. Klaassen's pure soprano carried above the others, accompanied by Josie's pleasant alto. Adam and Frank's resonant voices drifted from across the aisle. Samantha experienced a tingle of pleasure. Obviously they all enjoyed singing, and even though there wasn't a hymnbook in sight, not a one of them seemed to miss a note or a word. They looked as familiar with church and its goings-on as they were with their own backyards. Her brow puckered as she considered if attending these services made them so different from people she knew back home, most of whom weren't churchgoers by any means.

Afterward, no one rushed to leave. They all milled around outside, gathering in small groups to visit. Samantha found herself corralled with Josie and a small cluster of giggling girls who peeked over their shoulders at a larger group of young men in which Adam seemed to be the center.

A husky youth with a shock of red hair poked Adam in the chest, said something behind his hand the girls couldn't hear, then threw back his head and laughed. The other boys joined in, and Adam shrugged, pushing the toe of his boot into the loose dirt.

Someone tapped Samantha on the shoulder, and she turned to face a petite young woman with sparkling blue eyes, a tiny upturned nose, and full rosy lips. A wondrous mass of glossy black curls framed her face, contrasting shockingly with her bright eyes. She was by far the prettiest girl Samantha had ever seen, but the prettiness was spoiled by a haughty angle to her head, the hint of a superior glint in her eye, and a snooty twist to her lips. Samantha was immediately on guard.

"Aren't you the girl who tried to steal from the mercantile last week?" the girl asked.

Anger flashed inside Samantha's chest and created a rush of fire in her face.

Josie stepped forward. "Priscilla, this is Frances Welch, and she's staying with us." Josie's tone said far more than her words.

Priscilla tossed back her curls. "So nice to meet you, Frances." Her tone dripped vinegar. She held her chin at a pert angle, fixing Samantha with narrowed eyes. "But you didn't answer me. Was that you?"

Samantha clenched her fists. "It was me. But I don't see how it's any of your business."

Priscilla held up her hands in a mock show of apology. "Oh, dear, I didn't mean to offend you." A sly grin flickered over her face. "I heard Adam carted home another stray—this time one caught stealing. I just wondered if it might be you. I meant no harm."

Josie put her arm around Samantha's shoulders and tried to pull her away, but Samantha shrugged it off. "He didn't *cart* me home; he invited me. I'm not a stray. And I'm smart enough to know you *do* mean harm, all right. But you don't bother me any. I'm used to your ilk and worse. So you can just keep your wonderings to yourself."

Priscilla gave a little giggle and turned to the other girls who had the grace to duck their heads in embarrassment. "I seem to have offended poor Frances here. Actually, I envy her. Wouldn't I love to be chased down the street by Adam Klaassen and then be taken home by him. Oh, my." She fanned herself with both hands.

"Come on." Josie steered Samantha toward their wagon. "Don't pay any attention to Priscilla Koehn. She's nothing but trouble. She's had her eye on Adam since we were in pinafores, but if Adam ever so much as *looks* at Priscilla, I declare I'll never speak to him again."

Becky clomped along beside them. "Give Adam credit for some sense. He knows Priscilla's nothing but a fickle flirt."

Samantha sent a withering glance over her shoulder. Priscilla stood within the circle of girls, jabbering away. "Makes me no never-mind," Samantha spat out. "But *she* better stay outta my way."

Samantha seethed all the way back to the farm, and not until the dinner dishes were cleared and the scripture cake served did she relax her tense jaw. By then her teeth ached from being tightly clenched, and she wished she'd never stepped foot in that church. Her speculations that churchgoing was what made this family unique were completely wrong. That awful Priscilla attended church, but she didn't possess the sweet spirit that marked the Klaassens. *It has to be something else, but what?*

The family retired to the parlor after dessert to relax and enjoy the one day of the week that wasn't filled with endless chores. Mr. and Mrs. Klaassen sat together on the camelback sofa with Sarah snug between them, drowsing against her father's chest. Teddy and Arn sat on the floor near the bay window, each with a leaflet in hand, reading. Josie ran an embroidery needle through a piece of muslin in a wooden hoop, creating a circle of flowers, and Becky leaned over her shoulder, providing unasked-for advice.

Frank disappeared upstairs for a nap after stating his plans to use the buckboard later to visit his girlfriend, Anna Harms. Adam perched on the seat of the bay window, trying to read over Arn's shoulder. Jake and Liz had joined the family for Sunday dinner and now shared the narrow courting bench across from the sofa. With Liz's extra girth, it was a tight fit, but neither of them seemed to mind.

Samantha sneaked upstairs and changed into her own set of clothes—clean, but still as oversized as ever and of course nothing like the frock she wore to church. She returned and stood in the parlor doorway, unwilling to intrude upon the family scene but also reluctant to stay away.

Laura motioned for her to come in. She gently pushed Sarah onto Si's lap and scooted over to create a slice of space. "Here, Frances, sit down. Liz and I were just talking about you."

Samantha prickled. Had they heard what Priscilla said after church?

"We wondered if you'd decided yet whether to stay and work for Liz," Laura began.

Samantha released a sigh of relief. She slid into the edge of the sofa, her hands in her lap. "I'm not sure. . . ."

Liz sent a beseeching look in Samantha's direction. "I'd love it if you could, Frances. Truthfully, even though the baby isn't here yet, I could use your help now. I'm so big, it's hard just to pull myself around. Jake has had to take on many of my chores—"

"And he's not complaining." Jake placed a kiss on his young wife's temple.

Liz smiled at him and patted his hand. "Which he's done cheerfully, but it makes for an awful lot of work for one person." She shifted her gaze to Samantha again. "He has his own work to do, and he really doesn't have the time to spare for mine."

Jake linked his fingers through Liz's. "She's right, Frances. I've kept up so far, but mostly because of the rain we've had. Now that things are drying out and we'll be starting harvest, Liz needs someone close at hand. We'd both appreciate it—a lot—if you could help us out."

Samantha hesitated, looking from Liz to Mrs. Klaassen. As much as she needed the money, should she stay in one spot for so long? She didn't know how to ask how long she'd be needed without having to explain her reasons.

Jake said, "As for wages, I was thinking four dollars a week. We can raise that after the baby's born, as I'm sure your workload will increase then."

Samantha gawked at Jake. "Oh, no. That's more'n enough. That's plenty, even *after* the baby's born. I just—well, I don't know how long I can stay around here. How long do you reckon you'll need my help?"

Liz and Jake looked at each other. Liz shook her head and shrugged. "I'm really not sure. I've never had a baby before. Mother was up and around in three weeks or so after her children were born. Could you stay that long?"

Samantha chewed her lip. Three weeks . . . Pa could cover a lot of territory in three weeks. And that baby wasn't even here yet. But if she had three weeks' worth of wages in her pocket, maybe she could buy a train ticket and get clear across country. Pa'd *never* find her then.

"I'll hire on," Samantha blurted. "I'll just go with you folks when you go home tonight and stay till the baby's born and Liz's back on her feet."

"Wonderful!" Liz broke into a relieved smile and leaned against Jake, who squeezed her shoulders and beamed down at her.

Laura Klaassen patted Samantha's knee. "Thank you, Frances. You're an answer to prayer."

Those words wove a web of pleasure around Samantha's heart. Heat rose from her chest to her face, and she ducked her head, too embarrassed to meet anyone's gaze. Had anyone ever said something as kind to her before? Face aimed downward, she made a silent vow to prove the woman's confidence in her was well placed for the time she remained here. She'd leave them with no regrets for having placed such trust in her.

Chapter Nine

*S*amantha easily settled in with Liz and Jake. Neither of them was much older than she—Liz only twenty and Jake one year older than that—but they seemed eons older in life experience.

They lived in a small, square house with a room that served as both kitchen and parlor, a back bedroom, and a small pantry lean-to on the ground floor. A narrow stairway split the little house down the middle and led to two small attic rooms. Since the upstairs rooms were tucked in under the rafters, the ceiling slanted on either side of the door, ending with a four-foot-high wall. Across from the door was one small four-pane window, the frame of which was painted white and covered with a bleached muslin curtain.

The walls and ceiling had been plastered by Jake and his father, and wide pine planks formed the floor over which Liz had thrown several small rag rugs for color and warmth. Next to the door in the room Samantha used was a narrow bachelor's chest that held her meager belongings—Laura had insisted she bring along the borrowed clothing from her time at the Klaassens—and a white iron single bed pressed beneath the eave. Beside the bed was a small washstand with a china pitcher and bowl, both of which carried chips but were more than serviceable. The room, though unpretentious and without unnecessary trappings of any kind, was paradise to Samantha.

Samantha's room was to the left of the stairs, and Liz had been fixing up the other one for the baby. But poor Liz was so awkward and heavy now, it was too hard for her to get up there.

So it became Samantha's job to finish the curtain hanging and furniture placement. Liz had already painted the walls a pale yellow, and Jake had moved a handmade cradle that had been used by several Klaassens, a dresser, and an oak rocker into the room. Samantha hung the curtains of goldenrod calico and arranged the furniture, delighting in her part to ready the room for the new little one.

Liz spent most of her time in the kitchen rocker, stitching sheets and tiny gowns and flannel diapers. The pile of baby things grew in the basket beside Liz's feet over the course of the day, and in the evenings Samantha carried everything upstairs, cradling it in her arms with great care, to put it all away.

Samantha's days, though quite full of duties, were pleasant. Some of the work was hard; she was responsible for all the housecleaning, the gardening chores, washing clothes, feeding the chickens, and milking the cow. Since she had been largely responsible for her own little house back in Wisconsin since she was quite young, she found no difficulty in meeting the demands of her new job, but she'd never realized how pleasant tasks could become when performed for people who appreciated your efforts and weren't adverse to saying so. At night she fell into bed blissfully exhausted with words of thanks echoing in her ears. She'd never been happier.

"Frances," Liz said on the fourth morning of Samantha's employment, "how would you like to make blueberry preserves today?"

Samantha hunched up one shoulder. "I never done—did—that before. I don't reckon I could do it on my own. Might mix something up."

Liz heaved herself with difficulty from her rocker and swayed across the floor. She placed her hand on Samantha's shoulder. "I realize I've been more than just a wee bit lazy lately, but I would not expect you to do something as time consuming as making blueberry preserves on your own."

Samantha's lips twitched into a small smile. "Well, if you're helping, I reckon I can do it. Should I pick the berries now?"

Liz nodded. "Yes. It's been wonderful to eat fresh berries this summer, but they won't keep through the winter unless they're made into preserves, so we better hop to it. I'd pick with you, but I just can't take the heat these days—makes me so dizzy. Besides, bending over . . ." They looked at each other and laughed.

Samantha had never considered the miseries that went along with carrying a child. She glanced at Liz's swollen belly, hoping it was all worth the trouble. "You just sit and stitch on some of your baby things. I'll fetch a basket from the cellar and get to pickin'. It won't be so bad in the morning—sun's not so high and hot yet."

The humidity was certainly high, though, Samantha realized, and by nine o'clock her clothes bore damp patches from perspiration, and sweat ran down her forehead in rivulets that stung her eyes and tickled her temples. Strands of hair worked loose from her braid and fell across her damp cheeks. She longed to stop and fetch a cool drink, but determination kept her hunched over the plants, pulling ripe berries from their hiding spots among thick green leaves, stopping occasionally to swat a mosquito.

She'd filled one basket, and was well on her way to filling a second, when a shadow crossed her path. She shielded her eyes with one hand and looked up, expecting Liz had come out to check how things were going. But Adam stood over her wearing his familiar straw hat and easy grin. "Well, you're certainly hard at it," he commented, leaning over to pick a handful of berries and bring them to his mouth.

Samantha shoved back the errant wisps of hair flying around her face. What a sight she must be, her hands as dirty as her overalls, and and hair standing on end. But if Adam thought she looked a mess, he gave no indication.

"Use a little help?"

Samantha watched his teeth bite through the fruit. A tiny spurt of juice came out the side of his mouth and ran down his chin. He brought the back of his hand up to catch it, grinning all the while. Samantha surprised herself by asking, "With picking or eating?"

Adam's eyebrows rose toward the sky, and after a moment of dead silence, he snatched the hat from his head, banged it against his knee twice, and let out a whoop that startled Samantha as much as her teasing must have surprised him.

"Maybe a little of both." He lifted out another plump blueberry, but this time he offered it to her.

She looked at the berry held with the tips of his fingers, then up into his smiling face. His brown eyes sparkled at her in a friendly manner. Hesitantly she gave a quick flash of a smile in return, took the blueberry, and popped it into her mouth. The warm sweetness exploded against her tongue, and she closed her eyes. "Mmmm."

When she opened her eyes again, Adam was still beside her, his eyes glued to her face, his hat back in place on his head.

"So, Frances . . ." His unwavering gaze warmed her more than the sun beaming overhead. "Do you want my help?"

Her heart pounded hard beneath the bib of her overalls. "Uh, are you sure you can spare the time?"

"Wouldn't be here if I couldn't."

Samantha let her gaze sweep across the remainder of the berry bushes. "There is a heap of picking to be done."

With a nod, Adam scooped up a basket and headed to the opposite side of the patch. Samantha watched him go, flustered yet pleased that he had come. She gave herself a little shake. *Quit thinking that way about him. If he knew how your thoughts were flying, he'd turn tail and run. Now get to work.*

Reluctantly, she turned back to her task, allowing herself only an occasional peek at her helper.

Adam stood side by side with Frances at Liz's sink. He sorted and removed any stems from the berries then dropped them into the sink basin for Frances to wash. Her hands moved steadily between the sink and a large kettle, her lips tipped into a slight curve that might be contentment. Adam had a hard time keeping his focus on the berries. What a change her days with Liz and Jake had already brought to the girl's demeanor.

Although Frances was still wearing those overalls and ungainly shirt, she'd pulled her hair back into a sweet, feminine braid tied with a bit of yellow yarn. Her lips, which she'd usually kept set in a grim line, formed a gentle curve that softened her entire face. Steam from the kettle raised a sheen of perspiration, highlighting the pale freckles dancing across the bridge of her nose. Sunlight slanted through the window above the sink and brought out the golden shimmers in her red-brown hair. Curling dark lashes threw a soft shadow on high cheekbones, and her blue eyes were almost luminous in the bright light. What a pretty girl she was.

Adam smiled to himself. He'd known Liz would be a good influence on Frances. Only thirteen months separated him from Liz in age, so he was closer to her than his other brothers and sisters—agewise and otherwise. The two favored one another in looks, with their brown eyes and sandy hair that insisted on curling. Both were good-natured as well as deep thinkers, and sometimes found they knew what the other was pondering without saying a word.

Adam glanced quickly again at Frances. Being with Liz had erased the deep furrow of distrust from her brow. Twice he had heard soft chuckles as she and Liz exchanged idle chitchat and Liz offered instructions on the task at hand. The sullen exterior had all but disappeared, and while Adam couldn't say she seemed cheerful, she did appear to be peaceful. Frances had needed gentling as well as encouragement, and clearly Liz had offered both. He intended to give his sister a very long, very grateful hug for working this small miracle in his small foundling's attitude. Of course he would never say "his foundling" out loud.

Adam handed the last of the berries to Frances, then turned to Liz. "They're all ready for the pot. Finally!" He swiped his hand across his brow. "Should we cook them now?" He liked the sound of that "we."

Liz stopped the clack-clack of her knitting needles. "Yes, but mash them a bit first so they'll cook faster. Measure equal parts of berries and sugar, then boil them until the sugar is dissolved and the juice looks clear and shiny." She gestured to the tiny lean-to off the kitchen. "I have a second boiler pot out there. Would you get it, Adam, please? You'll be able to go twice as fast with two kettles. And, Frances, you know where the sugar is. I hope there'll be enough left in the barrel to finish the preserves today. Jake and his sweet tooth . . ." She shook her head, smiling indulgently. "I go through more sugar for the two of us than Mother did with all of us underfoot."

Adam and Frances moved to obey. Adam nearly tripped over her, and he caught her shoulders to keep himself from stumbling. Her face lifted and their gazes collided. His heart gave an odd hiccup. Something flickered in her eyes—apprehension? Awareness? He stepped aside quickly, his face flaming. She scuttled toward the pantry, and he ducked into the lean-to. He swept a shaky hand through his hair, giving himself a mental kick. He needed to be careful. *No sense giving her ideas* . . . or himself, for that matter.

Pot in hand, he returned to the kitchen, determined to help with the preserves and then go home before he made a *complete* fool of himself. He stood by while Frances scooped rinsed blueberries into the pots cup by cup, counting out loud along with her. He measured out a matching number of the sugar, then lifted both pots onto the stove. The heat of the stove combined with the heat of the day made the room nearly unbearable. Adam went around propping open the front door, the lean-to door, and all the windows in the house as well.

Liz watched him over the snarl of yellow yarn filling her lap. "I realize we need the breeze, dear brother, but now the dust will come through here and ruin the cleaning job Frances completed yesterday afternoon."

"Then I'll shut it back up." Adam reached for the window above the dry sink.

Frances grabbed his sleeve. He shot her a startled look, and she pulled back quickly. Clasping her hands against the bibbed front of her overalls, she licked her lips. "C-can you just leave it open? The breeze feels good, an' I can always dust again. I'd rather feel cooler. The air an' all . . ."

Liz cleared her throat. Adam flicked a glance in her direction and caught a worried pinch in her brow. Heat rose in his cheeks that had nothing to do with the temperature in the room. Turning away from his sister's questioning look, he saw Frances pull the collar of her flannel shirt away from her neck as she stirred the cooking preserves with a long-handled wooden spoon.

Sympathy replaced the awkwardness of the previous moment. "I bet you're really warm in that getup. Wouldn't you rather change into something else?"

"Don't have anything else. Your ma tried to get me to bring the two nice dresses she borrowed to me. . . . Not so good for workin' in, I told her."

Adam turned to Liz. "Don't you have an old summer dress Frances could wear for these chores? She's cooking faster than the berries are."

But now Liz wasn't paying any attention to him. She drew in a breath and clutched at her distended belly with two hands, dropping the half-finished baby afghan to the floor.

"Liz!" Adam darted across the kitchen and knelt beside her chair. He took her hand, and she clung hard, her eyes closed and lips forming a thin line. It seemed a lifetime passed before his sister relaxed her hold on his fingers. Little beads of sweat had popped out across her forehead, and a weak smile creased her face.

"Oh, my, that one was a whopper."

Adam frowned. "Whaddaya mean, *that* one?" Realization dawned. He scrambled to his feet. "You're having pains?" At Liz's nod, he stepped back, his fists on his hips. "How long has this been going on, missy?"

"Awhile."

"A*while?*" Adam threw his hands wide, fear and irritation fighting inside his chest. "Why, tell me, have you been messing around here, preserving berries and who knows what else, for Pete's sake? You should be in bed—"

"Adam, you sound like a mother hen." Liz shook her head, her expression calm. "I hope you're ready to calm down now and quit your scolding, because you're about to become an uncle."

Adam gulped. Cold sweat broke out over his body. "You mean . . . it's *time*?"

She laughed, increasing his ire. "Yes, it's time, and don't look like that, Adam. You didn't think I was going to carry this baby forever, did you?"

"Well . . . well . . ." Adam's anger dissolved, but he couldn't gather his thoughts.

At the stove, Frances had swung around, spoon in hand, with berry juice dripping onto the kitchen floor.

"Watch out, Frances—the spoon is making a mess on the floor," Liz said. She gave Adam a pointed look. "Help me into bed, then get Jake for me. I want him here. After that, run for Mother. I'm not having this baby without her."

Adam remained rooted in place, muscles too stiff with shock to move.

Liz pushed herself out of the rocker and slugged Adam on the arm. "Adam! For goodness' sake, stop acting like a ninny. You've been around at enough birthings to keep your wits about you this time."

Adam grabbed a deep breath. "Oh! Yes. Of course." He placed a shaky arm across her back and guided her to the bedroom. She sat on the edge of the bed, and he lifted her feet as carefully as if they were formed of spun glass, settling them on the mattress.

She nestled against the pillows. "Thank you, Adam."

"Now I'll get Jake." He moved to the door. "And then Mother." He returned to the side of the bed. He didn't know what to do with his hands, so he stuffed them into his trouser pockets.

Liz sighed. "Adam, Jake is in the east field, and Mother is probably at home in her kitchen. Do you think you can find them?"

Adam darted to the door again. "Yes, sure, I'll get them. I won't be long." Then he stomped back and delivered a kiss to his sister's forehead. "Take it easy, Sis."

Liz touched his cheek, a smile on her face. "*You* take it easy—I'm fine, really. And Frances is here with me, you know."

Samantha stepped into the doorway, the wooden spoon clutched in both hands. "What—what can I do for you?"

Liz smiled. "Stir the blueberries, Frances. I can't abide burnt preserves."

Chapter Ten

*I*f anyone had stopped to think about it, they might have found it amusing that the only calm person in the little house was Liz, who had the best reason for being distressed. Samantha knew by the low moans escaping Liz's throat that having a baby wasn't easy, but so far Liz seemed to take the whole thing in stride. Between those labor pains, as Liz called them, she smiled at her husband, squeezed his hand, and assured him that she was fine. Whenever another one hit, Jake leaned over his wife, his face contorted, seemingly in pain himself.

When Adam had returned, he'd brought not only Laura, but Si and Josie as well. Samantha watched Adam pause just long enough to peek in at Liz, with Jake now by her side, then rush off again to fetch Dr. Newton. Liz had told him to slow down or he'd give himself heat stroke, adding with a teasing smile that she wanted the doctor focused on her and the baby, not her brother. Adam had quipped back, "You always did have to be the center of attention," and Liz had laughed, then grabbed her midsection, face contorted again.

Samantha was relieved of her berry stirring by Josie, who said she absolutely *had* to have something to do, so Samantha busied herself hauling in water, heating some on the stove, and bringing extra sheets down from the *Schrank*, the shelved wardrobe that sat on the small landing at the top of the stairs. Mrs. Klaassen had indicated these items would be helpful, but no one else seemed to have the ability to go beyond planning to doing.

Josie stirred berries. Mr. Klaassen paced back and forth in the kitchen, hands behind his back, his brow furrowed. Mrs. Klaassen hovered beside Liz's bed, wiping her daughter's face with a cool cloth and murmuring to her in German, words Liz seemed to understand.

Jake kept a grip on his wife's hand, and his face grew more pale with each pain. He asked repeatedly, "When will Doc Newton get here?" No one had an answer.

Samantha, her tasks completed, stood at the window and watched for Adam to return. When she finally spotted him on horseback, followed closely by the doctor's little black buggy, she turned around excitedly. "Adam's here. The doctor, too."

Mr. Klaassen gave a huge sigh and went to the bedroom doorway to relay the news.

Although Adam pulled up first, the doctor beat him to the door. He was a small man with a narrow pencil line of a mustache, green eyes, snub nose, and short-cropped hair that stuck up in the back. His suit was rumpled as if slept in, and his wire-rimmed glasses sat on the tip of his nose in a way that made him appear absent-minded.

He acknowledged the people waiting in the main room of the house with a single nod but didn't slow down for pleasantries. He passed straight to the bedroom. "Jake, kiss your wife, then kindly leave. We'll all do better without you." As Jake reluctantly rose to obey, the doctor said, "Laura, please stay. I'm sure you'll be a comfort to Elizabeth here. And a help to me."

Jake paused in the doorway, and the doctor promptly shut the door in his face. Mr. Klaassen put his arm around his son-in-law's shoulder. "Come sit down, son. Liz is in good hands, and fretting and stewing won't speed things up any."

Samantha hid a smile. Mr. Klaassen was better at giving advice than he was at taking it; as soon as he got Jake settled at the table with a cup of buttermilk from the icebox, he took up his pacing again.

Adam entered the house, sweaty and breathless and smelling of horses. He went to his father. "Is Liz all right?"

Mr. Klaassen barely paused in his back-and-forth trek across the narrow floor. "The doc is in there, and your ma. Liz'll be fine." He paused to squeeze Jake's shoulder on the way by.

Josie turned from the stove. "Frances, where are Liz's canning jars? These preserves are ready to pour."

"In the cellar," Samantha said. She hated the underground cellar with its cobwebs and damp smell. With a little shudder, she reached for the cellar door at her feet.

Adam hurried over. "Let me do that."

Samantha nearly sagged in relief. "Thank you."

As soon as Adam retrieved the wooden box full of canning jars, Samantha slipped them into a large pot of boiling water along with their lids. After the jars were sterilized, Josie filled them and Adam sealed them tight. No banter accompanied their task. All ears were tilted toward the bedroom door, listening for any sound that would give a clue as to what was taking place behind that closed door.

The sparkling jars of preserves marched across the wooden work table like jewels. Lunchtime came and went without anyone even asking about eating. To Samantha, it felt like the whole house was laying in wait.

Late afternoon Mr. Klaassen and Adam headed out to take care of the milking and feeding the chickens and geese. Jake insisted on following them, though Samantha could tell the poor father-to-be was torn. Josie promised to fetch them immediately if anything happened. Josie and Samantha put together ham sandwiches and cut up radishes and carrots to go along with them.

"I'm not hungry," Josie admitted, piling vegetables into one of Liz's serving bowls, "but no one's had a bite since breakfast. We'll not be good for much if we don't eat."

The men returned and ate the simple meal. Samantha nibbled at half of a sandwich. She might have been eating sawdust for all she noticed it, but she did feel better after having a little something in her stomach.

Mr. Klaassen leaned back in his chair to let Josie reach his empty plate and glanced at the ticking clock on the wall. "After five . . . I guess I'd better run home and check on the children, then—"

A sound cut through the quiet kitchen. Every head turned toward the closed bedroom door. Jake jumped up and placed both hands flat against the paneled door, his face nearly pressed against the wood. Adam half stood, hands tensely pressing the tabletop. Mr. Klaassen covered his mouth with a shaky hand, and Josie reached blindly for Samantha who clutched at her, thankful to have something to hold onto.

Samantha had never heard a noise like that before. Low, guttural—a harsh, anguished sound that cut through the hearts of everyone in the room.

The doctor's voice, tense and authoritative, carried from behind the door. "Come on, Liz, bear down. Push, girl! I need your help."

Jake pressed his forehead to the door. His hands curled into tight fists and thumped at the wood softly. Si went over and placed a hand on the younger man's taut back. Adam crossed to stand between Josie and Samantha, and Josie turned into his chest, leaning against him. Samantha, so caught up in dismay of what could be happening to Liz, unthinkingly moved into his embrace. His arm coiled around her, holding her snug against his side. They stood thus, silent and straining for any further sound that could reassure them.

Then it came—a new, soft, mewling sound that brought joyous smiles to the faces of the listeners. Josie hugged Adam, crying against his neck.

Adam chuckled shakily. "It's all right now. No need to cry." But tears glinted in his brown eyes. A lump filled Samantha's throat. She swallowed hard, trying to dislodge it.

She suddenly became aware of Adam's arm around her waist and stepped quickly away.

The bedroom door opened, and Mrs. Klaassen stepped out. She moved directly into her husband's arms, a weary smile on her face. With her cheek pressed to Mr. Klaassen's chest, she held out her hand to Jake. "Congratulations, Papa, you've got a fine-looking son."

Jake took a deep breath and then smiled so wide the room seemed lit by his happiness. "Can I see him—and my wife?" He turned toward the bedroom door.

"The doctor will call you in just a moment." Mrs. Klaassen stepped away from Mr. Klaassen and wrapped Jake in a hug.

Samantha stood to the side while the others buzzed happily, congratulating Jake and asking Mrs. Klaassen how things had gone. Their happy news sharing ended abruptly, however, when the doctor's voice called out. "Mrs. Klaassen, come here—quickly! I need you."

She shot a panicked look at Mr. Klaassen before disappearing once more into the bedroom and closing the door firmly behind her. Everyone froze in place, not daring to look at one another. Liz's moaning, a baby's weak cry, and the doctor's and Laura's hushed, frantic voices carried from the other room.

Samantha thought her heart might burst, it banged so hard against her ribs. What was happening in there?

Mr. Klaassen stretched his arms wide. "Jake, Adam . . ." His voice, gravelly with emotion, held authority. "Come. Josie, Frances—you, too. Come close. We will pray."

Samantha skittered to the circle and took hold of Josie and Adam's hands. They bowed, their heads almost touching, hands squeezing tightly. Samantha, unfamiliar with praying, wasn't sure what to do, but she found her thoughts begging someone, someplace. *Oh, please, please, let Liz be okay. And the little baby, too. Keep them both safe for Jake—he loves them and needs them so much.*

It seemed hours passed before a creak announced the opening of the bedroom door. Samantha spun toward the opening with the rest of them. The doctor stepped out and released a heavy sigh. He pulled a wrinkled handkerchief out of his pocket and wiped his face.

Jake crossed to him, his fingers woven together. "Dr. Newton, Liz—is she . . . ?"

Dr. Newton reached out and put a hand on Jake's shoulder. "Liz is fine, Jake. She's had a rough time of it. The baby was breech. She'll be down for a while, but she'll be fine."

Jake blew out a relieved breath, then looked straight into the doctor's face. "The baby . . . my son—?"

"That wife of yours is sure one for surprises," the doctor responded with a shake of his head. He expelled a huff of laughter. "Go on in. I think she should be the one to share the news." He headed for the door, still shaking his head and chuckling softly.

Jake frowned in confusion. He stepped into the bedroom and crossed quickly to the bed. Samantha trailed behind the others, straining to peek over their shoulders. Jake sat on the edge of the bed, his broad back blocking Liz from view, but his shout nearly raised the rafters. "Why, Liz Stoesz! No *wonder* you were as big as a house."

A tinkling laugh—Liz's—rang out. "No shouting. You'll wake them."

Samantha's gasp was echoed around the circle crowding against the doorway. *Them?*

The group surged forward. Mr. Klaassen rushed to his wife's side, and Adam and Josie followed, stopping at the foot of the bed. Samantha came more slowly, afraid of intruding but unable to resist. She stood close to Josie and gaped at the extraordinary scene.

Two tiny bundles snuggled securely in Liz's arms. Liz looked pale and weak but undeniably happy. "Can you believe it, Mother? Twins."

Jake beamed. "Two sons, Simon. Liz has given me *two sons*."

Mr. Klaassen leaned in and deposited a kiss on Liz's sweaty forehead. "They're just beautiful, Liz."

Liz smiled. "Yes, they are, Papa. The most beautiful babies ever."

Samantha thought they were about as attractive as newborn baby birds, but she kept the comment to herself. Besides, it didn't seem to matter much what they looked like. They were fine, and Liz was fine. Her heart bumped in her chest. Someone had heard their prayers.

Liz adjusted the blanket more snugly around the baby boy on her right. "We do have a small problem, though."

Jake's eyebrows raised. "How on earth can we have a problem?"

She touched the fuzzy dark hair on the head of the baby on her left. "This one is Jacob Andrew. He was born first, so he should be given the name we chose. But we can't name his brother Amanda Joy, now can we?" A hint of teasing had entered Liz's otherwise frail voice.

Jake laughed and stroked the cheek of the unnamed baby. "No, I suppose we can't." The baby puckered up a tiny mouth and twisted his head within the confines of the blanket.

"So we have a problem," Liz said.

"Not much of one." Jake turned to Adam. "Uncle Adam, how would you feel about having a little namesake?"

Adam looked dumbstruck. "A—a namesake? Why, I—I—."

Liz touched Jake's hand. "Perhaps Adam would like to save that for his own little boy someday, Jake."

Adam shook his head. "No, Liz. I mean, yes, maybe someday I'll have a son, but I never considered naming him after myself. I'd be honored to have the baby given my name."

Jake turned back to Liz. "Little Jacob Andrew was named for my pa and me. How about we name his brother for Adam and your pa's middle name? Adam James?"

Mr. Klaassen nodded sagely. "I like that idea."

"That sounds fine." Liz yawned behind her hand.

Mrs. Klaassen waved her hands at those gathered around the bed. "Come now, everyone out. Liz has labored harder today than any of you, and she needs her rest." She leaned over the bed to kiss first Liz, then the heads of each of her new grandsons. "*Schlop Die gesunt, kleine mudder,*" Mrs. Klaassen whispered.

Josie whispered to Samantha, "She means 'sleep well, little mother.' "

Liz's eyelids drifted closed.

Everyone quietly left the room, Samantha once again trailing behind. When Adam reached the door, he paused and looked back. A smile lifted the corners of his lips, and somehow Samantha knew he was looking at his little namesake.

He turned to her. "It's something, Frances, having a baby named in your honor," he said, his voice low. He placed a palm on his chest. "I feel so proud. And responsible." Sucking in a breath, he lifted his chin. "I want to always be the kind of example little Adam can look up to."

Samantha, observing the determination in Adam's eyes, experienced a funny swelling in her chest. Adam was so unlike the men she'd known before. He could be moved by the coming of a baby, and he wasn't ashamed to show it. He seemed more manly than any of the tough, hard-nosed men in her past.

She closed the bedroom door behind the little group, sealing the new mother and babies away together. Mr. and Mrs. Klaassen each gave Jake a hug, and then Mr. Klaassen asked Adam to hitch the horses back up to the wagon. "We need to head home and share the good news with the others."

Josie caught her mother's hand. "Ma, can I stay here tonight? I can help Frances, and I'd like to hold one of the babies yet before I go home."

Mrs. Klaassen looked at Jake. "Is it all right with you?"

Jake nodded. He stood so tall and proud. "That's fine. She can bunk with Frances, and—." He slapped a palm to his forehead. "Oh, no!"

Everyone started, and Mr. Klaassen bolted forward and grasped Jake's arm. "What's wrong?"

Jake blinked twice, his jaw hanging open. "I just realized—I'm going to need another cradle."

Chapter Eleven

*S*amantha settled into a routine as comfortably as a pair of old slippers. Her days were filled with household chores and garden work that she found to be mostly enjoyable. Her nights were sometimes disturbed by the sound of a tiny cry from downstairs, then another one, but she just put her pillow over her head and went back to sleep.

Liz devoted her time to caring for the two small boys who grew more plump and attractive each day. Samantha loved those times when Liz called to her to hold one of them while she nursed the other. They looked so much alike that most couldn't decide which was Andy and which was A.J., as Jake called them. Liz, however, could determine which one was fussing when a pathetic, hiccupping wail trailed to her ears. These first weeks of their life, they shared the bedroom with their parents, tucked side by side in a dresser drawer set securely on a small table. And Jake was busy fashioning another cradle for when the two would move to the bedroom across from Samantha.

She grew, too, during the last days of summer, in contentment and self-confidence as she successfully handled the responsibilities bestowed upon her. And she did earn that four dollars a week. She'd never canned vegetables before, but with Liz in her rocker, handing out instructions in her patient voice that reminded Samantha so much of Mrs. Klaassen, Samantha put up quart jars of green beans, tomatoes, carrots, and corn. She even pickled beets. She made herself overcome her fears about the cellar, and she couldn't help but smile when she had all those winter provisions lined up on the wooden shelves down below.

She baked bread for the family's consumption, washed loads and loads of tiny flannel diapers and gowns, gathered eggs, kept the house clean. . . . The workload was never-ending, but not once did she complain. When she dropped into bed at night, exhausted, it was a happy exhaustion that she'd not known a person could feel. It was so wonderful to be needed, and to be appreciated, to maybe even be loved. . . .

One thing bothered her, though—living a lie all this time. Samantha admired Liz and Jake and the whole Klaassen family so much, and she wanted to be honest with them and confess she wasn't Frances Welch. At first it had seemed clever to fool them, but as she'd gotten to know them and be accepted into their loving family unit, her conscience pricked each time one of them called her Frances. She longed to tell them who she really was, but one fear always stopped her. Her pa. If they knew her real name, then the sheriff would send her name down the line, and sooner or later Pa would arrive to take her back home.

Home. Already this place, Mountain Lake, Minnesota, was far more home than the house where she grew up had ever been. Even when Gran was alive it hadn't truly been the kind of home where the people within its walls loved and respected one another. Samantha hadn't even known that kind of family was possible until coming to the Klaassens. Gran's loving presence had made those early years bearable, but Samantha knew now all that she had missed.

Whenever her conscience started bothering her again, she got busy with something else and sent those uncomfortable thoughts far away. She wasn't willing to give up what she had now—not just yet.

Harvest was well under way by the second week of September along with the beginning of the school year. Samantha watched children walking along the road early in the morning, swinging their tin lunch pails and carrying books and tablets. Deep inside she couldn't help but envy them. When Josie stopped by on the way home in the afternoon for a visit with her nephews, she reported anecdotes from the school day, and Samantha secretly wondered what it would be like to go, too.

She'd been a better-than-average student at the school in Milwaukee. But with the kind of life she lived, she was always a misfit. School was a lonely place. Samantha wondered if things would be different here, going with Josie, Arn, and the others. Then she remembered Priscilla Koehn and decided it was best to stay away. Besides, once harvest ended, Liz wouldn't need her any longer. Another four weeks or so, and she'd need to move on.

But where?

Adam loved harvest time. Being outside in the fields, smelling the scent of fresh-cut grain, bantering with the men with spirits as high as his, working hard and sweating much. . . . He couldn't help himself. Farming was in his blood, and he'd been quite young when he knew he would be staying near the family homestead and farming with his father, taking over when Pa decided he was too old to continue. Adam had helped with harvests since his thirteenth birthday, delaying school the first weeks until the work was done. It had never bothered him to work rather than be there at the start of school. He always caught up and never felt at a disadvantage; his education was in the fields too.

Arn, now fifteen, didn't share Adam's enthusiasm for farming, however. Adam occasionally caught the younger boy looking off toward the schoolhouse during those days when harvesting and school overlapped. He was expected to help with harvest, but he wasn't required to enjoy it. Although Arn was fast developing the husky build of his farm-loving brothers, he didn't possess the farmer's heart. Adam figured when Arn was grown, his vocation would be closer to Daniel's than Pa's. Another man might feel threatened by the realization that his son didn't want to follow in his footsteps, but Adam knew Pa would support Arn's decision in whatever job choice he made, as long as he was satisfied with it.

Adam scraped fallen stalks of wheat together with a long, wooden rake, his thoughts wandering to Liz and Jake's house. He remembered holding little Adam James for the first time. The baby had fit snugly in the crook of his arm, a warm and soft bundle with a certain smell better than his mother's best meal. When he had touched a finger to the baby's palm, A.J. had curled his tiny hand around Adam's work-roughened finger. Liz explained it was a reflex reaction, but Adam preferred to think the little boy was accepting him as his uncle, the one for whom he'd been named.

He remembered something else: when he'd looked up right then, he'd caught Frances watching him with an expression on her face he couldn't quite read. Gentle, tender, and maybe a little sad. When their eyes met, she'd colored prettily and looked away, fussing with her braid in a peculiar way. Had he embarrassed her somehow? The girl remained a puzzle in many ways.

The sullen, defensive girl he'd tackled in the street seemed to be long gone. This new one—although never overtly outgoing—now could offer a warm smile and engage in conversation. He reflected on the morning in the blueberry patch when she'd teased him a little bit. She was uncommonly pretty with that wild mane of hair and unusual pale blue eyes. If the new, warmer, more open side of her was for real, he could imagine being attracted to her. . . .

The thought brought Adam up short. He stopped raking. *Attracted?* Yes, she was appealing, both in looks and personality. That spunk was still there, and from someone so small it was both cute and endearing.

But could he think of her *that way?* An image—the shy way she behaved when he spotted her observing him with the baby—filled his mind. He swallowed. Could it be possible that *she* was thinking of *him* that way . . . ?

"Adam?" His father's voice cut into his thoughts. He turned his head to locate Pa.

"It's not lunchtime yet, son. Keep 'er moving."

Adam nodded and began raking in earnest. He'd have to give his feelings for Frances Welch some serious consideration. *When the work is done.*

⌒⊙

Wednesday evening at supper time, Jake paused with fork in hand and sent a serious look across the table to Samantha. "Frances, starting tomorrow, I'm afraid you're in for it."

Samantha's stomach turned a flip. She looked up from cutting a bite of her chicken. "What do you mean?"

Jake chuckled. "Don't look so worried, goofy. I'm not planning to string you up by your fingernails. But after the next few days, that might look pretty good, just to get out of the work. Next Monday the harvest crew will begin in my fields. That means you and Liz will be responsible for fixing them breakfast, lunch, and two snacks during the day. It's a heap of cooking, and Liz is still pretty tied down with Andy and A.J. So the majority of the work will fall to you."

Samantha breathed easier, then swallowed. "I'm okay at cooking for *us*, I guess." She glanced across the bowls and serving plates filling the center of the table. The fried chicken was crisp and tasty, the boiled potatoes and gravy passable, and she'd flavored the green beans with some chopped onion. Even her bread was getting to be as good as Liz's had ever been. "But I've never cooked for that many people before. . . ."

Liz reached across little Andy, who nearly dozed at her breast, and patted Samantha's arm. "Now, Frances, one thing you need to keep in mind; when those men come in, they're so hungry you could feed them boot leather. They wouldn't complain as long as you provided salt and pepper to season it. You're a fine cook, and I'll help you judge amounts so we're sure to have enough. I cooked for the last two harvest crews, and I wasn't any older than you the first time. You'll do fine."

Samantha nibbled her lower lip, still uncertain. "Well, if you can supervise, I guess I can do it." Andy had fallen asleep, his little mouth drooping open as he relaxed. She reached for the baby. "Give Andy to me. I'll carry him up to bed so you can eat your supper without droppin' anything on him."

Liz laughed softly and relinquished her bundle. "Thank you. It would be nice to finish my supper without having to lean over a little body."

Samantha cuddled Andy close as she mounted the stairs. It felt good, holding him. At first she'd been nervous to even touch the babies, but Liz had assured her they wouldn't break, and soon she learned the enjoyment of doing things for them. Of course Liz took care of most of their needs, but there were times, like now, when an extra pair of hands was very useful.

Useful. Samantha savored the word. Before coming here, she'd felt more useless than anything. As she tucked Andy into his cradle, Samantha hummed softly. She rubbed Andy's tiny back until she was sure he was sound asleep. Smiling, she leaned down and placed a kiss on the slumbering infant's moist neck, then turned to the other cradle.

Baby A.J. lay on his side, his nearly transparent eyelids quivering. As Samantha watched, he stretched one arm upward toward his nose, curled his hand into a tiny fist, then let it relax again, bringing the arm back down. His rosebud mouth puckered, and he made a soft sucking sound. He was waking, and no doubt would soon squall to be fed.

To be sure he wouldn't disturb his sleeping brother, Samantha scooped him up and tiptoed out of the room. She paused at the top of the stairs, holding the baby nearly beneath her chin, breathing in his scent. Andy and A.J. looked alike—two peas in a pod, Mr. Klaassen laughingly called them—but over the weeks Samantha had learned which was which by observing their distinctive personalities.

A.J. wasn't quite as demanding as his brother—when Andy wanted something, you'd better get it quick or prepare for a storm! A.J. seemed to enjoy snuggling more than Andy, and he was more relaxed—easier to placate. Although she felt stirrings of love for both little boys—in their helplessness, their darling little faces, how could she not?—she admitted to herself that she found herself favoring little Adam.

She walked slowly downstairs with the now-awake baby, who peered up at her curiously. His tiny dimpled hand grazed her cheek, and she tipped her face—better to feel the softness of his palm. Jake certainly had named this baby aptly. He seemed to have inherited his uncle's mild disposition and loving spirit.

Samantha sat back down at the table, A.J. cradled in her arm.

Liz looked over. "Is he ready to eat now?"

"He was waking up, so I brought him down in case he decided to howl." Samantha pressed her cheek to the baby's downy hair. He wriggled, nestling closer, and she smiled. She was learning the joy of touching and being touched by the tiniest of teachers. "I'll hold him while you finish up, long as he stays quiet."

Jake held out his arms. "Here, let me have him, Frances. I've not been around enough during the day lately to really enjoy my boys. I'll hold him while you get the clean-up started."

"Well, I guess his papa can have him," Samantha quipped as she slowly rose and handed little A.J. to Jake.

As she started to pick up the dishes from the table, Jake added, "You'll probably want to turn in early tonight. We're working you extra hard these days until harvest is done."

Samantha nodded. That's why she was here. But *when the crops are in, what then?*

amantha woke promptly at five o'clock Monday morning, the crowing of the rooster signaling the sun's arrival and the dawn of another day helping Liz. She yawned, snuggling into her pillow for an extra few minutes of rest. Then she remembered today was the start of the harvest crew coming to work in Jake's fields. Throwing the covers aside, she hooked her heels over the edge of the mattress and pulled herself out of bed. An all-over stretch completed, she squinted into the early morning gloom.

Her fuzzy gaze located a shadow . . . of something . . . next to the door that hadn't been there the night before. She rubbed her eyes and looked again. A dress. Curious, Samantha lightly ran across the floor and pulled the frock from a nail next to the doorjamb. Holding it toward the little bit of light flowing through her window, she checked it over. Pink-and-white-checked fabric proved faded at the elbows, and the skirt bore a short, stitched-closed tear. So it wasn't new. *Must be a hand-me-down from Liz.*

She fingered the collar, trying to decide what to do. She glanced to the overalls and flannel shirt draped over the small chair in the corner. The bulky clothes were so hot and uncomfortable. And they needed washing—again. It was hard to get the heavy materials dry enough to wear the next morning. She held the dress against herself, imagining how much cooler it would be than the britches and shirt.

The decision made, she slipped out of her nightgown and into the dress. As she fastened the buttons up the front, she noted it was a bit loose, but she could easily take it in if Liz loaned her a needle and thread. She pulled on stockings and boots, then tiptoed down the stairs, wincing at the one that squeaked. Liz was already at the stove, measuring coffee into the blue enamel pot. She turned when Samantha entered, and a smile lit her face.

"You found the dress. Does it fit?"

Samantha smoothed the skirt. "Pretty much."

Liz crossed to Samantha and pinched the fabric, pulling it away from Samantha's waist. She chuckled. " 'Pretty much,' she says. At least two sizes too big!" She placed her hands on her hips and shook her head. "You're much smaller than I ever remember being, even before the twins added to my girth. But it'll do, I suppose, in a pinch. I can take it in for you when I get a minute."

Samantha toyed with the buttons, a question hovering in the back of her mind. She'd been here for several weeks already, shuffling around in her makeshift clothing. Why was Liz giving this to her now? Before Samantha lost her nerve, she blurted a simple question. "Why'd you give it me?"

Liz's cheeks blazed pink. She said, "I should have done it much sooner, Frances, but, well, Ma said you seemed really determined to wear . . . your own clothing, so I was a little shy about bringing it up." She turned back to the stove to move the boiling coffee off the burner.

"So why now?" Samantha pressed.

"Frances, I need to tell you something, but—but I don't want to hurt your feelings."

Samantha shrugged.

Liz lifted a skillet onto the stove's top and fidgeted with the handle, her lips pursed in an embarrassed grimace. "Jake is rather old-fashioned, and while he likes you very much, he—well, he's a little uncomfortable with you wearing boys' clothes," she finished in a rush.

Samantha felt herself bristling, her defenses rising. "Well, those are all the clothes I've got. I've been so busy, I haven't had time for dress sewing."

Liz stepped toward Samantha, her hands reaching without touching her. "Oh, Frances, I know we've kept you awfully busy, and neither of us is faulting you for the clothes you wear. It's more my fault than anyone's. It's just that—well, with the harvest crew here and all, Jake was hoping I might be able to persuade you to wear one of my dresses." Liz blew out a breath and lifted her hands, palms up. "Some of the men might snicker and poke fun, and we'd feel terrible if you were . . ." She started over. "We'd feel a lot better if you were in a dress. There."

Samantha stared at Liz in amazement. Not once had she imagined that Jake didn't approve of her overalls. They were hot and uncomfortable, but they were the only clothing that was hers. Well, actually, they were "borrowed" too. And while she'd been wishing she had something else to wear, Jake and Liz had been secretly wishing the same thing. Amusement chased her defensiveness away, and she released a bubble of laughter.

Liz offered a lopsided grin. "You aren't upset with me?"

Samantha shook her head. "No, I'm relieved I won't have to drag myself around in those durn overalls one more day."

Liz laughed too and threw an arm around Samantha's shoulders for a quick squeeze. "I'm glad, too." And they shared a smile.

Samantha stepped away from Liz's embrace. "I'll get to the milking now." She scooped up the bucket beside the kitchen stove and headed outside. The sun formed a bold white arc on the horizon, flooding the fields with a shimmer of gold. Samantha paused to admire the sight. A smile tugged at her lips. It'd be a golden day for sure. And she sure would be cooler.

❧

Samantha lugged back a pail of milk, and promptly at six o'clock, as Liz had predicted, stomping feet on the front stoop alerted Samantha to the harvesters' arrival. She poured batter into the sizzling pan as Jake threw open the door and shushed the men's greetings with a finger against his lips. "The babies are still sleeping." The men nodded their understanding, walking in as if on eggshells.

Samantha hid an amused grin. Grown men tiptoeing with hunched shoulders and tightly pursed lips looked rather funny. But they wasted no time seating themselves. Normally there were only four chairs at the round table, but Jake had hauled in some old nail kegs and wooden boxes from the barn to create makeshift seating. Eight of the men crowded around the table, their elbows pressed together. The rest caught a seat wherever they could and balanced plates on their laps.

Liz and Samantha served up fried eggs, fried potatoes, pancakes, *zwieback*, and coffee. Samantha stayed beside the stove, frying more pancakes as needed, while Liz made her rounds refilling coffee cups, holding out a jar of preserves for sweetening the *zwieback*, and carrying plates back and forth between the stove and the men needing "just a couple more o' those pancakes" or "a good-size spoon a' them potatoes, please."

Samantha glanced over at the table to see Adam watching her, but he looked away. She would have liked to ask after Mrs. Klaassen, Josie, Becky, and the little kids—but there wasn't the time between the requests for refills.

As Liz prepared to fork the last pancake onto her father's plate, one of the babies upstairs began to tune up. She flicked a glance at Samantha. "Uh-oh . . ."

Samantha took over Liz's tasks, and Liz darted toward the stairs, wiping her hands on her apron as she went.

Mr. Klaassen ignored the pancake on his plate, grinning from ear to ear. "I was hoping they'd wake up before we headed out. Haven't seen those little guys in over a week."

Since it was now unnecessary to be quiet, a big-boned man named Elmer Harms laughed heartily. "I betcha they're growin' like weeds, huh, Jake?"

"Oh, sure," Jake said. "We'll have them out milking cows in another week or so."

The men laughed, then all eyes turned toward the stairway as Liz descended, a baby on each arm.

Samantha moved out of the way as several of them forged forward to take a look at the twins, reaching out thick fingers to poke at tiny tummies or ruffle their downy hair. Andy and A.J. seemed to take it all in with big, curious eyes for about two minutes before deciding being wet and hungry outweighed being cute and entertaining. First Andy opened his mouth to yell, and A.J.—no doubt startled by his brother—joined in. The men backed off, and Liz shut herself in the bedroom with the babies to change their diapers and give them breakfast.

The group began filing out the door, placing empty plates on the dry sink as they went. Adam was last in line. He paused, offering Samantha an apologetic look. "I guess you're the whole cleanup crew, huh?"

"I guess so." Samantha surveyed the pile of dishes, forks, cups, and skillets. She hoped there'd be time to get everything washed before she had to make lunch.

"I'd stay and give you a hand, but . . ." He gestured toward the open door. Out in the yard, men were clambering into a waiting wagon.

Samantha gave a little sniff and waved both hands at him in dismissal. "Oh, go on, do your work and let me do mine." She softened the command with a teasing grin.

He bowed at the waist, his eyes showing a mischievous sparkle. "Yes, Your Highness." He headed for the doorway, but before stepping through he paused and glanced over his shoulder. "By the way, you look right nice this morning, Miss Frances."

Fire ignited in Samantha's face. Overwhelmed by the emotions his simple comment raised, she spun, presenting her back to him. She held her breath, willing her galloping pulse to calm. When she felt she could speak, she turned to thank him for his kindness. An empty doorway greeted her eyes.

She dashed to the door and peered out in time to see the wagon roll out of the yard, a puff of dust rising from its wheels. She couldn't distinguish Adam from the other workers. Crestfallen, she shuffled back into the kitchen. Then she squared her shoulders. Liz had said Samantha would need to take a snack to the fields midmorning. She'd make sure to thank Adam then.

Cheerfulness restored, she set to work washing up, humming a little tune she sang to the babies when she was sure no one could hear her.

Despite the hearty breakfast, Adam's stomach was growling well before noon. Pa had assigned him the task of following the reaper and forking cut stalks into the hay wagon. His arms ached, straw and dust clung to his clothes, and the sun baked his head. He wished he knew how long it would be till their morning break when he could rest in the shade of the hedge apple windbreak, enjoy a drink of water, and eat a sandwich

. . . or whatever Liz might send out. And eagerness to see Frances again nibbled at the corners of his mind. Well, more than nibbled—it was taking over.

An image of her at Liz's stove, the rosy flush in her cheeks matching the pale pink checks of the dress, filled his mind's eye. She'd looked so pretty, thick hair pulled back into a wavy tail, neat apron tied around her narrow waist. Her weeks in Mountain Lake had put a little weight on her reed-thin frame, and although she was still slender, she now looked healthy rather than half starved.

But more than her physical changes held Adam captive. The relaxed curve of her lips and the spark of teasing in her eyes made his pulse stutter. What would she look like—and how would he react—if she ever completely released her guard and returned a full-fledged smile? He tried to imagine it, but a picture wouldn't form. How he wanted to coax a real smile to her lovely face.

A shrill whistle cut through Adam's reflections, and just ahead Ed drew the team pulling the reaper to a halt. Adam saw Jake at the edge of the field, waving his hands. "Come on in! Snack's here!"

Adam squinted against the sun and then frowned. Frances—astride Liz's sorrel mare—had brought out the promised snack, but she was wearing her old overalls and shirt again. He leaned the hay fork on the reaper and trudged in, apprehension swirling through his gut. Had his compliment embarrassed her enough to return to those clumsy britches and plaid shirt?

She unhooked a burlap bag from the saddle horn and handed it to Jake, then slid down unassisted. Strands of hair had pulled loose from the piece of yarn and blew around her cheeks. She stayed near the horse, placing paper-wrapped sandwiches into the men's hands as they filed by, her gaze low.

At each man's thank you, she offered a brief nod. Adam received his sandwich and paused, hoping she might look up, but she shifted her gaze behind him as if looking for the next worker to be fed. Disappointed, he moved out of the way so Lucas, Jake's youngest brother, could step up.

To further Adam's frustration, Lucas opened his sandwich right there in the sun next to Frances, one arm draped over the saddle's smooth seat and the other gesturing with the sandwich. Adam sat in the shade with the other men, his gaze pinned on Lucas talking so easily and friendly-like with Frances. She lifted her chin, crinkling her nose when the sun hit her full-face, and Adam watched her lips move as she answered Lucas. Lucas laughed hard at whatever she'd said, and jealousy smacked Adam with such force he couldn't finish his sandwich.

He leaped up, determined to figure out how to send Lucas away from Frances, but before he made it halfway to them, Jake sidelined him with a smack on the shoulder. "All right, everyone, let's get back to it!" he called.

With a small groan, Adam turned his steps toward the field. But he angled his gaze over his shoulder, keeping watch on Lucas. He clenched his teeth together when he saw how Lucas linked his hands, offering Frances a leg up into the saddle, and she accepted. Astride the horse again, the empty bag curled in her fist, she gave a little wave—to Lucas!—and pulled the reins so the horse aimed for the road.

Adam watched until the horse disappeared in a puff of dust, but Frances never looked back.

Chapter Thirteen

*A*s Samantha rode back down the road toward Liz and Jake's place, she reflected on the brief conversation with Jake's brother, Lucas. She'd never engaged in idle chitchat with a young man before, and even though she'd had trouble thinking of responses to what she recognized as his flirting, she'd found their little exchange enjoyable. His attention had given her a lighthearted, pleasantly female feeling that was new and exciting.

The moment she returned, Liz called over her shoulder, "I put the pies you fixed up this morning in the oven, but there's much to do to be ready for lunch. And I've soon got to feed. . . ."

Samantha heard the rest of the sentence as she headed for the stairs. She'd asked Liz earlier if it would be okay to change into her overalls so she could ride astride Liz's horse, and Liz quickly agreed. She was sure Jake wouldn't mind when he realized her reason. But the flannel shirt and heavy overalls felt even heavier and more cloying than ever, and the pink-checked dress beckoned to her.

"Where are you going?" Liz called to her.

"I'm gonna change—"

"There's not time for anything but cooking, Frances." Liz's voice and face held an uncharacteristic note of impatience. "Those men'll be hungry and won't want to waste daylight hours waiting for us to put lunch on the table. Let's get busy."

With a sigh, Samantha changed direction and got to work readying the two fresh-killed chickens for the stew pot. While the chickens simmered, Samantha set up a makeshift table in the side yard, placing several long planks over a pair of wooden sawhorses. Perspiration rolled down her forehead as she surrounded the table with the chairs, boxes, and kegs the men had used at breakfast time. Oh, how she missed the coolness of that loose-fitting dress! On the other hand, dragging planks and sawhorses around seemed to call for overalls.

The wagonload of men rumbled onto the yard promptly at noon, and, after washing up at the pump, they gathered around the improvised picnic table for their lunch of the stewed chicken, corn on the cob, sliced tomatoes, pickles, mashed potatoes, *zwieback*, coffee, and apple pie. Samantha tripped around the table in her ungainly overalls, making certain the cups stayed filled and the men's needs were met.

Unlike breakfast's low murmurs, the men now chatted and laughed boisterously, telling wild stories about hunting trips and other harvest experiences, and ribbing Frank Klaassen about having to spend so much time away from courting his Anna. Frank took it well, though his ears glowed red. Samantha had determined his temperament wasn't as even as Adam's, and it looked like the men were having a good time trying to get him riled.

"Yeah, yeah, Frank," one of the men—Samantha thought his name was Girard—hollered from his end of the table, "ya' can't be away from 'em too long, or they lose interest. Gotta keep plyin' 'em with sweet talk and posies. Can't do much o' that when you're workin' mornin', noon, and night." The man slapped his knee and guffawed.

Frank gave the older man a quick frown. "Reckon not."

The man across the table from Frank pointed with his fork. "'Course that Anna, she's still a schoolgirl. Got her days pretty well filled up with book learnin'. The mornin's shouldn't be much of a problem—ya' just needs to worry 'bout the evenin's."

"Uh-huh, you got that right." Girard apparently enjoyed being in the middle of things, as he jumped in again, twinkling eyes pinned on Frank. "I heard the new school teacher, man named Reimer, is not too bad to look at, an' not a whole lot older'n Frank here. Anna bein' free these days might look a mighty good prospect. . . ." Another loud laugh.

Frank's lips formed a tight line, his shoulders bunching.

Adam cut in, his voice calm. "I'm sure Frank and Anna have things pretty well arranged between them."

Samantha nearly heaved a sigh of relief when Girard shrugged and turned his attention to his plate.

The man named Ed poked Adam with his elbow. "How 'bout you, Adam? You got things 'arranged' with some special young lady?"

Samantha paused, coffeepot clutched in her hands as an odd feeling tiptoed through her middle. She held her breath, awaiting Adam's response. But instead it was Lucas who called an answer from across the table.

"Adam may not have much to do with it, but that pretty little Priscilla Koehn seems to be workin' on arrangin' somethin' with him. She sure was eyeballin' you at church a Sunday or two ago, Adam." He spun, fixing his smile on Samantha. "You were talkin' to her, Frances. Did she say happen to say anything to you about likin' Adam?"

Samantha gave Adam a quick glance. To be a part of the group, she would have liked to join in the teasing—but the strange feeling that filled her at the idea of Adam with some special gal held her tongue. She finally said, "Maybe she did, and maybe she didn't. A lady wouldn't be tellin' secrets, so keep me out of it."

The men laughed loudly, and one of them elbowed Lucas. "Not many females around who won't spread a good piece of gossip. Reckon we got ourselves a real special one here. 'Course, it's hard to tell if she's a lady or not, since she's covered head to toe in a pair of men's pants."

The men roared again. Samantha scowled, wishing she could whack the man over the head with the coffeepot. He should leave her and her britches alone!

Ed's neighbor whistled and leaned toward Adam. "You could do a lot worse than Priscilla Koehn, Adam, boy. Priscilla's a mighty lovely little lady. She'd look right smart on your arm."

Samantha stifled a snort. Adam had more sense than to get himself involved with a shallow little flirt like Priscilla. She cocked an ear to catch his reply.

"You fellows might oughtta concentrate a little harder on your plates before those of us more interested in eating than yapping finish it all and you end up without second helpings." While the rest seemed to consider that prospect, Adam motioned to Samantha. "Frances, I sure would appreciate another piece of pie. Did you bake them?"

Samantha nodded, heart pounding.

"They're every bit as good as Mother's."

Pleasure raised gooseflesh across her arms. She retrieved the pie pan and hurried to his side. As she scooped a sizable wedge onto his plate, he said in a near-whisper, "I liked the dress, but I suppose it would be hard to ride Tess in it."

Suddenly she got a mental picture of the dainty Priscilla with her perfect curls and impeccable clothing. Priscilla wouldn't be caught dead wearing a pair of men's oversized overalls. That same feeling—which she now recognized as jealousy—flooded her as she imagined Adam and Priscilla walking arm in arm.

The feeling welled up and spilled out in a tart hiss. "My britches are better suited to a lot of things, horse riding included." She stuck her nose in the air, turned on a bare heel, and thumped back into the kitchen. Once inside, her anger deflated. She placed her hands on her warm cheeks and berated herself. Why had she responded like that? He'd complimented her on how she looked in the dress, then complimented her pies. And she'd returned the favor by being peevish.

Samantha sighed. What an addlepated fool she was, repaying a kindness with a fit of impatience. But maybe she could fix it. Quickly, before she could change her mind, she dashed up to her room and changed back into the dress. She took an additional few minutes to brush her willful hair into a neat braid and formed a bow of yarn at the curling end. Back down she ran, only to step out into an empty yard, save Liz who was cleaning up.

Samantha's heart sagged. She had wanted Adam to see that she could be a lady. It was as close to an apology as she could make herself give. But she was too late. He, along with the others, had already headed back to the fields. A lump filled her throat as she considered how her golden day had ended.

With a sigh, she moved to the table and began to stack dirty dishes. And if she carried Adam's plate a little tighter than the others, it was no one's business but her own.

The harvest crew spent five days in Jake's fields before all the wheat was cut, raked, threshed, and scooped into baskets to be transported to the railroad. The days passed in a blur for Samantha, who kept so busy she almost felt as if she walked in her sleep at times. She'd worn Liz's dress continually after the first day, sitting sidesaddle for the trips out with snacks, but Adam hadn't made any further comment, and she found herself growing irritated with him for not noticing and with herself for worrying so much about it.

When the next Sunday arrived, Liz, Jake, the twins, and Samantha were invited to have dinner with Laura and Si. Samantha started in about wanting to stay at the house rather than go to church, but Liz took her aside. "I could really use you there, Frances. It's Jake's turn to lead the singing, so I'll be left holding both babies. Please, won't you come along and help me with the boys?"

Samantha grudgingly agreed and sat on the bench beside Liz, cuddling little A.J., who slept contentedly through the whole service. Not until midservice did she realize Liz's mother would have gladly held one of her grandsons while Jake was at the front of the church. Apparently church attendance was important enough to Liz for her to use some wiles to get Samantha there. She shot a glance at Liz and caught her employer's attentive expression as she listened to the minister. Samantha turned her focus to the front.

Her earliest church experiences had taken place when she was quite young, so she didn't have many memories from that time. But she did seem to recall the preacher at Gran's place of worship doing a lot of Bible thumping and thundering at his congregation. This minister, Reverend Goertzen, was so soft-spoken, one had to strain to catch his words.

Samantha found her attention captured when the man started reading from the book of John. "'Greater love hath no man than this, that he lay down his life for his friends.'" He paused to look around at the little congregation. "This, then, is what our Lord and Savior did for us: He gave up His own life, that we might have redemption for our sins. He claimed us as His friends, even before He knew us. How humbling to think that this perfect person, God's holy Son, could love us enough to die for us."

Samantha shifted in her seat. Humbling, the minister said, and he was right. But the preacher couldn't possibly mean her when he said "us." After all her wrongs, she surely didn't deserve the love of God.

The minister continued. "We wonder, how can we deserve that kind of love?"

Samantha nearly gasped. Had he read her thoughts? She leaned forward, eager to hear what he'd say next.

"And, people, I can tell you, none of us deserves it. We can't earn it by doing kind deeds or dropping hundreds of dollars into the offering plate on Sunday morning. No matter how we try, we can't live a perfect life and work our way into God's favor. We're sinners; we were born sinful, and we do many wrong things. . . . But yet He loves us. He loves us enough to die for us."

Samantha shook her head, disbelief clouding her mind. Why would the perfect Son of God go to all that bother? And certainly not for her.

Reverend Goertzen smiled, lines crinkling around his gentle eyes. "He loved us because He created us. He saw in each one of us the potential to be like Him. But He knew that sin would drag us down, keep us from being what we could be. So how do we get past that sin? How can He look past it?"

The minister's gaze roved over the congregation, and Samantha ducked her head, fearful he could see inside to the sins hiding there.

"Remember what the Scripture said," he went on. " 'Greater love hath no man than this . . .' I wonder how many of us would be willing to bear the punishment for our brother's sin. Or our neighbor's wrongdoing. Yet we claim to love our brothers and our neighbors. But we don't love them with the kind of love God has for us. Not until we invite the Lord Jesus Christ to be the king of our hearts can we love one another with that kind of love."

Samantha frowned. *What on earth does he mean?*

"Brothers and sisters . . ." Reverend Goertzen placed his palms on the homemade wooden podium and leaned forward, his expression fervent. "We can go to church, we can tithe our income, we can help our neighbors, but until we accept Christ's gift of love and receive Him into our lives and hearts, all that goodness is ashes in the wind. Until Christ's love is inside of you, you remain apart from Him. And His death was in vain."

Samantha braved a glance at Mrs. Klaassen, seated on the other side of Liz. She carried the love of which the minister spoke in her heart. And so did Liz and Jake and Adam and Josie. . . . They all had Christ's love. Samantha was sure of it. And that was what made them different from most other folks. That's what made them reach out to her in kindness even when she'd tried to steal from them. When she was living a lie.

Her heart thumped wildly in her chest as a strong desire caught her. I *wish I could be like them*. . . .

Chapter Fourteen

*S*amantha hardly noticed when Jake lifted A.J. into his own arms. She blindly followed Liz through the narrow aisle, nodding when spoken to but her thoughts fixed elsewhere. The preacher's final words were whirling through her mind. "Jesus loves you—every one of you, and He is holding out that love to you this morning," he said, his voice low but clear. "Take His love, His forgiveness, with you as you leave here this morning."

Out in the sunshine, Josie skipped over and linked arms with Samantha. "Want to ride home in the wagon with us instead of going with Liz, Frances? I haven't talked to you in ages."

Samantha moved along in silence.

Josie tugged at her arm. "Frances? Are you sleepwalking?"

Samantha gave herself a shake and forced her attention to Josie. "I guess I was daydreaming. What did you say?"

Josie laughed. "I asked if you want to ride home with us. It'll give us a chance to catch up on things. You won't *believe* what happened at school this last week."

Liz smiled and waved her on when Samantha told her about Josie's invitation, and she climbed into the wagon with the Klaassen family. Once they were bouncing along toward their farm, Josie poked Becky. "Tell Frances what Priscilla did last Thursday." She leaned over to Samantha and said, shaking her head, "Wait till you hear this."

Becky scooted closer and cupped her hand over her mouth with a giggle. "That Priscilla!" She kept her voice low. "She was in such trouble with our teacher, Mr. Reimer. He made her stand with her nose in the corner for fifteen minutes. At lunchtime she was so mad she was almost spitting."

"Never mind that." Josie glanced around the wagon and whispered, "Tell Frances why she was in trouble."

Becky's dark eyes sparkled as she related the tale. "Last Thursday Mr. Reimer gave us an assignment to write an essay about the future, what we were planning for our lives. We each had to read ours aloud to the class. So Priscilla writes this lovey-dovey poem about how she was"—Becky's eyes fluttered upward, and she clasped folded hands beneath her chin— "going to be a farmer's wife and 'live with the most handsome farmer around all my life.'"

Becky dropped her simpering pose. "It went on and on, and she even drew pictures to go along with it of a man and woman in wedding finery, with the words 'I do, forever and ever' written underneath the picture. And in a half circle over the man's head, she wrote Adam's name, and her own name over the woman's."

Josie cut in. "Mr. Reimer was really angry. He said school assignments weren't to be wasted on such foolishness. He gave her a failing grade and made her stand in the corner like a six-year-old. It was so funny."

Samantha forced herself to join in the laughter with Josie and Becky, although thinking about Priscilla and Adam in the same breath gave her a stomachache. Priscilla was so sure of herself. What if the self-confident girl convinced Adam he should give her a further look? Samantha shifted to peek at Adam, who sat at the back of the wagon with Sarah snug at his side, reading a Sunday school paper to her. He glanced up and caught her eye. He smiled. She looked away, flustered and confused.

She hadn't spoken to him after that encounter over her clothing. He'd been at Jake and Liz's house every day of that harvest week, but she'd kept her distance, too embarrassed to face him. And he hadn't sought her out either, which had gotten her dander up. If he felt bad about being hissed at, he sure didn't act like it. Maybe she shouldn't feel guilty about it, either. She had enough other things to feel guilty about without worrying about stepping on Adam Klaassen's toes.

As the wagon pulled into the yard, she remembered how the minister had said if people refused to accept Jesus' love, it was as if they were saying Jesus had died in vain. If it was true that Jesus had died for everyone, then that included Samantha O'Brien, and she was guilty of more than just fibbing about her name or trying to steal some groceries—or filling her pockets with the Klaassens's food while they were saying grace, no less!—she was guilty of letting Jesus die for a person who wouldn't repent. Although the concept of someone loving her enough to die for her was new, something about it sent down roots deep into Samantha's heart. Observing the Klaassens, how they lived and loved each other—and even her—Samantha had seen firsthand the difference Jesus could make in someone's life.

Then Priscilla's smirking grin flashed into her memory. From the way Priscilla behaved, Samantha presumed Jesus died in vain for that young woman. She gulped. She wanted to be like the Klaassens, not like Priscilla, but how could she change things? Her thoughts came to an abrupt stop when someone tapped her on the shoulder.

Adam stood outside the wagon bed, his hand extended to her. "Want a help down?"

To her surprise, the others had all left the wagon and were halfway across the yard. Her heart fluttering, Samantha nodded.

She placed her hand gingerly in his much larger one, inwardly hoping he didn't notice how it trembled. With her other hand, she braced herself on the wooden side of the wagon bed and hopped down, stumbling just a bit on the landing. Adam held her arm till she had her footing.

She tried to step away from Adam's grasp, but he closed his fingers around her arm and gave her a serious look. "Frances, I feel I owe you an apology."

Samantha wanted to pull free and run, but the fervent look in his eyes kept her rooted to the ground. "W-why?"

"I'm afraid I hurt your feelings when I commented on—well, on your overalls."

His sincere expression pierced Samantha through the center of her heart. She looked down, unable to look into his caring face.

"I didn't mean to make you uncomfortable," he said quietly, "but I think that's what I did, and I'm sorry."

Samantha fidgeted. She owed him a bigger apology, but her tongue felt swollen. She couldn't form the words to get started.

Adam ducked down to look eye to eye with her. "Will you please forgive me? So we can be friends again?"

Heat flooded Samantha's face. He'd said they were friends. She had to say something! Gathering her courage, she peeked at him through her eyelashes. The hint of a smile showed on his lips. The sun had already put little crinkles around his eyes from squinting. He was so handsome, and it was so hard to talk to him. But his sincerity tore at her heart. She had to put him at ease.

"There ain't—there isn't anything to forgive." Her words escaped in a raspy whisper. She swallowed, and when she spoke again the rasp had disappeared. "You didn't say anything wrong. But I did." Ducking her head again, she admitted, "I'm sorry I yelled in your ear. I was feeling, well, unladylike, wearing my overalls, so I acted unladylike. I'm sorry too."

Adam released a big breath. "Whew!"

She looked up at him, startled.

He grinned. "Well, I feel better." He sandwiched her hand between his palms. "Do you?"

She bit the insides of her cheeks to keep from smiling. She nodded.

"Good." He abruptly released her and took a little step backward. "I'd better get these horses taken care of, and you'd better catch up with the others or there won't be any dinner left for either of us."

With another nod, she turned to go. But she took only three steps before stopping and turning back. "Adam?"

He paused, one hand on the harness. "Yes?"

She took a deep breath and finally managed to say the words she'd wanted to say for weeks. "That day I was trying to steal from your uncle's store—and we . . . tussled. . . ." Her glance skittered away briefly and heat nearly scorched her cheeks. She turned her eyes back to his and continued bravely, "I called you a honyocker. You're not a honyocker. You're a really nice person, and I shouldn't have said it."

Adam's ears turned red. "Aw, I would've expected to be called something worse than that for sitting on you like I did. Let's just call it even, okay?"

Happiness exploded through her and found its way to her face. She beamed at him. "Thank you."

He stared at her, amazement dropping his jaw. "I was right. . . ." He swallowed, making his Adam's apple bob. "A smile truly can transform a person."

Samantha stared back, uncertain.

He gulped again. "You're beautiful, Frances."

Delight nearly lifted her feet from the ground. He'd said she was beautiful!

But then shame sent the rapture into hiding. He'd called her Frances. . . . There was more she had to confess.

Picking up her skirts, she turned and raced for the house.

Chapter Fifteen

*A*s Samantha had learned was customary on Sundays among the Mennonite Brethren, they enjoyed a cold lunch of *zwieback*, sausage, cheeses, and pie. A simple meal allowed the women more time to get to church and to rest afterward, and Samantha found she appreciated the extra time it left for visiting.

Several times during the meal, she looked up from talking with Josie or the younger girls to find Adam watching her. Each time he would smile briefly then turn his attention elsewhere. But then when she'd look, his gaze would be on her again. It gave her a funny feeling—a light, quivery lifting up inside that pushed at her heart. A not unpleasant, feminine feeling. And at the same time, it frightened her in ways she didn't understand.

When they'd finished eating and everyone had stacked their plates for washing later in the day, the women congregated in the parlor, cooing over the babies and chatting about their harvesting activities and the like, while the men congregated at one end of the porch to talk more harvest along with the war in Europe. Samantha eventually wandered outside and headed to her favorite spot, the porch swing on the other end near the lilac bushes. Adam and Teddy stumbled upon her a few minutes later. Teddy was cuddling a yellow and white fur ball.

Samantha exclaimed, "Oh! A kitten . . . he's so sweet."

Teddy dropped the kitten into Samantha's lap. "Wanna keep that one?"

She stroked the tiny head, and the kitten set up a loud purring response. "Are you sure . . . ? Is it all right?"

The boy shrugged. "He's my favorite, but there's four more I can go play with, so it's fine."

Samantha flashed a grateful smile. "Thank you."

Teddy trotted off toward the barn, but to Samantha's discomfort—and mixed in, a feeling of gladness—Adam didn't follow. Instead, he settled into the opposite end of the swing.

The fluttery feeling returned with Adam so near, rendering her tongue-tied. She had never experienced such a response to anyone before, and her confusion grew. Instead of looking at him, she turned the baby kitty onto its back and teased it with one finger.

Adam planted one foot on the porch floor and set the glider into gentle motion, rocking the swing slowly up and back, up and back. He reached out to poke at the kitten too, and it squirmed around, curling tiny paws around Adam's forefinger and biting down on the tip.

"Ouch!" He jerked his hand back and put the finger in his mouth.

Samantha laughed, then quickly covered her mouth. She rubbed her hand against the kitten's tummy. "Shame on you, baby, attacking poor Adam that way. Why don't you find someone your own size to pester?"

Adam snorted. "Size has nothing to do with it when you've got teeth like razors." He examined his finger. "I was just trying to play, and he goes for blood."

Samantha swallowed another giggle. The kitten yawned, showing off a little pink tongue and minuscule teeth, before curling himself into a ball on her lap and drifting off. While the kitten drowsed, Adam's foot kept the swing moving in a rhythmic squeak. Through the window came the muffled sound of voices; from the other end of the porch the men were talking about whether America would get into the war; from the barn drifted the occasional snort of a horse and boys laughing. From the distance, whip-poor-wills called and mockingbirds answered. The scents of cut wheat, marigolds, and grass mingled, creating a heady perfume. The September sun sent golden shafts of light through the porch railings, creating a series of shadows marching across the porch floor and across Samantha's lap, where a little yellow and white kitten continued to nap.

Adam released a contented sigh, and Samantha sneaked a peek at him. He sat with his eyes half closed and his lips tipped into the hint of a smile. Another pang of remorse shot through her for misleading him into believing she was someone she was not. How quickly would his contented expression change if she opened her mouth to admit her name was really Samantha O'Brien and not Frances Welch, as he believed?

Focusing her attention on the kitten, she bit down on her lower lip to hold the confession inside. Living a lie wasn't easy—for one thing, it was hard remembering to keep the lie straight, but further, it pricked her conscience sorely, especially now that she had grown to love this wonderful family. But would it be better to spill the truth, even if it meant she'd be sent back to Pa? Having gotten a taste of happiness, she was more than reluctant to lose it. Besides, soon harvest would end. Jake would be around home most days, and Samantha's help wouldn't be needed any longer. She'd be free to head on down the road, and the Klaassens would never know they'd been deceived.

The thought provided no comfort. She realized moving on would be even harder than keeping her secret had been.

Adam gave a huge yawn and raised his arms to stretch, his hands balled into fists. He swiveled his gaze and grinned at Samantha. "Think maybe I'll go in and help myself to another piece of rhubarb pie. Want to have one too?"

Oh, how Samantha wanted to accept his invitation. But time with Adam would only lead to greater heartbreak in the future. She pointed to the kitten sleeping peacefully in her lap. "I'll just stay put till this little one wakes up."

Adam rose, and the swing jerked sideways. The kitten's eyes popped open, and it flexed its little paws. Adam grimaced an apology. "I guess I disturbed your guest. Since he's awake, why don't we walk him back to the barn to his mama? You can come have a piece of pie after all."

Samantha had no more excuses. She scooped the little kitty against her chest as she stood. "All right, but instead of rhubarb, I'd like the apple pie. I've never cared for rhubarb."

Adam held his hands wide, palms up, and shook his head in mock dismay. "Don't care for rhubarb? How'd you manage to get this far through life without developing a taste for rhubarb?"

Samantha stepped off the porch. "I'd rather eat hay than eat rhubarb."

Adam laughed as he caught up with her. "Well, then, you're in luck, because right this way is a very large supply of hay. You can just eat all you want. Just like our cows."

Samantha couldn't help but chuckle at that mental image. Despite her intention to stay at a distance from Adam, she grinned at him and shook her head.

He grinned in return, looking warm and approving.

A wistful thought drifted from Samantha's heart. I *wish harvest could last forever, so I could stay on working here forever.* . . .

◌

After a supper of leftovers from the noon meal, Liz, Jake, and Samantha placed Andy and A.J. into baskets softened with quilts and climbed into the buckboard to head back. As the wagon rattled along, Liz sent her husband an inquisitive look. "What were you and Frank discussing so seriously in the corner of the kitchen before we left?"

"Thomas—Henry Enns's oldest boy."

Samantha looked up from tucking A.J.'s blanket a little more securely around his chin. The concern in Jake's voice made her concerned, too.

"He ran off and joined the army. With the United States coming in to the war last April, he thinks he should go over there and help out."

Liz drew in a quick breath and curled her arm through Jake's, leaning against him.

Jake went on grimly. "Henry's pretty well beside himself. Thomas is nineteen, though, and doesn't need permission to go."

Samantha didn't know much about the war in Europe. She'd picked up bits and pieces of conversations here and there. She knew the wheat prices were higher than they'd ever been and that farmers were exempt from the draft since they were needed to produce wheat. But hearing of someone she knew, although only slightly, going off to fight made her chest go tight. She patted A.J.'s tummy absently as she listened.

She heard Liz murmur, "Has Henry spoken with Reverend Goertzen? Maybe he could help."

"In what way?" Jake's tone took on a hard edge Samantha had never heard from him before. "Talking to the minister won't change anything. The boy's gone. He'll be holding a gun—and somebody will be shooting back. Henry's worried sick, and no amount of talking—even to the pastor—will eliminate the worry."

Samantha noticed Liz squeeze Jake's arm, and he released a heavy sigh. "I can't imagine having a child fighting somewhere.

Before we had the twins, I never gave much thought to such things. Being a father myself makes me understand Henry's anguish. I never want to experience the pain of seeing one of our boys march off to war."

Liz, silent, laid her forehead against his shoulder. He placed his free hand on her knee and left it there. Her hand covered his, and their fingers interlaced.

As Samantha observed the pair, a lump rose in her throat. How must it feel to love and be loved by someone? Even though Liz and Jake were sharing feelings of sorrow for a friend, Samantha found it beautiful to behold. Would she ever know such beauty for herself?

Her thoughts skittered back to the minutes she and Adam had shared, side by side on the porch swing in the quiet afternoon. Other images flashed through her mind: Adam ardently arguing with his uncle on her behalf; holding tiny A.J., a soft expression on his face; teasingly offering a blueberry, then laughing with his head thrown back; comforting Sarah when she stubbed a toe; redirecting the conversation of those farmers when they were trying to rile his brother. . . .

She held her lips tightly together, battling tears. How she wished her situation were different—that she belonged here, that she wasn't living a lie, that she was worthy of the love of someone as special as the Klaassens . . . as Adam. She gave a quick shake of her head. She might as well wish to be the queen of England. Samantha came from a world where wishes never came true.

Chapter Sixteen

*T*he reminders of summer drifted away like the clouds in an azure sky, replaced by a lovely, mellow fall that pulled at Samantha's heartstrings with its earthen colors of mahogany red, pumpkin orange, and golden yellow. Many times she stopped on the narrow stoop at Jake and Liz's front door, arms often full of clean, dry clothing from the line, and drank in the pleasant changes in nature. She'd never seen so many colors before. Fall arrived in Milwaukee too, but in the city it was different from out here in the country with all the open spaces and towering trees and wild breezes carrying wondrous scents Samantha couldn't even name.

Although harvest on the Stoesz farm had already ended, Samantha stayed on. When Samantha tentatively brought up the subject, Liz begged Samantha to stay until Jake had finished his part harvesting the neighbors' farms and was home again. Liz insisted she simply couldn't do without her, it was so exhausting trying to keep up with the needs of two babies at once. Samantha agreed to stay. Truthfully, she didn't need an excuse to stay. She'd been in Mountain Lake for several months now with no sign of Pa. She was finally allowing herself to relax and bask in this new sense of security. And the longer she stayed, she told herself, the more money she could put aside for traveling later on.

One sunny Saturday afternoon in late September, the rumble of a wagon's wheels on hard-packed ground carried through the open front door. Liz set down her mending and crossed to the door. She flashed a smile to Samantha, who stood at the table kneading bread dough.

"It's Ma and the youngsters."

Samantha quickly cleaned her hands on her apron and ran to the doorway. She watched Adam help his mother to the ground. Teddy, Sarah, Becky, and Josie leaped out the back and charged toward the house. Sarah waved a brown paper-wrapped package, and the others were clamoring so that Samantha couldn't distinguish one voice from another.

The ruckus awakened the twins, who joined their indignant cries to the merry exclamations of the Klaassen siblings. By the time Mrs. Klaassen and Adam stepped through the door, Samantha wanted to clap her hands over her ears. Adam glanced over the fray with a frown, then placed two fingers in his mouth and blew. The piercing whistle stopped the commotion instantly, even stilling the babies for one startled second. All gawked at him, open mouthed.

"That's better." He strode across the room and took little A.J. from Samantha's arms, turning the baby against his shoulder. "It sounded like a gaggle of hungry geese in here." He patted the baby. "No wonder you were bawling, isn't that right, A. J.?"

Liz handed Andy to her mother, shaking her head. "What on earth was all that racket about, pray tell?"

"This! This!" Sarah waved the package over her head.

Teddy added, "It's a present for Frances."

Samantha's eyes grew wide and fastened on the slightly lumpy package wrapped in brown paper and string. "For *me*?" She pressed her hand to her chest.

"Yes." Becky gave Sarah a little nudge. "Hand it over, Sarah."

Sarah thrust the package into Samantha's arms, then danced up and down in excitement. "Open it! Open it quick, Frances!"

Samantha held it gingerly, unsure of how to behave. She couldn't remember the last time she'd been given a present. "But . . . but . . ." She shook her head, confusion making her tongue stumble. "It's not my birthday or Christmas or anything. W-what's it for? Why'd you all—?"

"It's a thank-you present," Josie put in, slipping her arm around Samantha's shoulders and beaming.

Samantha stared at her friend, then let her gaze travel over the circle of smiling faces, finally settling on Mrs. Klaassen's. " 'Thank you?' For what?"

Mrs. Klaassen's warm smile flooded over Samantha like warm honey. "For all the help you've given Liz. She tells us you've worked as much as two people these past weeks, and we're so grateful you are here for her and for the twins. The gift is a little something to show our gratitude. From all the Klaassens."

Samantha blinked quickly against the tears gathering in her eyes. She swallowed the lump in her throat and looked down at the crumpled brown paper, squeezing it with both hands. It was soft, with a funny little bump in the middle. A *thank-you present to show their appreciation*. She swallowed again, harder this time. They didn't understand. Instead of them thanking her, *she* should be thanking *them*.

They'd given her a place in their family, made her feel wanted and needed, had shown her more kindness than she'd ever known in her entire life. And now they were *thanking her*? Overwhelmed by emotions she couldn't put into words, she clung to the package while her heart thudded hard in her chest.

Sarah had taken to jumping up and down once more. "Open it, Frances!"

"Yes, do," Josie said, giving Samantha's shoulder a squeeze.

Adam's low voice reached Samantha's ears. "Give Frances a minute, girls. I think we've taken her by surprise."

Samantha lifted her eyes to his, and the gentle smile above A.J.'s downy head seemed to say, *It's okay. Just relax and enjoy this.*

"Well . . . Well . . ." She directed her words at Adam. Slowly, her pulse ceased its reckless pace. "Let me sit down first."

Teddy jerked out a straight-back chair from the table for her, and Samantha sank into it before her quivering knees gave way. The youngest two Klaassens crowded close, getting in the way while Samantha tugged the string loose. She placed it on the table, taking care to form a coil. Then she carefully pulled the brown paper aside slowly, savoring the anticipation.

As she pulled the paper back, she had a glimpse of roses and vines on a pale yellow background. She took a deep breath, then held it. Opening the wrapping completely, she discovered two neatly folded lengths of fabric—rose-print calico on top, and a piece of sky blue gingham on the bottom. Sandwiched between them, two spools of thread and a small wooden tube of sewing needles created the bulge.

"Oh, my . . ." Samantha's breath eased out slowly. With one finger, she traced a vine weaving between the calico blooms. "It's beautiful. They both are."

Mrs. Klaassen said, "I hope you don't mind that we picked out the fabric for you. We thought about taking you into town and letting you choose your own, but that would have spoiled the surprise. If you don't care for either of them, we can certainly exchange them for something else."

"Oh, no!" Samantha couldn't take her eyes off the fabrics in her lap. "These are just perfect. But—" At last she looked up, fixing an uncertain gaze on Mrs. Klaassen. "I've been paid for my work here. I don't understand. . . ."

Josie shrugged, a grin bringing out her dimples. "It's a bonus. One which you have richly earned, dear Frances." She laughed. "Besides, we figured you might be tired of wearing

Liz's old too-big hand-me-overs." Josie grinned at Liz, who returned the favor with a mock glare. "Now you'll have a Sunday dress *and* a work dress all of your own."

Samantha pressed both palms onto the soft cotton fabrics, reveling in the crisp newness. *Two dresses. One for Sunday and one for everyday.* She couldn't wait to start cutting out pieces and threading the needle and turning these wonderful fabrics into clothes. She wanted this more than she'd ever wanted anything.

But a heavy weight bore down on her, forcing her brows into a frown. She looked into the happy faces surrounding her. "This is—this is so wonderful. But I just don't know. . . ."

Mrs. Klaassen curled her hand over Samantha's shoulder, the touch warm and tender. "What's troubling you, dear?"

Samantha swallowed and gave her head a brief shake. How could she tell them that they'd already given her much more than she ever expected to receive in life? And then there was the secret lie she was living. . . . She didn't know how to respond. Ducking her head, she finally said, "I don't want to take more'n I deserve."

Mrs. Klaassen's hand slipped around her shoulder and tightened briefly. "There's about as much chance of that happening as—as Sarah here suddenly sprouting a mustache."

Samantha lifted her face and caught the teasing glint in the woman's eyes. Humor had diffused the emotionally charged moment. She managed a nod, a quick little grin in Sarah's direction, then met Mrs. Klaassen's gaze squarely. With all the sincerity she could muster, she said, "Thank you very much."

The woman's face lit up in a smile, and she leaned down to deliver a two-armed hug. Samantha didn't pull away. She didn't return the embrace, but she leaned into it, savoring it.

"Now . . ." At Liz's admonishing voice, Mrs. Klaassen released Samantha and stood back, giving her a chance to regain her composure.

"If you all will clear out of here," Liz said, "Frances and I can restore some semblance of order. We'll dish up gingerbread and whipped cream for anyone who wants some. Shoo now, kids—out of here till we call."

With a whoop, the three youngest dashed outside. "Let's play tag," Teddy shouted. "I'm it!" Mrs. Klaassen carried the babies up to their bedroom to finish their naps. Adam announced he was going to go say hello to Jake in the barn. Liz scurried to the icebox for the cream.

And Samantha remained in her chair, emotions reeling. She scooped up the folds of fabric and lifted them to her nose. A delightful aroma—clean and fresh and *new*—filled her senses. Pressing the bundle close to her heart, she finally rose and carried the gift up to her room. Still hugging the package, she peered out her little window and caught a glimpse of Adam striding toward the barn. As she watched, he paused and turned his face upward, almost as if he knew she was there. . . .

Her breath caught when he saw her. A smile brightened his face, and he lifted his hand in a wave. After a moment's hesitation, she waved in return. Then, her heart light, she laid the fabrics on the end of her bed and hurried back down to join the family.

Every spare minute of the following two weeks, Samantha holed up in her under-the-eaves bedroom, stitching feverishly. Gran had started her on sewing when Samantha was just a little girl, and then she continued making her own clothing while she was growing up, though never with brand-new fabric. When a neighbor took pity on her and gave her some cast off, she had remade it into a dress for herself.

Now she created a pattern by tearing apart one of Liz's threadbare dresses and modifying some pieces to fit her slimmer frame. Finally she attached the final button and donned her favorite—the morning-sunshine yellow covered with delicate pink roses and trailing deep, green vines.

She turned this way and that in front of the little mirror on her dresser, trying to get a glimpse of the whole thing. She blew out an exasperated breath. The mirror was just too small. She reached out to shift its position, angling it sharply downward, then looked again.

Someone knocked at the door, and Josie stuck her face around the opening without waiting for an invitation. Her eyes widened as she stepped fully into the room. "Oh, Frances, you did such a good job. It's beautiful—*you* are beautiful."

Samantha, embarrassed yet pleased at Josie's praise, fingered the tiny stand-up collar she'd embellished with a bit of white lace purchased with her very own money. "Does it look all right? I can't see the whole thing at once."

"Yes, it fits just right." Josie handled Samantha like a large doll, turning her in circles. "Even the buttonholes are perfect, and the gathers on the skirt are nice and even," she exclaimed. "And look at the lovely puff at the shoulder of the sleeves. You look like an angel, Frances."

Samantha wasn't accustomed to such compliments, but pleasure flooded through her. She toyed with the skirt, her head bent.

Josie tugged at her wrist. "Come downstairs. *Tante* Hulda is here with Mother and Liz, putting her stamp of approval on the twins. You remember, Uncle Hiram's wife. Come show off your creation."

Samantha drew back. "I don't want to show off, Josie."

Josie laughed at her. "I don't mean you will really be show-ing off, silly. Mother will adore this dress, and even *Tante* Hulda will be impressed."

So Samantha allowed herself to be led down to the kitchen, where she blushed self-consciously under Mrs. Klaassen's along with the girls' and Aunt Hulda's exclamations of admira-tion. "That's a lovely dress, Frances," Aunt Hulda said in her thick, husky voice. "The colors make you look healthy." Aside, to Mrs. Klaassen, she whispered too loudly, "That girl is too thin." Then she waved a pudgy hand at Samantha. "Come closer, child. Let me check the stitching."

Reluctantly Samantha obeyed the somewhat intimidat-ing woman, allowing her to scrutinize Samantha's handiwork. Hulda muttered, "Mm-hm," and "Ah," under her breath as she tugged at the skirt and sleeves and turned Samantha this way and that. At last she settled back in the rocking chair, crossing heavy arms across her ample bosom. She peered up at Saman-tha from over round lenses sitting precariously on the end of her nose. "Well, Miss Frances, you've done a commendable job. You've obviously sewn before."

Samantha moved away now that the inspection was over. "Yes, ma'am. I was taught to sew a long time ago, by my great-grandmother."

"She taught you well." Hulda pursed her her lips and squinted at Samantha. "I don't suppose you would be inter-ested in sewing for profit?"

Confused, Samantha turned to Mrs. Klaassen for help. "She means, would you be interested in sewing for other people, who would pay you?" Mrs. Klaassen explained.

"Pay me to sew?" Samantha thought the idea ludicrous. Who would pay her to do something they could easily do themselves?

Hulda said, "Many of the women in town do not enjoy sewing or feel inadequate in their ability, so they either buy from a catalog already made"—she snorted, waving her dimpled hand in a gesture of derision—"or hire someone to sew for them."

Samantha gaped at her. "Of course—of course I'd be willing." The idea of earning money appealed to her. "But I don't know if I'm good enough to sew for others."

Hulda gave another short laugh. "There's no doubt you are good enough, dear. I could put a sign up at our store by the dress goods, offering your services. We would capture customers quickly if we hung a sample garment. . . ."

Without thinking, Samantha placed her hands protectively against the skirt of her dress.

An understanding smile creased the older woman's face. "But I suppose we could do without. Just wear this dress to church on Sunday, and we shall have business. Mark my words."

Samantha looked from Josie to Mrs. Klaassen to Hulda. Worry scurried around in the back of her mind. "I'm not sure Mr. Klaassen or—or the sheriff would approve of me working out of your store. After all—" She ducked her head in embarrassment. "I did try to steal from there. . . ."

"Nonsense." Hulda shrugged. "Water under the bridge. Hiram wouldn't hold a grudge, especially when the venture will prove profitable to him as well." Her eyes sparkled with mischief. "We do have the fabrics available for sale, and even after the ladies pay you to sew, they will spend less than they would on a ready-made dress. Anyone can see the advantages there. No, Hiram won't argue. I'll bank on it . . . and he'll take it to the bank." She laughed at her own cleverness.

Samantha thought about having access to the many fabrics and laces at the store, cutting and stitching until a finished dress emerged from only assorted shapes of material. She thought of earning extra money that would keep her far away from her pa. She thought of being able to stay in Mountain Lake, close to the Klaassens. *Close to Adam* . . .

She smiled at Hulda. "If you think it will be all right, I'll try it."

"This is just wonderful!" Josie scurried over to wrap Samantha in an impulsive hug.

"Now sit down here by me," Hulda ordered, "and have some applesauce cake to celebrate our new business venture."

Still basking in the warmth of their confidence in her, Samantha eagerly joined the others for cake and chatter. As she daintily smoothed the skirt of her fine new dress across her knees, she wondered with a spark of unfamiliar vanity, *What will Adam think when he sees me in this?*

Chapter Seventeen

*A*dam couldn't stop a rush of jealousy as he watched Lucas Stoesz hotfoot it across the churchyard at the approach of his older brother's buckboard. Lucas hurried around to the back and helped Frances down. Adam caught his breath at the sight of her in the trim-fitting dress she had made from the rose-covered fabric Ma and Josie had chosen. The perky flowered bonnet added an appeal and a maturity to her appearance that made Adam feel as if someone had socked him hard in the midsection. The feeling was all mixed up with another much less brotherly, and he carefully guarded his expression as he followed his family into the church and settled himself on the familiar bench.

Out of the corner of his eye, Adam saw Lucas steer Frances in next to Liz, then lean down to whisper something in her ear before straightening. Frances, pink-cheeked, lifted a bashful face to Lucas's and nodded slightly. A huge grin split the young man's face, and he unabashedly winked at Frances before moving down the aisle to sit with his father.

Adam's brows pinched together. *That Lucas is just a little too sure of himself.* Samantha didn't have a father or other family member around to look out for her. It was Adam's duty as her benefactor, so to speak, to provide protection when needed. He was uncomfortable with the idea that protection from his brother-in-law's sibling would be necessary, but he knew Lucas well enough to be concerned. Lucas had always been more reckless than wise.

Rev. Goertzen stepped up to the pulpit, and Adam turned to the front of the church. The minister's somber expression—so different from his usual Sunday morning smile—caught Adam's full attention. Apparently he wasn't alone, because the sound of stirring and soft murmurs drifted across the congregation.

"Brothers and sisters . . ." Tears glittered in Reverend Goertzen's eyes. "I must begin our time together this morning with some distressing news. I have just come from the Enns farm. Henry and Marta received a telegram yesterday, informing them that their son, Thomas, was killed in a training accident."

Shocked gasps came from every corner of the church. Adam clutched the edge of the bench, almost dizzy at the terrible news. *Thomas . . . gone?* The sound of a woman sobbing quietly came from behind him.

The pastor continued, "This morning, I ask that we unite our hearts in prayer for the Enns family. They are much in need of comfort. Shall we pray?"

After the service, which was more brief than usual, Pa and Ma asked Adam to take the children home in their wagon, and they rode with several other couples to the Enns farm to spend the afternoon with Henry and Marta. Jake and Liz decided to go over to the Klaassen farm rather than heading to their own little house alone. At this time of sorrow, they needed one another.

Liz, Josie, and Frances set out lunch, but no one ate much. Sarah and Teddy couldn't really understand the impact of what had happened, but they must have absorbed the tense currents because they reflected the somber moods of the older ones around them. After pushing their food around on the enamel plates for a while, Liz sent the two youngsters out to the barn to entertain themselves with the kittens, and she supervised the little cleanup that was needed. The afternoon stretched before them, with very little conversation to fill the sorrowful hours.

Adam joined Frank, Arn, and Jake on the porch, as was their custom on nice Sunday afternoons, but restlessness drove him to the yard. He needed to think. He needed to do something. He decided to take a walk to clear his head. But he really didn't want to be alone. Frances and Josie were on the porch swing, and he crossed the yard with long strides and paused at the foot of the steps.

"I'm going for a walk. Anyone want to come along?"

Josie shook her head. "I'll stay around in case Liz needs help with the twins. Why don't you go ahead, Frances? You've been doing a lot of extra duties lately. A walk would do you good."

Frances looked from Josie to Adam, indecision in her face.

"I'd like the company," Adam said, trying to keep his voice matter of fact.

"I suppose I'll go then." Samantha pushed out of the swing. "It's awfully warm for fall, isn't it? Must be Indian summer."

"Nah, can't be Indian summer until after the first hard frost."

"Well, how about a walk to the lake? Is it very far? We could dip our feet in the water and—."

"Lake?" Adam frowned.

"There must be a lake. The town's named—"

"Oh!" Adam released a short huff of laughter, but he quickly stifled it when she drew back, her brows drawn together. "There isn't a lake," he said. "Then why—?"

"There was a lake here when the town was founded," Adam explained, motioning for her to join him, "but since most of the people who chose to make Mountain Lake their home wanted to farm, the town leaders drained the lake. In 1905 or 1906, I think. So it's all farmland now."

"Hmmm," was all she said, but she looked disappointed as they started to move away from the porch.

"But with the north pasture cut now," Adam offered, "it'll be easier to walk there. Shall we go that way?"

She clasped her hands behind her back with a shrug. "That's fine."

So Adam set off, Frances moving quietly at his side. Neither spoke, and Adam discovered he didn't mind walking along with Frances in silence. A light breeze whirled leaves across their path and gently rubbed the tips of empty branches together. The fall sun beamed down, and Adam could see it bouncing off the glossy strands of her hair and bringing out reddish glints.

Such a beautiful day . . . and such heavy thoughts. A sigh shoved up through his chest.

Frances flicked a glance at him. "You're thinking about your friend, aren't you?"

A lump filled Adam's throat. "Yes." He couldn't say anything more.

She sighed too. "I didn't know Thomas—I'd only seen him in the churchyard with you and the other young men. But he'd looked young and healthy and full of life, and now he's gone." Her voice cracked. "It doesn't seem fair."

No, it wasn't fair, but lots of things weren't fair. It seemed especially wrong when Thomas hadn't even been in combat. Uncertain how to respond, Adam remained silent. Samantha set her lips in a grim line and continued to trudge along beside him. Their shoulders bumped occasionally as they moved across the uneven ground, and he considered putting more distance between them but decided against it. He found a level of comfort having her near enough to touch, even if the contact was brief and impersonal.

The wind picked up, and she nearly tripped when her skirt tangled about her ankles, but Adam reached out and caught her arm, keeping her from a likely tumble. She gave a small smile of thanks, stepping back to smooth her dress. He glanced over his shoulder, stunned by how much distance they'd covered. They should turn around and go back.

He gestured toward the house. "Should we—?"

"What is that?" she interrupted, pointing in the opposite direction.

He followed the line of her finger. "What?"

"Over there." She squinted. "It looks like the front of a shack getting swallowed up by the hill."

Adam shaded his eyes for a moment, then dropped his hand and grinned at her. "That's Grandpa Klaassen's dugout."

She sent him a curious look. "Dugout?"

"It's the first house built on our land. When Grandpa and Grandma settled here, he didn't have time to build a proper house before winter hit, so he just dug into the side of a hill, stacked some logs for a wall, and made a house out of the hole. I haven't been out there for years. Want to take a peek?"

She gave an eager nod, so Adam caught her elbow and steered her toward the small dwelling. As they drew near, a smile of wonder grew on her face. "Oh, my. It *is* a house dug right into the side of a hill! I've never heard of such a thing."

Adam planted his shoulder on the warped door and pushed hard. A discordant creak sounded as he forced it open. The smell of earth and neglect greeted his nose. Frances leaned forward, peeking into the dark, musty space, and then jerked back. Her expression turned dubious.

"Will there be . . . are there critters . . . in there?"

Adam shrugged, hiding a grin. "Maybe."

She inched backward, nervously twining her fingers together. Adam was sure she had no idea how cute she looked with her nose all wrinkled up with worry. Stifling a chuckle, he stepped into the dugout. He waved his arms around, breaking down cobwebs and scattering dust everywhere. A glance around the room confirmed no dangerous animals had taken up residence. He turned to the open doorway with a smile.

"It's safe. C'mon in."

Hesitantly, Frances stepped over the dirt threshold. She immediately sneezed.

Adam pursed his lips in sympathy. "Not too clean, though, is it? Dark, too. Maybe I can open the shutters."

The oiled paper windows had long since rotted away, but sturdy wooden shutters still protected the openings. Adam forced them outward, and a negligible amount of light made its way into the room, followed by the sweet fall breeze. He stood in the shaft of light from the window, looking around the small room. An old table still remained along one wall, and a pile of old clothing, mouse eaten and filthy, lay discarded in a corner. Frances kicked at it, sending up a puff of dust. She covered her nose and moved nearer the door where the air was fresher.

"Josie and Liz used to play house out here." Adam wandered the small space, remembering. "I came out here a lot, too, as a kid. I thought it was a neat hideout. It doesn't look like anyone's been around for a long time, though."

He stood back and watched Frances ease farther into the room. She slid her fingers along the smooth dirt wall, raising her face to examine the sturdy overhead beams of the ceiling. Lowering her gaze, she moved over to the shelves wedged into the back wall of the dugout. A row of grimy glass jars still rested there. She lifted one down and cradled it in her palms.

"The place is not large, as you see," he told her, "but there's ample room for a bed, table, and a couple of chairs."

She gave an approving nod. "A fine little house," she said. Her gaze drifted in a circle, her lips turned up in a smile. Returning the jar to the shelf, she moved across the floor to the fireplace centering the side wall. She squatted down, peering into the dark shaft. Then she fingered the outer structure of the fireplace.

She sent a glance over her shoulder to Adam. "What are these?"

Adam walked over and hunkered down beside her. "Mud bricks. Formed of mud, grass, and cow manure."

She jerked her hand back and brushed her palms together.

He bit down on the inside of his cheeks to keep from laughing. "The Mennonites formed bricks of those materials in Russia, so of course Grandpa would do the same thing here. The bricks are amazingly strong. They built entire structures of these mud bricks."

Keeping her hands in her lap, she examined the fireplace again. "Clever . . . but, well, a little unusual."

Adam nodded.

Slowly she turned her head and looked into his face. Sunshine slanted across the floor, painting the two with its yellow glow. Only inches apart, he glimpsed his own reflection in her irises. Tiny particles of dust danced around them like glittering bits of sunshine.

Emotion glimmered in her eyes—an emotion he couldn't define—and suddenly she sucked in a sharp breath. Averting her eyes, she jolted upright and swished dust from her skirts. Adam rose, too, both disappointed by her abrupt withdrawal and relieved. What had he been thinking?

She began a casual stroll around the room, her hands linked at her waist. "So . . . this was your grandparents' home?"

Adam chuckled, "Grandma called it her badger's den. She joked that when she'd married Grandpa, back in Russia before they immigrated here, he had been worried about his penniless state, but she had assured him she could be happy living in a hole in the ground as long as he was in it with her. So Grandpa put her word to the test."

Frances laughed, the sound giving Adam's heart a lift. "Your grandma must be fun."

He bobbed his head in agreement. "Both of my grandparents are wonderful. I miss them."

"Are they . . . ?"

Adam understood the abbreviated question. "Both are well and living in Minneapolis. My oldest brother, Daniel, lives near them in the city. He keeps an eye on them. They always visit at Christmastime. Maybe you'll meet them then."

Her brows puckered briefly, and she again took up her slow perusal of the space. "Did your parents live here, too?"

"Nope." Adam leaned on the wall, observing her. "Grandpa built the house we live in before Pa and Uncle Hiram were born. Then, when Grandpa had a stroke and couldn't farm anymore, he split the land between Pa and Uncle Hiram and took Grandma to the city. Uncle Hiram found out he wasn't that interested in farming, so he sold Pa his half of the farm and opened up his mercantile."

Frances paused, sending him an interested look. "Your family's been on the land for quite a long time. . . ." She tipped her head, one strand of hair curling around her cheek. "Will you stay on the farm, like your pa has done?"

Adam answered promptly. "Sure will. Pa's already told me this north pasture and the east field will be mine, and the other side will go to Frank. There's enough land to support more than one family here, and I have no desire for city—or even town— life. Daniel and Arn are welcome to it."

Samantha nodded, a lilting smile lifting the corners of her lips. "Farming takes strength of body and spirit—being at one with the land. It seems to me you have all the requirements to be a farmer." She turned her head away as if embarrassed, but her words pleased him more than he could really understand.

He finally said, "I know what I want—what God wants for me. And I'm not afraid to work for it." Satisfaction welled in his chest. "When I inherit this land, I'll also inherit the knowledge and commitment of the people who've gone before me. They've given me a good, solid base on which to build, both physically and spiritually."

She sighed. "I envy you, Adam. What a wonderful family history you have." Her eyebrows scrunched together. "I hope you know how lucky you are."

Adam knew well how lucky he was. How blessed. Being in the dugout again brought back many memories of childhood, listening to his grandparents' stories. He came from a God-fearing family, and he was proud to be a part of it. Watching Samantha move around the small space, poking her nose into corners and swiping at the dust motes in the air, he had to wonder about her background—who her people were, where she'd come from. Time had passed, but none of them were any more enlightened than they had been the first day she arrived and tried to withhold her name.

Curiosity got the best of him. "Frances, do you have grandparents?"

She stiffened and froze in place, her gaze aimed at the shelves on the wall. Then slowly she turned, her face down. "No, not anymore."

"Parents, then?"

"I'll wait for you outside." Without looking at him, she skittered out the door.

Remorse tangled Adam's insides into knots. She'd been enjoying herself. He'd been enjoying her enjoyment. And then he'd chosen to pry, ending their time of easy camaraderie. He sighed and closed the shutters, reminding him of how Frances sealed herself away from all of them. What deep pain held her captive? Would she ever trust them enough to let someone in?

As he stepped into the sunshine again, a prayer winged from his heart. *Lord, shine the light of Your love and healing into Frances's soul. Replace her pain with joy.* He couldn't help his young friend, but he knew who could. He'd trust God to meet Frances where she was and to give her what she needed.

nce again, Samantha fell in step with Adam. Her heart ached. This day had started out with such promise. With only a little prompting from Hulda Klaassen, her new dress had gotten just the reaction at church they had hoped for; she'd noticed Adam watching her with an expression of interest; and Lucas Stoesz, who was admittedly handsome, had openly flirted with her and asked to walk her home after the service. Even though she had no intention of taking Lucas up on his offer, she'd settled onto the church bench feeling happy and accepted. But now the day seemed tarnished, battered, and scarred.

Although she kept her face aimed toward the farmhouse in the distance, images from her visit with Adam in the dugout played across her mind's eye. When they had knelt side by side in front of the fireplace, the sunlight streaming through the door had turned his hair to burnished gold, and green flecks appeared in his brown eyes. Looking into his face, a feeling as real as the ground now beneath her feet had coursed through her, catching her breath and causing her heart to flutter. Through her mind had flashed a mental image of her tending a fire and Adam returning home to her, belonging to her in the way that Jake belonged to Liz or Si belonged to Laura. It lasted only a moment—a wonderful, heartfelt moment—and then it was replaced by the realization that it was only a dream. A fantasy that couldn't—*couldn't*—come true. Because she wasn't who he believed her to be.

The weight of the secret seemed to fall on her with new force. She stumbled but caught herself before Adam came to her aid as he had before. Oh, if only she could be as open with him as he had been with her. But surely he'd turn away in disgust if he knew the legacy of her family—Pa's drunkenness, Davey's abandonment, the lie of her assumed name. She had nothing to offer Adam. As much as it pained her to continue living the falsehood, it was better for everyone if she continued to be Frances Welch, homeless and alone.

As she'd watched Adam secure the shutters of the little dugout, she had reached a sad realization. She did not belong here. She was not like the Klaassen family, not Adam's kind, and she never could be. Her foolish heart had been planting ideas in her head that could never come true. Adam's questions today proved the Klaassens would one day demand answers, and it would break her heart to confess how she'd misled them. She must move on—now, before her heart was so firmly planted that it could not be uprooted. She would talk to Liz. Soon.

They reached the house, and Adam lightly touched her back. "Go on in. I'm going to feed the horses." He trudged toward the barn without a backward glance.

Stung by his distance and abrupt departure, Samantha slowly entered the house. Mr. and Mrs. Klaassen sat at the table with Liz and Jake, and all four glanced up as she stepped into the kitchen.

"There you are, Frances," Liz said.

Samantha winced, the false name stinging like the lash of a whip.

"We're ready to go home now. We were just waiting for you."

Samantha nodded wordlessly and reversed her steps. Liz and Jake followed, each carrying a twin. They settled the boys in their baskets in the back with Samantha and then climbed onto the wagon's seat. Side by side. Shoulders touching. Samantha angled her gaze low to avoid witnessing the sweetness of their love for each other.

When they were back, Samantha prepared a simple supper of cold sausage, *zweiback*, and cheese. She began to clean up while Liz tucked Andy and A.J. into their cradles. When Jake went out to see to the evening chores, Liz sank into the kitchen rocker with a pair of Jake's socks and her darning needles in hand.

Now, Samantha told herself. She pulled out a chair from the table and sat. Hands clutched tightly in her lap, she took a breath, trying to gather her courage.

Liz glanced up from her mending and offered a tired smile. "It's been a long day, hasn't it?"

Samantha nodded. "Yep, and not an easy one for you folks." And she was about to make it more difficult. Guilt smote her, but she pushed the feeling aside. This had to be done. "I sure am sorry about Thomas Enns."

Liz sighed. Tears in her eyes caught the light. *Brown eyes, like Adam's.* "It's going to be terribly hard for Henry and Marta. Thomas was their oldest, and his signing up and leaving without their permission was awful enough without having to face the fact that he's never coming home again."

Never coming home again . . . Samantha understood the feeling all too well. A lump filled her throat. But she swallowed resolutely and forced the words she had to say from her stiff lips. "Liz, it's time I be on my way."

Liz's head came up sharply, her hands stilling. "Oh, Frances, no! You've become part of the family. And what on earth will I do without you?"

How good it felt to be needed. Samantha smiled sadly. "You'll do just fine, and you know it. The twins are sleeping through the night now, and there's just the Voths's wheat to be finished harvesting, so Jake will be here days again. I appreciate the job you've given me, but it's time for me to go."

Liz stared, eyes wide and distressed. It was hard for Samantha to meet her gaze. "Have I done something to offend you, Frances?"

"No, nothing like that!" Her guilt rose by the minute. "But when I took this job, it was for harvest. Well . . . harvest is over."

"But what about the deal you made with *Tante* Hulda? I thought she'd already gotten interest from two ladies for dresses. You'll sew those, won't you?"

In all honesty, Samantha had forgotten. "I—I don't know. I'll have to talk to Mrs. Klaassen about that. I just wanted to let you know what—what I am thinking."

Liz rocked, a speculative gaze pinned on Samantha. "You've been happy here, haven't you?"

Samantha wouldn't lie. She gave a miserable nod.

"Then what happened?" Liz frowned. "Did you and Adam have a spat this afternoon? If so, I'll—"

"No!" Samantha jumped from the chair. "Nothing happened. Nobody did anything to me." Her heart pounded so hard she wondered if Liz could hear it. "It's just like I said. The job is done. I need to move on."

Liz stared at her in silence for several tense minutes. Then she blew out a little breath and returned to her mending. "When do you want to leave?" She sounded terse. The tone bruised Samantha's heart. "Now. Before the cold weather hits. I need to be settled somewhere before the snow flies."

Once again, Liz dropped her hands to her lap. Her voice gentled. "Where will you go, Frances?"

Samantha bit her lower lip. "I'm not sure yet. The city, probably. Maybe Minneapolis. I can get work there." *And Adam's grandparents and brother live there, so maybe I'd run into him someday. . . .*

Liz lifted the sock. "All right,. I won't try to stand in your way. But will you at least wait until the Voths's wheat is in? It would help me a lot."

An agonizing war took place in Samantha's soul. Desire to stay battled with the need to escape. How she wanted to please Liz, who'd been so kind to her. But how even more she needed to get away before she and the others learned how they'd been duped.

"I . . ." Her dry mouth made her voice sound strangled. "I don't know." She turned and raced up the stairs before Liz could offer another argument.

As Adam hitched the team to the wagon Monday morning for the trip with Pa, Frank, and Arn over to the Voth farm, the clatter of hoof beats reached his ears. He turned to see Liz rein in her horse next to the corral. *What is she doing out so early*?

He met her halfway across the yard. "Liz, is something wrong? What—?"

"Frances is leaving."

He felt as though a lightning bolt had shot from the sky and seared his insides. "But—but she *can't* go!"

Liz stared at Adam's face, her expression apprehensive. "I don't want her to leave either, Adam, for strictly selfish reasons—she's such a help." She rested her fingertips on his forearm. "What are your reasons for keeping her here?"

Adam swallowed. How should he answer? What *were* his feelings for Frances Welch? Sympathy for her aloneness? Brotherly caring? Simple Christian concern for a fellow human being? Or did it go beyond any of those? Was it possible he actually *loved* the girl? The thought brought him up short. Had he ever really defined his feelings for Frances?

"Liz, I . . ." Adam stared helplessly at his sister.

Liz's eyes filled with compassion, as if she already knew the answer and understood the conflict involved. Adam, as a Christian man, would not become seriously involved with a non-Christian no matter how much his heart might wish him to. With a sad smile, she opened her arms, and he moved into her embrace. After a long hug, he pulled back and took Liz's hands.

"Sis, I don't want her to go. If she has no family, she needs us more than you've needed her. I can't let her know how I feel—and we can't pressure her. She'll run like a scared rabbit." Adam dropped her hands and turned away, running his fingers through his hair. "I know why she wants to go. She's scared. I scared her."

"How?"

Adam shook his head, anger with himself putting a bite in his tone. "Yesterday Frances and I went walking, and ended up at the dugout. We started talking about Grandpa and Grandma, and I asked her about her own grandparents."

Liz shook her head. "I can imagine her reaction, knowing how she's responded to questions about herself in the past."

Adam gave a terse nod. "She closed her mouth and wouldn't even look at me." He slammed his hands over the top rail of the corral. "After all my intentions to go easy with her, to let her open up to me on her own terms, in her own time. I wanted her to trust me. And then I had to go and open my big mouth."

Liz curled her hand over Adam's. "One simple question, and in the context of your discussion, could hardly be considered applying pressure. It sounds like the conversation moved naturally in that direction. We have a right to ask questions occasionally. If that makes her lack faith in you, then I think the problem lies with her, not you."

Adam appreciated his sister's attempt to absolve him of blame, but he couldn't accept it. "No, I frightened her, and I need to set it right. I'll talk to her."

"Do you think you should?" Worry creased Liz's brow. "Maybe it would be better to—."

"To let her go?" Adam frowned at his sister, then his shoulders slumped forward. He hung his head. "No, Liz, right or wrong, we can't just let her go. I've got to try."

The day crept so slowly at the Voth farm that Adam wondered if the sun stood still. But at last evening fell, the men returned to their own homes, and Adam was free to go speak with Frances.

The horseback ride over to Liz and Jake's proved chilly, a huge change from yesterday. Rain scented the air, and clouds sent a gloomy cast across the sky. Adam pulled the collar of his jacket tighter around his jaw and wished he'd grabbed gloves too. By the time he arrived on Jake's property, the clouds had parted to reveal the moon and a dusting of stars high in the sky.

Liz answered Adam's brief knock, gesturing him in with a wave of her hand. Jake looked up from the table where he was working some figures on a lined pad of paper. A grin broke across his face. "Hey, Adam. What brings you here at this hour? I hope it's a game of checkers."

Adam smiled but shook his head. "Not tonight, Jake. I came to see Frances."

Jake's eyebrows shot up. His gaze went to Liz, who'd moved to the stove and was fingering the lid on the coffeepot. Adam imagined him thinking, *So that's how it is.* Embarrassment gripped Adam, but he wouldn't back out now. He asked, "Is she in?"

"Up in her room. I'll give her a holler." Jake moved to the bottom of the staircase. "Frances? Company."

Adam stayed beside the door, watching as Frances descended. When she saw who was there, her steps slowed and a look of surprise—and maybe a bit of pleasure?—crossed her face. Then she settled her face in neutral expression and came the rest of the way down.

"Hi, Frances," Adam said quietly.

Looking wary, she avoided letting her eyes meet his. "Adam." She nodded but stayed a good five feet away from him, twisting a strand of hair that fell across her shoulder. She wore her blue gingham dress and looked very young, very uncertain—and oh so appealing.

Adam cleared his throat, painfully aware of his audience. "I wondered if you'd like to take a little walk to the corral. The night sky's real pretty. Get a breath of fresh air. . . ." He hoped the clouds hadn't clustered in again, or she might think he'd told a fib.

Frances looked at Liz. Liz shrugged with a little smile and pointed toward the hooks on the wall near the door. "If you go out, take a shawl. It's chilly tonight."

Adam lifted down a woolen shawl and draped it across Frances's shoulders, taking care not to touch her. He opened the door, and with a final solemn glance at Liz, followed Frances outside. They walked silently across the yard, their feet making crunching sounds in the dry grass. The air was crisp, the sky bright, as he'd promised. He wished they could relax and enjoy it. He wished he knew exactly what to say . . . how to say it.

They stopped by the corral fence. Frances clutched the shawl tightly with two fists and leaned her elbows on the top rail. Adam turned to lean against the fence backward, one foot propped up on a low rail. Both examined the sky for a few moments.

Adam broke the silence. "Liz tells me you're planning to leave, Frances."

She shot him a quick look. "Yes."

He could hardly hear her, but the single-word answer rankled. It reminded him of the days when she had first arrived, tight lipped and sullen. He thought she had progressed beyond that, and he expected more from her now. But if she wanted to be difficult, two could play that game. "Why?" His tone sounded stiff to his own ears.

She had turned her gaze back to the stars. "I really don't understand why it concerns you, but if you must know, I feel it's time. Liz doesn't need me like she did at first, and I need to find a job. My own place . . ."

Adam chose to ignore her assumption that it didn't concern him. "You have a job here in Mountain Lake—sewing for the mercantile customers."

Frances huffed, the sound fraught with frustration. "I need a job where I can support myself. I can't make enough sewing dresses now and then to pay for lodging and food and all of my other needs. So I need to move on."

"You *need* to, or you *want* to? There's a difference, Frances." He paused, but she remained stubbornly silent, refusing to look at him. He went on. "I suspect your leaving has less to do with needing a job than with simply running away."

She dropped her arms and gaped at him. "Running away? Running away from what?"

Adam let his foot fall, and he shifted to face her. They were less than two feet apart, and their breath hung heavy between them in the cool night air. "That's what I would like to know." His eyes locked on hers. He gentled his voice, genuine desire to understand writhing through his chest. "What are you trying to escape, Frances?"

She set her jaw and glared at him. "What are you saying, Adam?"

He met her anger with his own steady look. "I'm saying something happened to frighten you into leaving. I'm saying you're running like a scared rabbit instead of sticking things out."

Brown eyes met blue, and sparks flew from both.

She dropped her gaze first. "I'm not running away."

"Then why this talk of leaving when I know you've been perfectly happy here." Adam longed to pull her against his chest, to hold her tight and protect her. He clamped his arms against his sides and continued. "You have a place to stay, a job, people who care about you. Two little babies I know you love. Why not stay?"

Defiance flared in her eyes. "Just because you helped me out when I needed it doesn't give you the right to question me and tell me what to do."

Her obstinate attitude brought a rush of temper. It was on the tip of Adam's tongue to holler that loving her gave him every right to question her and expect a straight answer. But he couldn't shout out something like that in anger. And now wasn't the time, anyway, to be admitting he loved her. He released a huff of aggravation. "Well, *someone* needs to tell you what to do. You're not thinking straight, girl."

Her gaze narrowed. Her jaw clamped so tightly he heard her teeth grind together. "Nobody tells me I'm dumb anymore. Nobody!" She pushed off from the railing with a shove of her palms. "I've already overstayed my welcome here. I'm thankful for all your family's done for me, but the job is finished, and it's time to move on."

Adam forcibly calmed himself, remembering her reaction to his questions about her family. His voice took on a pleading quality as he attempted another tack, trying to placate her. "Frances, the other day at the dugout—"

She cut him off with a shrill snort of forced laughter. "You think *you're* responsible for my leave taking? You think *you* said something yesterday that makes me want to leave?" Her lips twisted into a cynical smirk. "You think too highly of yourself, Adam. This decision is my own, and no one else helped it along." She yanked the shawl tight across her chest and turned toward the house. "Good night, Adam."

"You sure are a stubborn little thing," Adam muttered under his breath. As she took a step toward the house, he reached out to catch her arm, intending to make her stay and talk this thing out. The moment his hand closed on her forearm, she released a panicked cry. Her arms flew upward, curling around her head, and she dropped into a crouch, pressing her face against her knees.

Adam stared in shocked silence. For a moment he couldn't move, just stood motionless, his eyes riveted as she crouched, arms protectively over her head. Moonlight bathed her, making her fingers glow white as she clutched the back of her neck. The incongruity of the moment—the beautiful, starlit night and her frozen, fear-filled reaction—struck hard. Compassion filled him, his anger dissolving as quickly as it had flared.

He dropped to his knees beside her, reaching out a tentative hand to gently stroke her tense back—once, then again. Her muscles quivered beneath his touch. He swallowed hard. "Frances? Hey, Frances, look at me."

Instead of raising her face, she pulled tighter into her cocoon, as if folding into herself both physically and emotionally. Adam stroked her back again, his fingers brushing as softly as a butterfly's wings. He moved gently. Persuasively. His touch heartbreakingly light. He kept his voice whisper-soft, tender as his touch.

"Frances, please listen to me. I wasn't going to hurt you. This is Adam, remember? I'd *never* hurt you, Frances." *Oh, Lord, what have I done to her?* "I was upset, yes, but I wouldn't hurt you. You believe me, don't you, Frances?"

Ever so slowly she brought down her arms, and she peered at him sideways through a veil of hair. The emptiness in her eyes pierced Adam more deeply than fury could have. "Come on now, Frances, stand up. It's okay now." His hands trembled as he held them out to her.

She jerked back from his offered hand, standing quickly and stiffly. She moved several feet away, still watching him with a stoic yet wary expression. Her hands grasped convulsively at the shawl. "I want to go in now." As if it took great concentration, she began walking toward the house, her steps measured and stilted.

Adam stood in place, watching her go. As she entered the house, closing the door without a backward glance, Adam felt his throat constrict. Now he understood her reluctance to talk about her past, to share anything of her upbringing. Horror seized his gut as he pictured her, hunkering into that pose that said clearly what she expected to happen next. He forced his fingers through his hair, squeezing the strands with his fists, frustrated and more angry with himself than ever. He spun, dug his fingers into the wooden rail of the corral fence, and raised his face to the heavens. *What a horrible life she must have led. And I reminded her of it. I made her think I would hurt her, that I could treat her like that. That I would ever harm a hair of her head.*

In time he calmed, but he couldn't face Liz or Jake. He crossed with heavy steps to his horse, leaped on, and grabbed the reins. He jabbed his heels into the horse's side. "Gee-up!" His voice was hoarse, tear choked. He whispered, "Good-bye, Frances." For he was sure that he had lost her now.

⌒౨

By the time Samantha had hurried across the kitchen to the stairs and reached her room, humiliation had replaced the numbing shock. She sank onto her bed, burying her face in her hands. When Adam grabbed her arm, there hadn't been room for reasoning. Her reaction had been pure instinct, her body acting without a thought. Her brain screamed for her to protect herself, and her body obeyed.

What must Adam think of me now? She curled into a ball on the straw-filled mattress. Now he knew. . . . His gentle hand on her back, the shimmer of sympathetic tears in his eyes spoke the truth. He knew what her pa had done to her. Her chest convulsed with shame. How could she ever face kind, tender-hearted Adam again?

Her throat ached with the need to cry, but her eyes remained dry. Samantha didn't cry. Her thoughts begged, *Oh, Gran, please help me now. Give me the courage to do what I must do. Give me the courage to leave this place and this man. Please, please.*

She lay in her bed, dry eyed and hurting, her arms wrapped tight around herself, wishing . . . wishing . . . wishing for what could never be.

Chapter Nineteen

*S*amantha sat shivering on the hard wooden bench at the Mountain Lake train depot, shivering. Was it cold or fear that made her tremble? She tugged the woolen shawl more snugly around her shoulders, trying to hunch down inside of it as best she could. She would purchase a ticket for Minneapolis as soon as the depot opened. She held her money in her fist beneath the shawl, waiting for the train to come and carry her away from the community and the family who had come to mean as much to her as her Gran had.

Guilt niggled at her as she considered how she'd sneaked out before the break of dawn. But if she'd waited to say goodbyes, there would have been an argument or at least a series of questions she couldn't answer. So she'd lain in her bed to be certain both Liz and Jake were still asleep before creeping down the stairs, avoiding the ones that she knew creaked. She needed some kind of wrap, so she'd left $2.50 of her hard-earned money on top of the hook before pulling the shawl around her and beginning the long walk into town. In the moments when she had hovered over little A.J. and Andy's cradles to bestow a farewell kiss, she'd almost changed her mind. The little boys smelled so sweet and tugged at her heartstrings in a peculiar way. It was *so* hard to leave. . . .

But she surely had to go. She knew that. Particularly after her disagreement with Adam. She closed her eyes, picturing his stricken face, his eyes sorrowful and sympathetic. She could only imagine what he'd been thinking as she'd cowered on the ground before him. Well, before any more of her secrets were revealed and Adam realized how he'd been fooled, she'd be off. She couldn't bear to look into Adam's eyes and see that expression of pain again.

Shivering, she shifted on the bench, feeling the consequences of the long walk on top of very little sleep. She checked the clock hanging above the ticket window. The train wasn't due for another hour or so. Maybe she'd lean her head back against the station wall, close her eyes for just a bit. . . .

⁓

"Jake! Jake!" Liz ran across the hard ground, apron flying and money clutched in her hand. Jake met her in the doorway of the barn. She fell into his waiting arms. "She's gone. She didn't come down this morning, so I went to her room to check, and she's gone."

"Now, settle down, honey." Jake rubbed her shoulders, his voice calm. "I'm sure she can't have gone far. We'll find her, don't worry. I'll head out—."

"No, she won't let you find her." Liz shook her head, tears springing into her eyes. "Look—she left this money on top of the hook where the shawls are—she took one of them with her." Liz began to sob. "She was so upset last night when she came in. I could see it. I should have gone up and talked to her. I should have—."

"Liz, don't you start blaming yourself." Jake gave her a little shake. "She's made it clear she was ready to go, and she went. I'm willing to look for her if that's what you want, but not if it's only because of some sense of guilt, because you have no reason for it."

Liz shook her head, swiping at her tears with shaking fingers. "It's not guilt, honest. I just can't let things go like this.

She was upset. . . ." Liz clutched her husband's hands, drawing strength from his firm grasp. She had someone on whom to depend; Frances had no one. The girl needed them. "Go get Adam. Adam will know what to do."

Jake delivered a quick kiss on Liz's forehead, then released Samson from his stall. "Don't worry, honey, we'll find her, and everything will be just fine."

Liz watched Samson gallop down the lane, Jake hunched over the horse's broad back. *Everything will be fine*, he'd said. How she hoped and prayed her husband was right.

She walked back to the house, praying as she went.

⌐○

Adam dug his heels into Bet's side, encouraging her to move faster. He should have guessed Frances would do something like this after the way he'd left her. What else could she do but run? She was no doubt scared to death of him now. He should never have grabbed her like that. It wasn't like him to lose his temper, but when faced with losing her. . . .

He had to find her. He had to set things right. He needed to assure her that he was nothing like whomever it was who had mistreated her so terribly in the past. As he moved at a fast trot toward town, the horse's hide warm against his legs, his thoughts drifted backward over the past months. Frances's odd behavior finally made sense. Having been mistreated, of course she would be leery and insecure. Of course she would be reluctant to talk about her past. What they had seen as sullenness had really been protective walls she'd built around herself—a necessary way to cope with the unthinkable.

He clenched his fists around the reins, resisting the urge to press Bet into a full-out gallop. *Lord, please let me find her, and* help her understand that she doesn't need to be afraid anymore. Give me a chance to show her how much I care.

⌒☉

The shrill blast jolted Samantha out of a sound sleep. She jerked upright, wincing as her cold, stiff muscles strained against her abrupt movements. Smoke smudged the sky above the trees; the train would be here soon. In a few minutes she'd be off to a new city and a new life.

But only dread filled her stomach. She knew she'd made the right choice, though. The Klaassens—especially Adam— would be better off with her gone. She could start over again, free from Pa and free from the guilty feelings from pretending to be someone else.

The ground vibrated as the train chugged into the depot. As the huge black engine screeched to a noisy stop, Samantha stood, scooping up her bundle of clothing. She had convinced herself that the two dresses she'd made were hers, since the fabric was a gift. Her reasoning hadn't made her feel much better, though.

She scurried to the ticket window, her bag clutched in her fist, and glanced at the signboard on the wall. She drew in a deep breath. "Ticket to Minneapolis, please."

The smiling stationmaster stamped a cardboard ticket. "That'll be three dollars."

Samantha slipped her hand into her pocket, and panic gripped her. Where was her money? She checked her other pocket, then rifled through her bag, her alarm mounting. "I—I seem to have misplaced my . . ."

The stationmaster's smile faded. "Miss, there are others waiting. Will you hurry, please?"

Samantha whisked a glance at a trio of impatient faces behind her. "I'm sorry. My money—it's . . ." She dug through the bag again, but no bills appeared. Her shoulders sagging, she stepped aside and allowed the others to press forward. She found her way back to the bench and sank down. When she'd fallen asleep, she'd been gripping the money in her fist. It must have blown away while she slept. Perhaps she could still find it. She searched underneath the bench and along the platform, but she found nothing except some old newspapers flapping in the breeze.

Discouragement overwhelmed her. Burying her face in her hands, she battled wailing in fury. Why must everything go wrong? The train would leave soon. A conductor walked up and down the track, checking cars, but maybe she could sneak onto a later one. Snatching up her small parcel, she tossed the bundle over her shoulder and moved off the platform. She'd rest on the other side of the depot—soak up the morning sun's warmth, and wait for the next train. . . . If she were lucky, she'd be able to climb into one of the boxcars without being seen.

❧

Adam reined Bet in hard next to the depot and swung down. His heart beat in hopeful double beats. He let his gaze move across the people milling on the wooden platform. Where was she? It made sense she'd take a train out of town. But was he too late?

Flinging Bet's reins around a hitching post, he stepped onto the platform, nearly colliding with a scruffy-looking man with several days' growth of gray whiskers dotting his cheeks. The man's tobacco-stained teeth showed behind his sneer. A foul odor rose from his dirty, wrinkled clothing.

"Excuse me, sir." Adam shifted aside so the man could pass.

The man grabbed his arm. "Where's sheriff's office?"

Adam pointed to the right. "Three blocks that way. Sign above the door."

With a bob of his shaggy head, the man turned and shuffled off. Adam resumed his search, trotting from one end of the platform to the other, searching the faces of every person on the wooden walkway and peering from the windows of the passenger cars. But Frances was nowhere to be seen. Frustration and fear fought against hope, and he turned back toward Bet. Then a flash of blue on the other side of the depot caught his eye. He moved quietly sideways, peeking around the wall, and there she sat huddled against the side of the building.

The relief nearly buckled his knees. He stumbled toward her. "Frances!"

Her entire body jolted, her wide-eyed gaze spinning to meet his. She pressed one fist to her mouth and held herself tightly against the lapped siding.

Adam thought his heart would burst from sorrow. He approached slowly, fearful of sending her into panicked flight. "Frances . . ."

Leaping to her feet, she grabbed her bundle and darted around him into the depot. He followed her to the ticket window where she slapped the counter and cried out, her voice desperately shrill, "I need a ticket. Please, I *must have* a ticket."

Adam, his chest tight and aching, stretched out his hand but stopped short of touching her. "Frances, please, I must to talk with you."

She shot him a glance so full of pain he felt it like a blow to his heart. She twisted back to the agent. "A ticket. Hurry, please. I'll—I'll pay you when—"

"Frances?" Adam inched closer.

She froze, her fingers digging into the wooden counter. A low moan escaped her quivering lips. She spun away and marched back out to the edge of the boardwalk, her back stiff. "Why . . . ?" Her voice trembled. "Why'd you have to come now? I was so close."

Her words pierced him. He eased up behind her, hands pressed once again tightly against his sides. "Liz sent me to find you. She was worried." He didn't add how much he'd been worried. "Why did you take off that way, Frances?"

Her shoulders rose and fell in shuddering heaves, but she didn't speak.

He leaned closer, his breath stirring the little coils of hair trailing beside her ear. "Frances, can we go somewhere and talk . . . please?"

She drew in a deep breath, tension emanating from every part of her body. Then her tight fist released, her bundle falling from her hand with a soft thud against the wooden walkway. Her shoulders slumped, her hands lifted to cover her face, and a heart-wrenching cry burst from her lips.

Once started, the sobs and tears struck like a gale force. Her shoulders shook, and tears rained down between her fingers.

A murmur of voices sounded from behind him, and Adam glanced back at a small gathering of curious onlookers. Frances was a private person; this public breakdown would humiliate her. Grabbing up her bag with one hand and slipping his other around her waist, Adam guided her behind the depot building to a small storage shed.

dam yanked the door open and guided Frances into the dark shed. It took only a few moments for his eyes to adjust to the dimness, but it seemed a lifetime passed as he stood listening to Frances's painful sobs. Hands on her shoulders, he eased her onto a closed keg and helped her sit. She doubled up and buried her face in her lap as she cried. Adam found another keg and pulled it close to her, seating himself with his knees nearly touching hers.

Years of comforting crying little brothers and sisters made Adam long to reach out and hold this distraught child-woman, to somehow end her suffering. But he sensed these tears were needed to cleanse her of too-long-held sorrows, deeper than he could fathom. So he cupped his hands over his knees and sat, silent and still, breathing the musty odors of grease, dirt, and mold, listening, praying, his heart aching for the pain being so wrenchingly expressed.

Gradually the wild crying began to quiet, changing from harsh to quiet sobs. Eventually, after what seemed an eternity, it faded to weak hiccups. And, with a series of shuddering sighs, the sobs died out.

Slowly Frances sat up, taking in one long, ragged breath. Adam reached into his back pocket for a handkerchief which he laid in her lap. She mopped at her face, then blew her nose noisily. With shaking fingers she explored her swollen eyelids. Lowering her hands, she sighed. "I haven't cried like that since I was six years old." Her voice sounded hollow and raw.

Adam dared give her knee a gentle squeeze. "Then I think it was about time."

She twisted the soggy handkerchief in her hands, staring downward. She went on as if he hadn't spoken. "Yes, the last time I cried like that was when I was six. When Gran died." Lifting her face, she said, "Have I ever told you about Gran?"

Adam shook his head, afraid to speak. She'd never told him about anything, as she well knew.

She gave a nod, her lips trembling, then began speaking in an emotionless, even tone that somehow was more chilling than her wild weeping had been. "You see, my mama died birthing me. Pa wanted to take me out and drown me like some unwanted kitten, but Gran wouldn't let him. She moved in with us and took over. She cared for me and Pa and my brother just like it was nothing. It was really something, though. She was past seventy when I was born, but she ran that household as well as any woman half her age. Wasn't easy, either, with Pa . . ." She paused, seemingly lost in thought.

Adam held his breath, wanting to ask questions but afraid of frightening her again, maybe into permanent silence.

In time she continued. "Gran was . . . Gran was a lot like your mother. Always smiling and kind, never finding fault or fractious. She had this soft lap just right for snuggling up in. She used to hold me after Pa would—after he'd. . . ." She swallowed.

The image of her huddled in a ball in the moonlight flashed through Adam's mind. He leaned forward and pressed his hands around hers, telling her without words he understood. She needn't say anything more.

She pulled in another shuddering breath. "Afterward, she'd hold me and comfort me, and tell me not to believe the things he said, that I *was* special, that I *was* good. When Gran told me that, I could almost believe it." Her tone turned wistful.

Still holding her hands, Adam prompted quietly, "Your Gran died when you were six?"

Frances nodded, her head bent. "Yes. She was Pa's grand-mother. You'd think he'd have been sad, but I think he was angry, because then there wasn't anybody to wait on him, ex-cept me and my older brother, Davey, and we couldn't do it good enough." Her face turned up toward his, and she looked earnestly into his eyes. "We tried, though. We really did." Another deep sigh sagged her shoulders. "But it was never good enough."

She pulled her hands loose from his grasp, leaning against the shed wall. "Davey stuck around for a while—about three years, I guess, after Gran died. But then he said he had to git. Told me to wait for him, told me he'd be back for me. He *prom-ised*." She bit her lip, blinking back more tears. "That promise wasn't worth much. I haven't seen him since."

Adam battled a wave of sorrow. She'd lost so much.

"A person shouldn't make a promise he might not be able to keep." The hurt in her tone sent another shaft of pain through Adam's middle. "I waited every night for seven years, hoping he'd come back and rescue me. Took me a long time to figure out no one was going to rescue me but *me*. So I made my own plans to leave. I ran off, but I didn't get far. Pa always caught up with me. . . ."

So she was a runaway, just as the sheriff surmised.

"Till this last time. I decided if I was going to get away, I'd have to be somebody else. So I stole some clothes out of a trunk in the cellar to make me look like a boy, and when Pa was sleeping off a drunk, I lit out. I just wanted to get away from Pa, like Davey had—as far away from Milwaukee as I could. I just wanted to escape. I didn't mean—" Her chin shot upward. Her throat convulsed.

"Frances, what is it?" He used his gentlest tone. "You didn't mean what?"

Tears flooded her eyes as she began babbling, almost hysterical. "Oh, Adam, I'm so sorry. At first I thought it was smart and funny, fooling you into thinking I was somebody else. But then I got to know all of you. I knew it was wrong, and I wanted to tell you. Honest, I wanted to. I didn't mean to lie to you. But I had to or you would send me home. Back to Pa. That's why I *had* to lie. Oh, please, can't you understand?"

Adam stared at her confusion. It had been obvious early on that she wasn't a boy. "I *don't* understand, Frances. What—?"

"I'm not Frances." She shook her head wildly, impatience pursing her lips. "I'm Samantha."

Adam sat back as if he'd been pole-axed. Samantha? Her name was *Samantha*?

More tears rolled down her cheeks. She leaned forward and clutched his hands, her cold fingers digging into his palms. "At first I was Frances to fool you and keep me from having to go back. But the longer I was Frances, the easier it was to *be* Frances, and after a while, I almost believed it myself. I hated it, lying to you—you all were so nice to me. But if I told you the truth, you and the sheriff could find out where I came from. And . . . and I'd have to leave. I'd have to go back." Desperation tinged her tone. "I didn't want to go back."

Adam's world spun. Not Frances, but Samantha. All this time . . . and she *had* been running—from her own family, though, not him.

Tears rolled endlessly down her cheeks as she pleaded with him, one hand wrapped around his wrist with a strength he wouldn't have thought possible from such a small person. "I don't expect you to forgive me, Adam. I couldn't expect that. But can't you please try to understand? You and your folks were nicer to me than anybody ever was—except for Gran, and maybe Davey. I couldn't tell you the truth. Not without you being able to send me home. And I couldn't go home. I just couldn't."

In flashes of thought Adam silently compared her childhood to his, balancing his secure home against her unstable one, his knowledge of being loved against her feelings of unworthiness. He possessed so many warm, wonderful memories of family and home and acceptance. He almost felt guilty for having been born into his family when Samantha had been thrust into such an abusive, angry environment.

He *could* understand. And he could comfort her now. He reached a hand to smooth the tangled hair from her tear-stained face. He ran his thumbs beneath her eyes, whisking away the tears, and spoke her name—her true name—for the first time. "Samantha, it's all right. I understand." Then he stated the words he knew she needed to hear. "And I forgive you."

Her face crumpled, but she held the tears at bay, looking at him for a long moment, an expression of gratitude shining in her swollen eyes. Then she threw herself at him, wrapping her arms around his neck and clinging hard. He returned the embrace, cupping the back of her head closely against his shoulder.

He closed his eyes and tilted his head to feel her warm hair firm against his cheek. As he held her, offering the comfort of his embrace, he prayed, *Help her, Lord. Heal her, please . . . and help me to know just what she needs.*

In time she pulled away, flicking a self-conscious smile in his direction before letting her gaze skitter elsewhere. She lifted his handkerchief and wiped her face once again. Crushing the sodden wad of cloth in her fist, she offered a wobbly smile. "Want to hear something funny?"

Smiling, Adam gave a nod.

"Gran believed like you do—that there's a God who loves us and watches out for us. I used to say my bedtime prayers when I was little: God bless everybody. Gran would listen to my prayers then tuck me in. Like your ma does with Teddy and Sarah."

Adam was grateful she had this small memory. At least there was something pleasant in her fractured past.

Her voice lost its blithe undertone as she continued. "When Gran left the room, I'd tell God I really didn't mean God bless Pa. I'd ask would God please make Pa go away. But instead of taking Pa away, He took Gran, and then Davey. . . ." She swallowed, pain again creasing her face. "Adam, do you think God took Gran and David away to punish me for those prayers?"

Adam captured her hands once more. "God loves you. You were only a little girl. He would never hold you responsible for those prayers."

"Then why did Gran die? And Davey never come back for me? I loved them both so much, and they left me."

Her voice, so full of wounded bitterness, shattered Adam's heart. He prayed for the right words to ease her pain. "Listen to me, Samantha. Your Gran was old. She was doing much more than she had the strength for, but she wanted to do it, because she loved you. You weren't responsible for her death. And David had reasons of his own for leaving. He wasn't leaving to get away from you, but from his own unhappy circumstances. I don't know why he didn't come back for you as he promised, but there probably is a good reason. Either way, you can't blame yourself."

"But Pa said—."

Adam squeezed her hands. "Your pa is a bitter, unhappy man. Maybe your mother dying so early made him bitter, maybe he was always that way. Some people seem to enjoy being un-happy. The only way they can make themselves feel better is to make everyone around them feel bad too. Instead of hating him, we should feel sorry for him. He must be very miserable to act the way he has. And by his actions he lost a son . . . and a very special daughter."

Samantha looked at him doubtfully. "Me? Special?"

"Yes, you." Adam stroked the backs of her hands with his thumbs, determined to help her understand. "Why, with all the people in my family, you'd think we'd never need anyone else. But we did, Samantha"—he let his voice linger on her name— "and there you were. You came into our lives just when we needed you. And you've been such a wonderful help to Liz and Jake and the twins. You're a good friend to Josie, and Sarah adores you." He raised her hands to his lips, pressing a kiss on her knuckles. "Samantha, you are loved by every member of my family." *Especially me.* But he held the words inside. The time wasn't right. She needed time for healing—from the inside out. "And as much as *we* love you, *God* loves you even more."

Samantha's chin quivered. "I want to believe I'm somebody special, and worthy of love but . . ."

"What's keeping you from it, Fran—Samantha?"

Tears swam in her red-rimmed eyes. "I lied to you. I pre-tended to be somebody I wasn't. And before that, I tried to—"

Adam gently placed two fingers over her lips. "And you think that makes you unworthy?" Her face told him clearly that yes, that's exactly what she thought. "Samantha, God sent his Son, Jesus, when we all were still sinners. You can't have any greater love than that. He didn't wait around for us to become perfect, then love us. He loves us just where we are—imperfect and floundering and needy. All we have to do is accept that love, and the whole world changes."

"You believe in that love, don't you?" Wonder bloomed on her face. "I can tell by the way you are with other people. All of you—kind and giving. I've never heard your mother or father say hateful things. They act the way I think God must be."

"That's because we've accepted the love of Jesus and asked Him to live with us, inside." Adam touched his hand to his chest, and he could feel his heart beating hard against his shirt front. "When Christ's Spirit is a part of you, you begin to be bent to His nature. 'Old things are passed away; behold, all things are made new.' And here's a promise you can hang on to forever—'I will never leave you nor forsake you.' Christ will be with you every day, helping you become the person you want to be—ought to be."

Samantha sat in silence for several long minutes. Adam waited patiently, praying quietly for the truth to become real to her. From her brief sketch of her childhood, he couldn't help but marvel at her resilience and courage.

The years of suffering had damaged her emotionally, but he knew her feelings of worthlessness could be changed with God's help. He prayed that he could get through to her, to help her realize that what he had, what the Klaassens and so many others had, could be hers only for the asking.

Samantha recalled words she'd heard the minister speak in church. She remembered signs of God's power she'd seen in the lives of the people around her. More than she'd ever wanted anything, she wanted the peace and happiness that Adam and his family had. And according to Adam, all she had to do was *ask*. It seemed almost too simple to be true. But Adam had said if she'd just believe, it could be hers, too.

I *believe. I do believe.*

"Adam?" She drew in a breath, pushing aside doubt or fear. "Will you please pray with me?"

Without hesitation, Adam dropped onto his knees beside the nail keg. Samantha joined him and, right there in the musty storage shed beside the train depot, Samantha asked Jesus to come into her life.

When she'd finished, Adam rose, holding out a hand. She took it, and he drew her to her feet. She gazed into his face. Did the warmth beneath her skin show? Could he see the joy blossoming through her heart? Looking into his compassionate eyes, she believed he could. Without even trying, a smile burst across her face. "Thank you, Adam."

Unshed tears brightened his eyes. "Thank You, Jesus." He gave her a quick hug. "Come on, Samantha. Let's go home."

Home . . .

dam swung himself onto Bet's broad back, then reached a hand down for Samantha. She hesitated only a moment before placing her hand in his and allowing him to pull her up behind him. With her little bundle fastened in front of Adam, she leaned against him, relaxed and trusting, her arms holding lightly to his waist.

As the horse moved slowly along the leaf-strewn road, the gentle swaying motion must have lulled her to sleep. Her head tipped forward against his back, and a quick look over his shoulder showed her thick lashes throwing a shadow across her cheek. Gazing into her peaceful face, he smiled. *Samantha.* The name suited her far better than Frances. *Samantha of the russet hair and cornflower eyes.*

The significance of what had occurred in the storage shed behind the depot brought a lift of joy to his heart he wasn't able to describe. Samantha now knew the Lord too. The barrier that had kept him from truly acknowledging his love for her was removed. His heart thrummed happily. Now he could—with a jolt he realized he didn't even know how old she was. Was she old enough to be betrothed?

He mentally scrolled backward in time. Her great-grandmother died when she was six, her brother had been gone for seven or eight years after staying home for—what? Three years after Gran's death? That would make her seventeen or so. Josie's age. . . . Taking another look at her relaxed face, he decided she seemed younger—especially in sleep. But her age mattered not a whit. If she was too young now, he'd just wait. He certainly wasn't so old he had to be married right away. And she was worth waiting for.

He experienced a rush of feeling for the young woman who lay so trustingly with her cheek pressed to his shoulder blade. She was a beautiful person with well-placed features. And that hair. It waved around her face in wild disarray, but he loved it. It was perfect for her—free and flowing and uninhibited. But more than her physical beauty, there was her inner beauty. Oh, she could be stubborn at times, but he'd seen her sweet, giving spirit. The stubbornness, he was convinced now, was just a cover for the insecurity she felt.

Compassion filled him—what an unhappy life she'd had before coming here. Somehow he would make it up to her. He would spend the rest of his life showering her with tenderness, giving her every happiness, if only she would accept him. If only she returned his feelings. . . .

The farm waited around the next bend. He should wake Samantha before entering the yard. He drew back on the reins, bringing Bet to a snorting halt. "Samantha?" He turned as best he could, giving her a gentle shake. "Samantha, you need to wake up."

She smiled sleepily, her eyelids fluttered, and then she straightened to meet Adam's gaze. A blush stole across her cheeks. "Not much company, was I?"

"Nope." Adam grinned, the temptation to tease too strong to resist. "And did you know you snore?"

Samantha jerked upright, her eyes round. "I do?"

Adam laughed. "Of course not."

She giggled, shaking her head in mock dismay.

Adam bobbed his head toward the house. "What say we get down and walk the rest of the way?"

She yawned and nodded agreement. "That would be best." He helped her slide off before hopping down beside her. They shared one last lingering look before Adam tugged at Bet's harness and they headed for the house. As they entered the yard, Samantha pointed to a buggy beside the barn. "Looks like you've got a visitor."

"Reckon so." Adam recognized the rig as John Jenkins', the town blacksmith who also rented it out. And wasn't that the sheriff's horse tethered next to it? "Go on up to the house while I take care of Bet. I'll be there in a few minutes."

Samantha sucked in her lips, her steps faltering. "They— they probably all know how I took off in the night, don't they?"

Sympathy welled in Adam's chest. "I'm sure they do, but they won't hold it against you."

She dipped her head and dug into the ground with the toe of her shoe. "Can—can I stay with you? Then we can go in together. . . ."

How could Adam refuse such a sweet request? "Come with me then." Her smile rewarded him. He enjoyed her company while he brushed Bet with a wide, short bristled brush, speaking his usual words of small talk to the horse as he worked. A barn cat rubbed against Samantha's leg, and she scooped it up, scratching its chin and making it purr.

She murmured silly things to the cat, and when she looked up and caught Adam watching her, her cheeks turned rosy. "Guess it's kind of silly, talking to a cat." She put the animal on the floor.

Adam shrugged. "No sillier than talking to a horse."

She gave a soft chuckle. "Then we're both silly."

Placing the brush on its shelf, Adam swished his hands together. "Two of a kind, that's us," he agreed, his throat tight as he considered the deeper meaning behind his simple statement.

They stood silently in the barn, oblivious to the purring cat and Bet's snorts of contentment. Nothing existed in those moments but Adam and Samantha. A question crossed his mind: *Should I?* In silent answer, he very slowly moved toward her, scuffing up bits of hay as he came.

He could see her draw in her breath and hold it as he approached, her eyes locked on his. He saw the question in her eyes: *Would he? Would he really?* . . . When he stood mere inches in front of her, he stopped, bringing up his hands to cup her upper arms. Her gaze flittered from his eyes to his lips, then to his eyes again. He watched the course of her blue eyes, and one side of his mouth quirked into a smile before he bent forward. "I love you, Samantha." He didn't wait but placed his lips softly—ever so softly—on hers.

When he straightened, she released in one *whoosh* the breath she'd been holding. Adam dropped his hands and stepped back. Bold crimson painted her cheeks, but she didn't avert her gaze. He had told her how he felt about her, he had kissed her, and she wasn't running scared. His heart turned over in his chest. He held out his hand. "Let's go see the folks."

She slipped her hand into his. "I'm ready."

They ambled toward the big house hand in hand. Adam opened the screened door into the kitchen and held it while Samantha entered. With a sharp intake of breath she stopped immediately inside the doorway. Adam peered over her shoulder.

Sheriff Barnes and the scruffy looking man Adam had encountered at the depot was sitting at the kitchen table with his ma and pa, sipping coffee. As the door slammed back into its frame, all four looked toward them.

The disheveled man grinned, showing his crooked yellow teeth. "Well, hello, girlie. Betcha yore surprised ta' see me here, huh?"

Samantha stood as still as if she were made of stone. Adam slipped a hand under hers and squeezed gently, a fearful understanding forming in his mind.

Ma stood slowly and moved toward them. Sympathy was clear in her eyes. "Adam, this is Burt O'Brien, from Milwaukee, Wisconsin. He's come to pick up his daughter."

Adam looked into Samantha's stricken face. His legs went weak. Why did her father have to come now? *I should have let her board that train.*

Sheriff Barnes pushed to his feet and crossed the room to stand beside Samantha. "Is this your father, young lady?" His tone was gruff, but his eyes looked sad.

When Samantha nodded woodenly, Adam put his arm around her stiff shoulders, hoping to comfort her with his presence. "Ma, Pa, I found Samantha at the train station. She agreed to come back home with me. We—."

Samantha's father blasted a snort. "*Home*? I hate to tell ya, sonny, but this ain't her home. She'll be a'certain to go home, though. Right now. With me." He lurched around the table and grasped Samantha's arm just above her elbow with grime-encrusted fingers and pushed her toward the door.

"Wait!" Adam leaped into their way.

"Wait fer what?" Burt O'Brien's harsh, grating voice scraped across Adam's ears. "S'pose yo're wantin' me to thank ya fer keepin' track o' my gal. Wal, fine. Thank ya. 'Preciate your hospitality." He spat the words, his taunting grin making a mockery of them. "Now lemme pass. I'm takin' my girlie home."

Ma and Pa followed as Burt pushed Samantha out the door. He stomped in a blundering gait across the yard, Samantha stumbling along as if in shock. Adam trotted beside them, wanting to stop the man but afraid to intervene. Burt O'Brien was a violent man. If Adam created a scene, Samantha could be hurt.

With a mighty shove, Burt forced Samantha into the buggy and climbed up awkwardly beside her. Adam ran around to the opposite side of the rig, reaching up to clasp Samantha's icy hand. "Samantha, I—" But what could he say? *I'll come for you.* Only an hour ago she had tearfully told him that people shouldn't make promises they couldn't keep. He wouldn't add another broken promise to all those made before. So he squeezed her cold hand and tried to tell her with his eyes what was on his heart.

Her lips wavered into the saddest smile he'd ever seen. "Adam, don't worry. I'll be all right." Then a smile reached her eyes, igniting an inner fire. "I have Someone stronger than me with me now."

Her bravery tugged painfully at his heart. Despite her determined expression, he sensed the fear in her stiffly upright position. *Oh, Lord, how can I help her now?* His Bible . . . he'd give Samantha his Bible. He waved both hands, inching sideways. "Wait, please, just wait a minute. Don't leave. I've got something—." He spun and took off at a run for the house.

He clattered up the stairs, his heart pounding so hard it hurt to breathe. He snatched the Bible from its spot on the bedside table and raced back out. The buggy waited, both passengers on the seat, with Pa and Ma at its side. Ma was telling Samantha's father about her good job working for Liz.

"That so?" O'Brien shot his daughter a speculative glance.

"Yes. She's done such a fine job," Ma continued, her eyes hopeful, "that we'd like her to stay and—."

"No." The man spat over the edge of the buggy, his brown-tinged spittle landing near Pa's booted foot. "She ain't stayin' here. She's got her own house to tend, an' she's gonna tend it. Now you folks jus' step back so we can git to the train station afore the next train goes without us." He raised his hands as if to slap the reins down against the horse's back.

Adam reached across Samantha to capture the man's grubby wrist. "Mr. O'Brien, please—just one more minute." The man scowled, but he held his hands still. Adam pressed the Bible into Samantha's lap. "Here are promises you can count on, Samantha." *They will keep you until I can make my own promises to you*, he tried to tell her with his eyes.

She looked down, and tears swam in her eyes. She clutched the book to her breast and nodded, smiling weakly through her tears.

"Hi-yup!" O'Brien brought the reins down on the horse's back, sending the startled animal into a trot.

Samantha turned backward in her seat, her face pinched and pale. But she offered a brave, tremulous smile, lifting her hand to wave. Adam took two steps forward, ready to chase down the buggy and bring her back.

Ma placed a hand on his arm. "Let her go, son. We have to let her go."

"But, Ma, that man—" Adam's voice broke. "He'll hurt her. I know he will."

Ma squeezed Adam's arm, the touch wrought with sympathetic understanding. "We have to let her go, Adam, and trust the Lord to watch out for her."

Adam looked to Sheriff Barnes for help, but the big man simply shook his head, an expression of regret in his face. "I'm sorry, Adam. She's underage—not old enough to be on her own. If her pa wants her home, I had to send her."

The buggy rounded the bend, carrying Samantha away. Adam pressed his hands hard into his jacket pockets, his jaw clenched. He'd only just gotten her—she'd only just become his. And now she was gone. It wasn't fair. *Oh, God, it isn't fair.* He looked down into his mother's empathetic face. "Ma," he choked out, but he could say no more. Lowering his head, he turned away and wept.

Chapter Twenty-Two

October passed, bleak and dismal with overcast skies and biting winds that matched Adam's somber mood. The first snowfall, usually an event of celebration, cheered Adam not in the least. Samantha's abrupt departure from his life—as sudden and unexpected as her entrance had been—left a hollow void he found impossible to fill. His days were full and busy, yet empty. The joy was gone. And he didn't know how to recapture it.

He haunted the post office, hoping and praying for some word from Samantha that would let him know how she fared. But nothing came, and gradually he came to accept that she wouldn't—or couldn't—write to him. The memories of their brief time together were no doubt as painful for her as they were for him. It was better to let go.

The day he overhead Sarah ask, "Mama, will Adam ever smile again?" he realized he must somehow regain his old, cheerful spirit. But how? He agonized, the image of Samantha cowering in fright after their brief argument haunting his dreams and creeping into his mind at odd times during the day. There were so many other images he could conjure—Samantha in her overalls picking berries with her hair wild around her piquant face; Samantha smiling blissfully as she cradled little A.J.; Samantha happily exploring the dugout; Samantha rising from her knees in a storage shed, her face shining. . . . Yet that horrible picture overwhelmed him.

Was she being abused now? Was she lying somewhere, bruised and broken, waiting for a rescuer? Those images tortured him until he wanted to scream at the heavens.

Adam needed a change. He needed a task so mind consuming that all thoughts of Samantha would be erased. He thought of his friend Thomas Enns and where he had gone. The idea of going off to fight, as Thomas had, filled him with dread, yet if he went, he felt certain he could rid his thoughts of Samantha. There were great risks involved, and his family would be in opposition to such a plan. Yet in his despondent state, the idea held merit.

He could enlist in the army. Frank and Arn, with Teddy's help, could handle the farm work so he didn't need to feel guilty about leaving his father short-handed. The plans fell into place in his mind. He would wait until after Thanksgiving. One last holiday with his family, and then he would go. The course of action decided, Adam made a determined effort to at least pretend to be his old, jocular self again. He wanted to leave his family with pleasant memories to recall while he was away. He didn't allow himself to dwell on the reason, but he knew it was just in case he didn't return. . . .

Back in Milwaukee, Samantha settled into her familiar routine. Household chores, caring for Pa's needs . . . The days were as she remembered—strained and bleak and joyless. She printed up a little sign and hung it in the post office, advertising that she would mend or construct garments for people. Before long, she had a steady business going, and she carefully hoarded away half of the money she earned. Pa took control of the other half, and most of it he squandered on drink. She read Adam's Bible daily, taking comfort in the words she found there. And as time passed, she discovered a peace of spirit within herself despite the outer turmoil in her life.

As she learned more about Jesus and His love for her, she began seeing her father in a different light. She understood that Jesus loved her pa, too, and if she wanted to be like Him, she must try to see her father through Christ's eyes. Instead of viewing him as hateful, she looked deep inside to a man so full of unhappiness that only hate could come out. Instead of reviling him, she began pitying him, and she prayed for him daily that he might come to know the peace she now held in her heart.

On Sundays she walked to the little church she had attended with Gran all those years ago. A new, young minister was serving there now, and his teachings were as gentle and mind soothing as Reverend Goertzen's. Samantha drank in the words spoken by the light-haired man behind the pulpit, reflecting on those words through the week. The more she listened and learned, the easier it was for her to bear Pa's ranting and raving. She was maturing into a spiritual young woman, and the changes did not go unnoticed by the young minister. However, as attentive as Samantha was to his teaching, she remained aloof to any other attentions. Her heart still remained in Mountain Lake.

Her mind carried her back to Mountain Lake often. She wondered how big the twins were, how Liz was feeling, if Sarah's front teeth were clear in and how that might have changed her looks, whether Hulda Klaassen had found someone else to sew up those dresses she was supposed to have made. . . .

But most often she thought of Adam, although she tried not to. She loved him more than she had ever thought possible, but the realization only brought heartache instead of the carefree joy she'd always imagined loving someone would bring. Some days she hoped she would find a letter from him, other days she was glad she didn't. This was her life now, and dreaming of other times and places served no useful purpose. So she immersed herself in her work, in her Bible reading, and her attempts to change her father.

One day as Samantha sat in a rocker near the small four-pane kitchen window, putting the hem in a petticoat, David weighed on her mind. He would be twenty-four years old now. Old enough to be married, maybe even have children. What was David like now?

She remembered him as a thin, pale youth, taller than Pa already at fifteen, with a headful of russet curls that refused to be tamed and her own pale blue eyes. Always somber, rarely smiling. Her brother . . . did David ever think of her? Ever wonder how she was doing? Ever think of returning for her?

She nipped the thread with her teeth and let the white cloth drop into her lap. It seemed sometimes that she had lost every person she'd loved. First Gran, then David. And Adam. It hurt most, losing Adam, because she'd had him for such a short time. Being yanked from him was like being wakened rudely from a happy dream.

The old Samantha would have engrossed herself in self-pity, but the new Samantha saw each loss as a means to strengthen her. She reminded herself that her Book of promises gave the assurance that all things work together for good. Adam had told her she could count on those promises.

She held to God's promises. Her life held meaning now, and purpose. It was only a matter of time before all things became good.

The week before Thanksgiving Adam broke the news to his father about enlisting in the army. They were in the tack shed, rubbing soap into two new saddles, when Adam interrupted the comfortable silence to announce his intentions.

Pa glowered. "You will do no such thing."

Adam put the soap aside and leaned forward, resting his elbows on his knees. "Pa, please, can't we talk about this?"

"Absolutely not." Normally mellow, Pa's voice took on a hard edge. "I forbid you to do such a thing."

Adam hung his head. He spoke to the spot of ground between his boots. "I'm not asking for your permission. I'm just telling you what I intend to do." He'd never defied his father before. His chest felt tight, but he wouldn't back down now.

Pa bolted to his feet, pacing back and forth twice in the small space. His breath came out in white puffs, his face set angrily, resembling a disgruntled dragon. "Don't think I can't figure out why you think you need to go. It's the girl, isn't it? It's because of Samantha."

Adam kept his head down, closing his eyes momentarily to mask the stab of pain the mention of Samantha had brought.

Pausing in his clomping progress across the floor, Pa clamped his hand over Adam's shoulder and shook it. "Answer me. Isn't it?"

Adam pushed aside Pa's hand and rose. "Yes. She's in my heart, Pa, and I can't get her out. I need to get away from here. I need to get my mind so wrapped up in something else that no thought of Samantha can intrude. I can't go on like this anymore."

"And you think taking up a weapon and facing an enemy bigger than your own mind will chase her out again?"

"Yes!" Angry tears threatened, and he set his jaw firmly to keep them at bay. He would not humiliate himself by breaking down now.

Pa huffed out a derisive snort. "I would've expected such rash behavior from Frank. He's been our impulsive one—acting first and thinking later. But you? You've always been reasonable and logical." Shaking his head, Pa scuffed his hand across the work table in the corner, seeming to forget Adam was in the room. "Fool boy. Foolish, heartbroken boy. Would never have imagined him threatening to march off to war. If it weren't for that girl . . ."

Adam's defenses rose. "Don't blame Samantha."

Pa released a mirthless laugh and turned to face Adam. "Oh, I'm not. I'm leaving the blame fully at your feet, son. She's not the problem. *You* are the problem. You're your own worst enemy right now." He tapped his graying temple. "Instead of using your head you're letting your heart misguide you. But I know you well enough to know eventually your head will convince your heart to do the right thing."

Adam thrust out his jaw. "I've been thinking. I've thought of nothing else since she left. And I don't know what else to do."

Pa pulled up a sawhorse and seated himself close to his son. "Listen to me, boy." He placed his thick, leathery palm on Adam's knee. "It's one thing to mope, but it's another to throw your life away. You have feelings for the girl. You're worried about her. I understand that. Even respect it. But how can making a foolhardy move like joining the army fix anything?"

Adam didn't have an answer, so he sat in stony silence.

Pa sighed and wiped a hand across his face tiredly, drawing his skin downward. He suddenly looked old to Adam, and it scared him. Pa slapped his hands down on his thighs. "You're twenty years old now, and if you mean to go, I reckon I can't stand in your way. But I can tell you to use the brain God gave you and think. Think long and hard on this before you go traipsing off. You accused Samantha of running away." He paused for a moment, his gaze boring into Adam's. "Just what do you call what you're doing?"

Adam didn't answer. There wasn't much to say when he knew, deep down, that his father was right. But he also knew, right or wrong, that he would go. Because he could think of no other way to rid his mind—and heart—of Samantha O'Brien.

With a heavy sigh, Pa pushed himself upright. He clapped one hand on Adam's shoulder. "I'm gonna go talk to your ma now. Tell her what you're planning. Ask her to pray." He chuckled, the sound sad. "I can tell you what she'll ask the Lord—to change your mind."

Adam whisked a hard glance upward. "About Samantha?"

Pa shook his head. "That'd be foolhardy on our parts. A person doesn't choose to love—it happens. And you can no more choose to turn off your love for Samantha than you chose to have it grow. But our understanding is one thing—giving our blessing to you drowning your sorrows in the horror of battle is quite another." Once again, Pa seemed to drift away. "No one said raising children was easy—and it sure doesn't improve with age."

With another squeeze on Adam's shoulder, Pa pulled his hand away. "Your ma and me are going to put you and your heartache in the Lord's hands, son. Just do one thing for me, will you?"

Adam kept his lips pressed tightly together, but he looked into his father's lined face.

"Heed His voice. Open your heart and your head, and *listen* for His leading."

Chapter Twenty-Three

The day after Thanksgiving, Adam stood on the wooden platform in front of the tiny depot building. His family gathered close, bestowing their good-byes in voices loud enough to be heard over the raucous rumbling of the engine waiting to depart. He was leaving, but not to Europe. Ma had suggested if he needed to get away, a visit to his brother and grandparents in Minneapolis would be much less drastic than enlisting to fight. Although initially resistant, he'd finally conceded that going to Minneapolis might be a good idea. Spending a few weeks keeping up with Grandpa and Grandma Klaassen might be just what he needed to clear his Samantha-filled head. And if not, the army would still be there when he returned.

"Give Daniel and Rose our love," Ma hollered next to Adam's ear, "and kiss little Christina and Katrina for me."

"I will."

Josie grabbed his arm, her mouth opened to speak. He turned to her with a smirk and cut her off, "And I'll give them the doll clothes you made the minute I arrive." She'd only reminded him seven times already. How could he forget?

With a playful grin, Josie punched him on the arm his arm. Then she hugged him hard, her arms curled around his neck. "Take care, Adam."

He planted a quick kiss on her cheek. "You, too—and stay away from Stephen Koehn until I get back." Adam laughed as she blushed and turned away. It hardly seemed that Josie could be old enough for young men to come courting, but she must be, for it was happening. But then, she was the same age as Samantha, and she——. He cut those thoughts off quickly. The purpose of this trip was to forget about Samantha.

Sarah tugged at Adam's coat sleeve, demanding to be lifted up for a hug. She gave him a noisy smack on the cheek. He lowered her to the ground and reached for Teddy, rubbing his little hat over his head affectionately. "Be good," Adam told the two youngest.

Next came Becky, then Arn who stood as tall as Adam now and insisted on simply shaking hands. His hug from Liz was longer and harder than the others, and he returned it with equal pressure. She pressed her nose against his, smiling into his eyes. "Come back happy," she said. He nodded.

Frank stood close, an arm curved around Anna. Yesterday at the height of celebration, they'd announced their intention to marry in February. Adam placed a gloved hand on Frank's shoulder, giving him a warm squeeze. "Take care of each other. I'll see you soon."

Last, Adam turned to Pa. Father and son clasped gloved hands, snowflakes flying wildly around their heads and cold air lifting their hair. They stood, a mere twelve inches separating them, for several long seconds before Adam lurched forward and found himself held firmly in his father's strong embrace. Pa bellowed in Adam's ear, "Be back in time for Christmas." Adam understood Pa meant for him to be back to himself again by Christmas. Without Samantha, would he ever be whole again?

The men pulled apart as the conductor bawled, "Bo-o-oard."

Arn grabbed up Adam's carpetbag and the whole family accompanied Adam to the steps that led to the railroad car. One more hug from little Sarah, and Adam hopped up into the car. He turned back for a last smile and wave before stepping inside the long box. He chose a seat then used his sleeve to clear a good-sized spot on the frosted glass. Pressing his nose to the open spot, he waved.

As the train started its chugging motion, Teddy ran down the boardwalk beside it, leaping off the end and continuing until Pa waved him back. Just before the train turned the bend, Adam glimpsed Pa slip his arm around Ma's waist and pull her snug to his side. Even from this distance, he recognized the shiny paths on Ma's face as tears. Pressure built in Adam's chest. *I don't want to hurt them, Lord*, he prayed as he settled into his seat for the journey. *But I don't want to hurt anymore, either. Help me, Lord. Please, help me.*

Thanksgiving had been just as Samantha expected. She had hoped that maybe—*maybe*—this year would be different. But she should have known better, she decided with a flash of cynicism.

She'd prepared a fine meal, using some of her saved sewing money to purchase a goose and stuffing it with a savory sage dressing. She'd prepared three different vegetables and baked bread, even stirred up a sweet potato pie in a flaky crust. But by the time Pa had staggered in, reeking of whiskey and mumbling belligerently, the food was cold. Some Thanksgiving it had been. . . . Although two days had passed, the sting of regret still clung to her heart. Samantha could not remember a holiday, ever, that had not been spoiled by her father's drinking.

She put a few dishes back on the warped shelving above the dry sink, and couldn't help but sigh. She had so hoped this Thanksgiving would be different. All the prayers, all the changes she'd made within herself, came for nothing. She rested her hands on the sharp edge of the dry sink and let her head drop low. Pa would never change. What was the use?

Suddenly an image of a family seated around a long trestle table popped into her mind. She could see their smiling faces, hear their laughing voices, and she was hit with a wave of melancholy so powerful tears spurted into her eyes. Oh, she missed the Klaassens and Mountain Lake. She missed them *so much. . . .*

She crossed the dim room to light an oil lamp and curl up in her familiar rocker, the old rocker in which Gran used to sit. She remembered well the security of cuddling up in Gran's soft lap and being rocked. She remembered, too, being cradled in Adam's arms that one time as they had ridden back to his house on Bet's strong back. What she wouldn't give to have one of them here to hold her now.

The front door rattled, startling Samantha out of her reverie. She heard a grumbled curse, and the sounds of the doorknob being violently twisted broke through the room. Pa was home. Samantha rose and hurried to the door to open it for him.

As he lurched through the open doorway, the stench of stale whiskey and cigar smoke drifted past Samantha's nose causing her to wince. He gave her a bleary glare. "Whatsamatter, girlie? Ain'tcha glad to see yore ol' man? Huh?" He laughed horribly, his breath making Samantha take a backward step.

"Come, Pa. Sit down and I'll get you some coffee." She guided him to the small table and helped him into a chair. He slouched drunkenly, watching Samantha through watery, red-rimmed eyes as she poured a cup of coffee and ladled out a bowl of vegetable soup. When Samantha placed the cup and bowl in front of him, he reached out with strength belying his drunkenness to grasp her wrist. A strange light shone in his blood-shot eyes, and his grin seemed somehow evil. Alarm bells rang in Samantha's mind. "W-what is it, Pa?"

Pa tightened his grip on her wrist and lifted his other hand to pinch a strand of her hair between two dirty fingers. "Jus' quite the li'l homemaker, ain'tcha? All growed up an' knowin' how to take keer of a man . . ."

An unnamed fear claimed Samantha. She twisted her arm, trying to pull away. "Pa . . . ?"

As suddenly as it had begun, his strangeness ended. Throwing her wrist away, he ordered thickly, "Oh, git away from me, girl. Git me some o' that bread to sop up this soup. Y'know I can't eat soup without bread."

Her heart thudding, she skittered to obey.

❧

Adam stood outside a large store in downtown Minneapolis, admiring the variety of toys in the window. Wouldn't his little nieces, Katrina and Christina, love those golden-haired dolls dressed in satins and lace?

During his three weeks in Minneapolis, he'd thoroughly enjoyed the time spent with Daniel and Rose and getting acquainted with his two small nieces. The girls were sweet and loving, dimpled and curly haired, and Adam found them irresistible. His grandparents were as pert and lively as ever, and many pleasant evenings were spent in their company. He'd even gone with Daniel to his law office several times and developed a respect for Daniel and his work.

But as much as he enjoyed his visit, he hadn't accomplished what he had come for—he hadn't managed to forget Samantha. The idea was ludicrous. How could he forget? But although she still hovered on the fringes of his mind, he no longer felt the stabbing pain of remembrance. Time in prayer with his wise, loving grandparents and with his older brother had soothed the edges of his tattered heart. Thanks to God's healing touch, thoughts of Samantha brought a gratefulness that she had entered his life and that they had been able to touch one another in a special way. Daily, he prayed for the Lord to keep her in His capable care, and he trusted that wherever Samantha was, she was at peace with herself.

Now he turned his attention back to the store window display. In the center of the toys, a tin train circled a metal track. Andy and A.J. would coo with delight if the train ran around their Christmas tree. He pulled out a folded wad of bills from his pocket. Counting it, he decided there was enough for two of the big, golden-haired dolls and the train. Maybe he could even get a doll for Sarah and a painted top for Teddy, as well as gifts for his other family members.

He stepped inside the warm store, glad to be out of the biting December wind. Minnesota wasn't known for its mild winters. He purchased the toys, asking the gray-haired man behind the wooden counter to wrap each gift. Smilingly the man began pulling out patterned paper and bright colored ribbons from beneath the counter.

"I'm going to look around a bit while you wrap those," Adam told the clerk.

The man gave a genial nod. "Certainly, sir, go right ahead. Take your time."

Adam browsed the store, picking up a round polished rock paperweight. He bounced it in his hand, envisioning it on Daniel's work desk. He found a kaleidoscope for Becky and spent a few cheerful minutes peeking into the brass tube, enjoying the varying designs that appeared as he turned the end.

On another table woolen scarves of every imaginable color caught his attention. He chose a blue one for Arn and a green one for Frank. For Pa he selected thick, wool-lined gloves of brown suede. Turning from the scarves, he spotted a glass-covered jewelry case. Broaches and necklaces, earrings and bracelets each set with colored rhinestones stretched across a background of black velvet. He selected a heart-shaped pin with a red center stone for Ma and dainty necklaces of crystal teardrops on gold-plated chains for Josie, Anna, and Rose. Moving on, he came to a large display of music boxes. He lifted the lid on the one closest to him, smiling as a tinkling melody spilled forth.

A saleslady came up behind him. "May I help you?"

Adam gestured to the boxes. "These are sure pretty."

"Yes, sir, they are." She fluttered her eyelashes, her smile flirtatious. "Any young lady would be pleased to receive one. Do you have a special young lady in mind?"

Samantha's face appeared before Adam's eyes. Yes, he had a special young lady in mind. But how would he get it to her? Buying one would be foolhardy, almost tempting fate. It was illogical, unreasonable, and probably even a waste of his hard-earned money. Adam said, "Yes, I do."

The saleslady seemed to deflate momentarily, but then she straightened and inquired brightly, "Which one do you think she would prefer?"

Adam's eyes drifted across the selections. There were at least fifteen music boxes, each with a different picture inlaid on the tops with what appeared to be bits of shell. His eyes roved, and one jumped out at him. It had a gold filigreed edge, with a cream-colored pearlized cover. A perfect opened rose, each petal set individually in varying shades of palest pink to deep burgundy, filled the center. It brought to mind Samantha's dress of roses and trailing vines.

He pointed. "I'll take that one."

The saleslady scooped it up and carried it to the counter.

Adam leaned against the wooden counter as the woman poked around somewhere below it, scouting for something. She finally stood, a scowl on her face. "I'd like to wrap it in paper and put it in a box, but I can't find a box." She headed for a door at the back of the store. "Stay here. I'll have our stockman look in the storage room. Surely there's something there that will hold your music box." Her pointed-toed shoes clicked purposefully on the tiled floor as she disappeared from view.

Adam gazed at the rose, a bubble of happiness pressing against his heart as he thought of Samantha's hands holding the music box. She would love it; he knew she would.

"We found one, sir." The saleslady approached, followed by a tall, slender young man. The young man held a stack of boxes in his freckled arms. "Just put those under the counter, David," the saleslady instructed the stockman.

She reached for Adam's music box, flashing a smile. "We'll get you fixed up in no time, sir." She set to work wrapping the box in a cloud of white tissue paper.

Adam watched the stockman bend to place the supply of empty boxes below the counter. There was something vaguely familiar about him. David, the woman had called him. Adam stared, trying to remember where he'd seen the man before. He was tall, his face freckled slightly, his head covered with auburn curls that seemed unable to behave. And his eyes were pale cornflower blue, just like—

Adam's jaw dropped. *David*. Could this be Samantha's brother who had run away? The stockman, his task completed, headed for the back of the store. Adam offered a quick apology to the saleslady then scurried after the stockman. "David?"

The man turned around, his thin face attentive. "Yes? May I help you?"

Now that he had the man's attention, Adam found himself tongue-tied. He couldn't very well accuse him of running away as a boy and leaving his sister behind. "I wondered . . ." The man waited, his expression wary. Adam released a nervous laugh. "Do you have a sister? A sister named Samantha?"

David's cornflower eyes narrowed, and his glance darted around the store as if seeking someone out. His eyes came back to Adam. "Why do you want to know?"

Adam recognized in the tall young man the same defensiveness that Samantha possessed. He found the physical resemblance and the familiar mannerisms uncanny. "I'm a friend of Samantha's. She told me about a brother named David, whom she hasn't seen in several years. I thought . . . well, I wondered if you might be him."

David stood still, staring off somewhere behind Adam, his face expressionless. For Adam it was eerie. It was as if seeing Samantha again, only not Samantha. But he couldn't squelch a bubble of hope. How excited she'd be if this was her brother.

The man finally shifted his gaze to look at Adam. "I'm sure there are dozens of Davids in the city." His voice sounded empty. Hollow. "I'm sorry, but I'm not the right one." He turned and hurried away, disappearing through a swinging wooden door.

Adam watched him go, frowning. He couldn't be certain the man was Samantha's brother—it could be wishful thinking on Adam's part that made him see the similarities between the two—but he got the impression that David *was* Samantha's brother and was unwilling to admit it for some unknown reason. Adam wouldn't press the issue now. He knew the name of the store, and he could come back. With that thought in mind, he gathered up his purchases and left.

Chapter Twenty-Four

*D*avid emerged from the back area of the store and rushed to the front windows, watching as the man headed down the snow-covered walkway with his arms laden with packages. David sighed, pressing his forehead against the cold glass. He thought back to that night seven years ago, when he had kissed his little sister good-bye and sneaked away, promising to come back for her. She'd been only ten or so then, a skinny little waif with too much hair for her slender neck.

Seven years . . . Samantha would be grown now, a woman. The man had said he was a friend. The man was well-dressed, polite, obviously from a good family. How would Samantha have met someone like him, coming from their part of town? What was she like now? Was she still with Pa? So many questions . . . And that man could have answered them, had David summoned the courage to ask.

He pushed away from the window, heading back to his work area. He thought of Pa. Had Pa changed at all? For Samantha's sake, he hoped so. Life with him had been unbearable. David carried the emotional scars of his childhood yet.

There had been no choice about leaving. He couldn't take it a day longer, he'd told himself over and over. But guilt overwhelmed him once more as he remembered leaving Sammy behind. He'd wanted to bring her with him when he stole away, but how could he? She was just a kid. She would've needed the kind of care he couldn't give, not on the run like he was. Did she understand how hard it had been for him to go without her?

David worried so often over the years, wondering if Pa had taken out his anger at his son's escape on the unwitting Samantha. The guilt had been horrible. Almost as bad as his pa's beatings. He'd promised to go back for her, though, and he had—three years later, after he'd established himself in the city. Pa had answered his knock at the door, and when David demanded to see Samantha, Pa only laughed. His father's voice echoed in his memory. *"She ain't here no more. Run off, just like you done. You ain't gonna find her here."* David's body jerked as he relived the slam of the door in his face.

His heart ached anew, wondering—just as he had then—where had she gone? How was she taking care of herself? That man who knew her could have answered David's questions, if only he'd asked. But after being David Bryant for so many years, he didn't know how to be—or if he even wanted to be—David O'Brien again. And why would Samantha want anything to do with him after he'd abandoned her?

Turning back to his work, David assured himself that his sister must be doing fine if she had a friend in that well-dressed, polite man. He didn't need to worry about her anymore. Still, it was hard not to be curious. His little sister . . .

♋

Adam deposited his purchases at the stately two-story home his brother and sister-in-law occupied. He spent a few moments fending off questions from Christina about the many ribboned packages before telling Rose he was going out again. He bundled up once more and caught a horse-drawn cab to ride to Daniel's law office.

"Daniel, I need your help," he blurted the moment he stepped through the door.

Daniel's eyebrows rose, but he set aside the papers he had been examining. "Professional or brotherly?"

Adam grinned. "Both, I guess. I was just at Smothers' Department Store, and I met a man . . ." Adam filled Daniel in, on how the man's name was David and how he resembled Samantha physically right down to the spattering of freckles across the bridge of his nose. "I'm certain the man is Samantha's brother, but he denies it."

Daniel leaned back and rested his elbows on the armrests of his chair, making a steeple of his hands in front of his chest. "So what do you want me to do?"

"I want you to find out if he *is* who I think he is—if he is Samantha's brother, David. Can you imagine what it would mean to Samantha, to have him back in her life? Why, she'd be beside herself with joy."

Daniel rocked his chair a couple times, his head cocked. "Adam, it would be a simple matter to check at the store, find out this David's full name. If his last name is O'Brien, I think that would prove to be too much of a coincidence to overlook. Then I would say he is Samantha's missing brother. But proving who is he and reuniting him with Samantha are two different things. Have you considered why he might have told you he wasn't the man you were looking for? Have you considered that perhaps he has no interest in being reunited with Samantha?"

Adam shook his head, baffled. Would a brother refuse to reunite with a sister? "I just figured maybe I caught him by surprise. I tried to be discreet, but to have Samantha mentioned after being separated for all these years . . . No, I'm sure if he really is Samantha's David, he'll want to see her."

"Well, then . . ." Daniel drummed his fingers on the desk, his tone less like a lawyer and more like a brother. "I think you need to consider something else. Samantha lost her brother a long time ago. From what you've said in the past, she feels abandoned by him. What will she think if she finds out he has been as near as a two-hour train ride all these years and never made the effort to come for her? Are you sure that wouldn't be more hurtful to her?"

Adam considered Daniel's question. The old Samantha—the sullen, withdrawn girl who had arrived at the Klaassen farm—would certainly be angry and bitter at the knowledge that her brother had been this close yet stayed away. But he couldn't help but believe the new Samantha would be willing to forgive. The new Samantha would make an effort to understand.

Adam blew out a noisy breath. "We have to take that chance, Daniel. Her brother is all she has in the world. She needs him in her life."

Daniel grimaced. "I hope you're right, little brother, because if I go poking my professional nose into this man's business and he is who you think he is, I am going to be opening one big can of worms."

Adam threw his arms wide. "Big brother, open away."

Chapter Twenty-Five

*S*amantha draped evergreen boughs and tiny red holly berries along windowsills and shelf edges. She had no tree, but this bit of greenery was almost as nice, she decided as she stepped back to survey her work. She placed two thick candles on the windowsill and swished a match along the underside of the sill, cupping the flame as she raised it to light the candles. She smiled at the result. Festive and warm.

Christmas Eve. Soon she'd leave to go to the service at church. She'd received a special invitation from the young minister, Reverend Johansen. It had taken her by surprise, but she'd recovered quickly, managing to smile in a friendly manner and thanking him without conveying any additional meaning. The blond, blue-eyed man had acted a bit disappointed by her casual response, but he hadn't pressed the issue. For Samantha, no one—not even a handsome, well-stationed man such as Reverend Johansen—could measure up to Adam Klaassen.

Her pa slept in his small bedroom. He'd staggered home almost two hours ago, having spent most of the afternoon at his favorite tavern. Samantha had helped him into bed, relieved when he'd immediately fallen asleep. His rumbling snore drifted through the closed door. He'd probably sleep the rest of the night.

She checked the small wind-up clock on the table. Almost seven. If she didn't leave now, she'd be late. She tiptoed across the wooden floor and tapped lightly on Pa's door. No answer—

just a snuffle and the squeak of the mattress as he apparently rolled over in his sleep.

Samantha cracked the door. "Pa? I'm going to the church now."

Burt made a growling sound as he came awake. He sat up groggily and turned his bleary gaze on Samantha, blinking as if to clear his vision. "Wha—whaddaya wan'?"

Samantha bit her lower lip. He was still pretty drunk. The nap hadn't done him much good. She stepped a bit farther into the room. "I'm going to the church now." She kept her voice low. Pa couldn't abide loud noises when he was coming down off of a drunk. "Can I get something for you before I go?"

Her final word must have penetrated the fog of Pa's alcohol-laden brain. He swung his feet over the edge of the bed, swaying and grabbing at his bedside table as he struggled to find his balance. "Go? You ain't goin' no place, girlie."

Samantha took a hesitant step backward. "But, Pa, it's just to church. I'll be home in an hour, and we can have some cider together."

"I said *no*!" He swung his arm, knocking the china bowl and pitcher from the table beside his bed. The subsequent crash made him clutch his ears in agony. "Oooh, my head. My head."

Samantha rushed to his side. "Are you all right, Pa? Here, let me help you." She reached for him, but he slapped her hands away.

"No!" His bellow echoed more loudly than the breaking china had. "Git away from me. Jus' leave—go on, git. Jus' go."

Samantha hovered, uncertain and scared. He was so unpredictable. "I—I'll clean up this mess." She gestured to the broken pieces of china scattered across the floor. "I don't want you to cut yourself." She knelt, beginning to stack the larger pieces together.

Pa stared at her glassy-eyed, mumbling. "Uh-huh, yup, you clean it up. Allus so worried 'bout 'er pa. Allus takin' keer o' 'er Pa. But she don' really keer. Not really. She don' really keer—nobody does, nobody . . ."

An ominous tone crept into her father's voice. Samantha stiffened. She understood what was happening, having lived it hundreds of times before. *Oh, God, please, not again . . .*

Pa lurched to his feet. "You don' really keer." He roared, his face near hers, his breath hot and foul smelling. His hand snaked out, and he caught her by the arm, drawing her to her feet and shaking her violently. "Ya left me. Jus' like yore ma, ya left me. Took off—you, an' Davey an' 'Livia. Ya don' keer. Yo're nothin' but a liar, S'mantha. A liar."

Samantha screamed as he released her to swing his arm. The back of his hand struck her hard across the cheek. She tasted blood, and she tried desperately to duck away. He raised his hand again, continuing his verbal barrage with loud curses. The second blow caught her on the side of the head, making her ears ring. In defense, Samantha brought up her arms to protect her face. Her elbow caught him under the chin and he stumbled. He fell forward, hitting the table as he fell and taking it with him.

Samantha scrambled sideways, crawling across the pile of the shattered china. Sharp pieces cut into her knees and the palms of her hands, but she paid no attention to the pain. She had to escape.

Out of her father's reach, she untangled her skirts from around her knees and rose clumsily to her feet. She looked back at her father. He'd passed out and remained on the floor as he'd fallen. The table lay beside him, one leg broken and hanging crazily. She slumped against the doorway in relief. She was safe. For now.

Samantha remained in the doorway, breathing heavily. The inside of her mouth was cut, and the sickening taste of blood filled her mouth. She touched her cheek. It felt swollen, and her fingers encountered a small amount of blood where he'd broken the skin on her cheekbone. Snow. That would bring the swelling down.

She staggered to the door, swinging it wide and breathing in the cold, clean air. She shivered but stayed where she was, letting the cold air wash her clean of the horror of the last few moments. It had happened so quickly. Finally she scooped up a handful of snow and placed it gingerly against her cheek. It stung, but she knew it would keep the swelling down.

Stepping back inside, she closed the door and leaned against it. The clump of snow began to melt in the warm room, and a trickle of wetness ran down her arm. Her palms and knees stung, her head ached, and she trembled weakly. She stumbled across the floor to wilt into her rocking chair. She set the chair into gentle motion. She would not be attending church this evening.

⌒〇

Adam sat on the window seat, bouncing little A.J. in his lap. "Giddyap, horsie, go to town. . . ." The chubby infant chortled as Adam chanted.

His family gathered in the parlor, wrapping paper scattered across the floor, happy smiles and cheerful conversation winging from every corner. Observing the scene, he sighed in contentment. What joy he'd discovered in releasing Samantha into the Lord's keeping. He'd also released Samantha's brother.

Daniel had checked into the background of the man named David who worked at Smothers' Department Store. The man, who called himself David Bryant, clung to his story that he had no knowledge of a woman named Samantha O'Brien. Adam still didn't believe him, but as Daniel had pointed out, it wasn't against the law to change your name or disown your relatives, so they had no way to force him into admitting the truth. Adam had left David Bryant his name and address in case he changed his mind, and all he could do now was hope for the best.

Coming home, he discovered, was bittersweet. Sweet to be among his dear family again, bitter because Samantha wasn't here to share in the homecoming. He hadn't placed the music box beneath the tree. It was hidden in his bedroom, under the bed behind the chamber pot. No one would look under there, he was sure. That gift was his promise to himself, to some-day find Samantha. And when he placed it in her hands, he wouldn't let anyone carry her away from him again.

"Adam, thank you." Sarah hugged the beautiful doll he had purchased in the city. "It's the prettiest one I've ever seen."

Adam teased, "Are you sure you're not too big to play with dollies?"

"Huh-uh." Sarah stared in wonder at the china face com-plete with two tiny teeth, the perfectly curled ringlets, and deep purple velvet dress.

"I'd rather have my kaleidoscope," announced tomboy Becky.

Adam grinned as, one by one, his family acknowledged the gifts he'd chosen for them. It was a good feeling, making them happy. Regret smacked as he realized how much his unhappi-ness had affected them. He made a silent vow to never again allow himself to become as despondent as he had been over Samantha's departure. No problem was worth distressing the people he loved. He needed to remember all of the lessons of his childhood—the most important one being that God is in control, and "all things work together for good."

At the Klaassen farm, Christmas day was bright with snow outside, and bright with happiness inside.

⌇⊙

In Minneapolis, in cramped quarters above the department store where he was employed, David O'Brien—known to his fellow employees as David Bryant—sat on a worn sofa and sipped a cup of weak tea. He stared out the curtainless window at the falling snow. It seemed the whole world was white. White—colorless—matching David's mood.

On the battered table beside the sofa rested a folded piece of yellow paper. He reached out a slender hand and fingered it for the hundredth time. All it would take was a telegram to this Adam Klaassen and all of his soul searching would end. Should he? Should he open himself up to this stranger—this man who claimed to be a friend?

He dropped the paper and sighed. A tired sigh. He was so lonely. It seemed he'd been lonely his whole life long. As a child he didn't have friends—not the way other children were friends, visiting one another's homes and playing after school. He'd held himself away from the other children, ashamed of his tattered clothes—although Gran had made sure they were clean tatters—and ramshackle house. And his alcoholic father.

Especially his alcoholic father.

He'd tried to hide the fact that his father was a drunk, but everyone had known. He'd heard the titters of his classmates when his back was turned, calling his father Ol' Burpy Burt. A stupid name—should have even been funny. But it wasn't. It had hurt. It still hurt.

At least he'd had Gran, and there'd been his little sister. He closed his eyes, sliding downward on the threadbare cushions and holding the now-cold mug two-handed against his stomach. How well he remembered the night Samantha was born. He'd been quite young—only seven—but he remembered.

The events of the night rolled in his mind. Mama crying out. Pa stomping around the room with a white face, cursing in fear. A doctor emerging from the bedroom and announcing somberly, "I'm sorry. There was nothing I could do. She hemorrhaged. She's gone." David hadn't known what hemorrhage meant, but he knew what the doctor meant when he'd said his mama was gone. Sorrow swept over him anew as he recalled throwing himself into the corner, weeping inconsolably at the loss of his mother. Gran came in and showed him a tiny, red-faced bundle. "This is your sister, Davey," she'd said. He'd only wanted his mama back.

His opinion had changed in a hurry though. Oh, he'd still missed and wanted his mama. But that Samantha. He smiled, remembering. She'd been such a happy baby. Pretty, too. She'd wrapped him around her little finger the first time she'd given him her spitty, toothless smile. As she'd gotten bigger, he'd thought of her as a friend. She'd followed him around endlessly, getting her nose in the way of everything he did and asking enough questions to drive a fellow to drink.

That expression sobered him in a hurry. He drew a hand through his hair. What kind of a life might they have had if Burt O'Brien hadn't been driven to drink? Try as he might, he couldn't remember a time when his father hadn't turned to drink to drown his sorrows. Gran had told him that Burt had once been a fine man, a good worker and provider for his wife and baby son. But he couldn't remember. Other memories crowded it out.

David scowled, his memories holding him trapped in another time. The night his mother had labored to deliver Samantha, Gran had begged Burt to fetch the doctor. Olivia was in trouble. But his Pa had complained that they couldn't afford a doctor. Gran had secretly sent little David after the old doctor against Burt's wishes. But it had been too late. By the time the doctor had arrived, Olivia had begun to hemorrhage—to bleed, David knew now—and there wasn't anything he could do.

Is that why Burt had started drinking? Did he keep himself in a drunken stupor to forget his guilt over his wife's premature death? He'd always blamed his children, but maybe . . .

David shook his head, sending the memories to the dark corners of his mind. Dwelling on the past accomplished nothing. Could he change any of it now? He pushed off the sofa and crossed to his dry sink, dropping the mug into a pan of oily water. He stood there, staring into the pan of unwashed dishes.

This, now, was his life. No better than the life he'd had before—alone and lonely. Did he really want to drag Samantha down with him a second time? His head shot up, his mouth dry, as another question wiggled through his heart. Would he be dragging her down? Maybe she was as lonely, too. Maybe . . .

A smile tugged at his lips as he pictured a tousle-haired little girl with adoring eyes turned in his direction. Oh, how he'd loved her. She'd been the best thing in his life. And he'd walked away from her. Would she be able to forgive him for that? Would she be able to understand why he hadn't returned?

David stamped across the quiet room to grab up the slip of paper bearing Adam Klaassen's address. Crumpling it tightly in his fist, he turned to stare again at the falling snow: great, fluffy flakes that coated everything, making the world clean and bright. Not colorless, as he'd thought before, but new and full of promise.

All right, then. He relaxed his fist, then smoothed the paper flat against his palm. He'd do it. He'd find out. If she wouldn't accept him, he'd be no worse off than he was right now. But he'd never know until he tried.

Chapter Twenty-Six

Two days after Christmas, Uncle Hiram's young assistant, Will Boehr, delivered a telegram to Adam. He read the stilted message—"Am Sam's brother. Would like contact. Please reply. David O'Brien"—and let out a whoop that startled the chickens into nervous flapping.

It took Adam a month's worth of telegrams and a trip to the city to finalize his plans to reunite David and Samantha, but it was well worth the time and expense. He and David dined together at a Minneapolis restaurant, and the two men talked for hours. David had been shocked to learn Samantha was still living with their father and was very eager to see her safely removed from their childhood home. By the time they parted, Adam felt as though he'd known David for years. And he was certain of David's love for Samantha.

He'd encouraged David to go with him to Milwaukee, but Samantha's brother feared his appearance would stir his father's wrath, and Samantha could get caught in a skirmish. Adam agreed it would be best for him to go after Samantha himself and bring her to Mountain Lake, where David would join them.

The last day of January 1918, Adam rattled across the country in a smoky train car, heading for Milwaukee. In his pocket he had the address provided by David to locate Samantha's home—or at least the home she'd lived in as a child. If she was no longer there, it would give him a starting point to begin his search.

He also had the Christmas gift he had purchased for her, the rose-topped music box. And a heart that beat out a message in time with the rocking rhythm of the train: I'm *coming, I'm coming.* *Wait for me, wait for me.*

David, he presumed, was on another train, traveling to Mountain Lake. The two men had decided it would be best for Adam to bring Samantha back to his own home for the re-union—a neutral territory, so to speak. David would stay in a room at the Commercial Hotel, and Frank would bring him to the farm when Adam returned with Samantha.

⁓𝕆

Only a few more hours and he'd hold Samantha close again. And this time, Adam had no intention of ever letting her go. Closing his eyes, he willed the train to move quickly.

When he disembarked at the Milwaukee station, a lineup of cab drivers waited along the curb to transport travelers. He approached a short, white-haired man who tipped his felt hat.

"Need a ride, sir?"

"Yes, I do." Adam jiggled the paper holding Samantha's ad-dress. "To Front Street."

The man rubbed his raspy chin with glove-covered fingers. "I reckon I c'n getcha there. Got any bags I c'n holp ya with?"

Adam indicated his single travel pouch. "Just this."

With a bright grin, the man snatched it up. "Wal, then, let's go."

Soon Adam was bouncing through busy city streets, peer-ing out anxiously as the horse skittered around new-fangled automobiles.

"Here, now, Tootsie . . ." The driver used a soothing tone when addressing the horse. "Y' keep yer attention where it belongs."

Adam smiled. It sure was different in the city—noisier, bus-ier. . . . The sky was tinged with a gray smoke, no doubt from the factories that dotted the outskirts of the city. There were more buildings than trees, more people than cows, and more automobiles than he'd care to deal with on a daily basis.

The driver of one auto turned a corner sharply, the nose of the vehicle dangerously close to Tootsie's nose. He grabbed the edge of the conveyance and let out a yelp of surprise.

"Crazy fool nincompoop!" The cab driver shook his fist at the vehicle driver. Then he turned an apologetic smile on Adam. "Pardon me, sir, but those young people and their autos. Nothin' but a menace, an' a waste o' road space, if ya ask me."

Adam nodded in agreement. Daniel and Rose were considering purchasing an automobile, but Adam felt more comfortable with a horse. A horse was safer, softer, and more companionable.

It took almost a quarter of an hour to reach the area of town where David had said his old home was located. Adam hopped out of the open-topped cab and held out a coin to the driver. "Thanks for the ride."

The man pocketed the money. "An' thank you, sir."

Adam stayed beside the curb as the horse named Tootsie carried its driver away. Alone now, he perused the area. Hardly a fancy neighborhood—most of the houses looked more like shacks—but somewhere Samantha was waiting. He began to walk.

He searched the street for someone who might be able to direct him, but no people loitered outside today—too cold. The wind bit his nose with its frosty breath. Adam turned up his collar and tugged the flaps of his hat low over his ears, but the chill wind still crept beneath the layers of clothing and made him shiver. He walked briskly, stamping his feet down firmly against the ground to warm them. He counted the houses on Front Street as he walked—two, four, six. . . . There—number nine. That's where David said he'd lived as a youngster with his sister and father. Adam's heart hammered in anticipation.

The house was much like the others on the street—small, squat, weatherworn. A stovepipe jutted from the narrowly sloped roof, emitting a steady series of coal-colored puffs. The windows bore faded calico curtains pulled to the side and tied with yellow ribbon. The ribbons—the bright splash of color— gave him hope he'd reached the right place. His heart caroming wildly in his chest, he stepped to the warped, planked door and knocked.

After only a few moments, the door squeaked open, and there she stood. Samantha. Warmth flooded his frame, joy exploding through his middle. The inside of the house was dark, shielding her in shadows, but he could make out her expression of happy surprise as her eyes widened.

"Adam!" Her voice expressed the joy coursing through his soul. "What—?" Then as suddenly as she'd brightened, her expression turned wary. She peered beyond him, her gaze bouncing around nervously. "W-what are you doing here?"

Adam's elation plummeted to concern when he got a good look at her in the sunlight. A sickly yellowish-green smudge marked her cheekbone, and blood-stained strips of cloth wrapped both hands. He caught her chin between his fingers and lifted her face, examining the ugly mar. "Samantha, what happened to you?"

She pulled away. "Nothing. Just a little accident." She wove her fingers together, he wide eyes holding a note of alarm. "Adam, as wonderful as it is for me to see you, you can't stay. Pa will be home soon, and—"

Adam gazed at her, dismay tangling his emotions in knots. Where was the happy reunion he'd envisioned? "But I've come all this way to see you, and to tell you—"

"Wal, wal, wal . . ." A third voice—harsh and grating—cut from behind Adam. "What've we got here? Comp'ny, huh? S'mantha, girl, why di'n't ya tell me you was 'spectin' comp'ny?"

Adam turned to face the same man who had carted Samantha away from him only two short months ago. By the drawl in the voice and his defensive stance—arms slightly akimbo, neck angled forward, and jaw jutting—Adam knew Burt O'Brien was in an ornery mood. He kept his own body angled to protect Samantha. Her shallow, frightened breaths filled his ears.

"Mr. O'Brien," Adam said, holding his tone steady yet firm, "my visit is a surprise. Samantha did not know I was coming."

O'Brien dismissed Adam's words with a wave of an ungloved, dirty hand. The man's coat hung open, revealing his grime-covered shirt. He wore no hat to fend away the cold, and his lank, gray hair stood up in the wind. His voice bore a menacing undertone as he snorted. "I ain't s'prised to see ya, boy. Knew that girl'd have comp'ny when I was out. When the cat's away . . ." And he laughed, baring his tobacco-stained teeth. He pointed past Adam's shoulder to his daughter, who cowered there, her eyes wide with fright. "You entertainin', girl? You looking' to treat this feller like yore man?"

Sickened by the man's implication, Adam stepped off the cracked concrete slab that served as a porch. "Now wait just a minute. You have no right—"

O'Brien charged forward and jammed one short, stubby finger into Adam's chest. "I got all the rights!" Adam winced. Up close, the man's stench was overpowering. O'Brien's watery eyes narrowed. "I got all the rights 'cause I'm her pa. Don't be tellin' *me* I got no rights."

Adam held up his hands as a sign of surrender. The man was completely unreasonable—no doubt hurting from a lack of alcohol in his system which made him worse than rip-roarin' drunk. Best to try and calm him. "I'm sorry, Mr. O'Brien. I just want you to understand that Samantha has done nothing wrong. I came here to bring her some news, and to deliver a Christmas gift." The mention of the Christmas gift reminded Adam that when he'd been delivered to Front Street, he'd been so anxious to get to Samantha, he'd mistakenly left his bag on the cab. *The music box.*

He turned to Samantha. "I brought you a gift, but I accidentally left it—"

A hand clamped on Adam's shoulder and spun him around. O'Brien glared at him, one fist balled and waving beneath Adam's nose. "Don't you go turnin' your back on me—treatin' me like I ain't even here. I'll teach you manners, boy!"

Before Adam could apologize, the older man planted his fist into Adam's midsection with an amazing amount of strength considering his age and obvious poor health. Adam doubled over, his breath escaping in a loud whoosh.

Samantha danced forward, trying to come between them. "Pa, don't!"

Adam threw out his arm to keep her back. "Go back in the house, Samantha."

O'Brien laughed and waved at Samantha. "Yeah, girlie, go in the house. Let us men handle this'un."

Samantha skittered backward but remained in the doorway, watching with wide, fear-filled eyes. Assured she was safe, Adam turned his attention to her father. "Mr. O'Brien, I don't want to fight you."

The man's face twisted in an ugly scowl. "No, you jus' wanna see my girl. Wal, ya can't, so jus' git on outta here. Git."

Adam held his ground, unwilling to leave Samantha alone with a man so clearly out of control. His hesitation must have stirred O'Brien's fury, because the man cursed and charged, fists flying. Adam fended off the older man's blows. Although unsteady on his feet, weakened from the cold and the alcohol that had damaged his system, O'Brien possessed the tenacity of a fire ant. They tussled, O'Brien pursuing and Adam deflecting blows rather than delivering any of his own. With conscious thought, Adam worked his way toward the street, well away from the house and Samantha. Near the curb, he caught the older man in a bear hug, intending to bring him under control, and the man's wild struggles toppled them both to the ground. They rolled several times and came back up again, their clothing coated with snow.

"Pa, stop it! Please!" Samantha danced on the porch, her face pleading. "Let him go!"

Burt pulled away from Adam, his heaving breaths sending heavy white puffs into the cold air, and glared at his daughter. He jammed his finger at her. "*You.* You brung this on! You wan'ed 'im to come, din'cha?"

Samantha covered her mouth with both hands and shook her head. Her huge blue eyes shimmered with unshed tears.

"Liar!" O'Brien sneered. "Yo're nothin' but a *liar*. Girl, I'm gonna—" He started for the house in his uneven gait.

Adam bolted forward. He couldn't let the man hurt Samantha again. Grabbing O'Brien by the arm, he swung him away from the house and toward the street.

O'Brien stumbled but caught himself before falling. He turned on Adam and doubled up his fist. "Why, you—"

The clatter of horse hooves on cobblestone intruded. Tootsie rounded the corner, her driver waving from the seat. "You there, sir, you left a package on board!"

To Adam, watching from the curb, the world suddenly took on an aura of unreality. O'Brien whirled toward the approaching buggy and stepped off the curb with one foot. Unbalanced, he fell heavily into the street. O'Brien's hands flew upward—a useless

attempt to protect himself as Tootsie reared, confused and frightened by the strange lump at her feet. Samantha's scream ringing
in his ears, Adam reached frantically for the horse's bridle, pulling her head down to keep her from stamping again.

The driver leaped out of the cab, crying out, "Oh, good lord
in heaven, what've I done?" He managed to back Tootsie away
from O'Brien, but the damage was done. The man's neck cocked
at on odd angle as he lay in the snow. His out-flung arms, the
palms facing up, lay unmoving in the dirty snow. A thin trickle
of blood ran from his ear. Adam knew he was dead.

Samantha's sobs cut through the air. She dashed toward
the street, her arms stretching toward her pa. Adam caught her
and pulled her tight against his chest. She clung, crying, re-
peating in a pathetic voice, "Oh, Pa . . . Pa . . ."

Adam's heart ached at her obvious distress. He stroked her
hair and pressed his lips against her temple. "Shhh, honey. He's
not hurting. And he can't hurt you now." He was holding her—
not the way he'd intended, but he had her in his arms. And as
he'd promised himself, he wouldn't let go.

Her warm tears soaked into his collar, her shoulders shaking convulsively. "He's dead, Adam. He's dead."

Adam could only hold her, rock her, comfort her. He placed
a kiss on the top of her head, on her russet waves that were as
untamable as the wind, letting his lips rest there as she sobbed
against his neck.

Neighbors came from their houses. Two men lifted O'Brien's
lifeless body and placed it in the back of the cab, which still
stood near the curb. The driver approached, twisting his hat in
his hands. "I'm so sorry." He touched Samantha's shoulder. "If I
can do anything . . . ?"

Adam spoke over Samantha's head. "Could you take the
body to the undertaker's? I'll make arrangements for burial later."

"Surely, sir, surely." His gaze drifted to Samantha, who burrowed against Adam's chest. "Will the little lady be all right?"

Samantha's sobs had quieted, but she clung tenaciously to Adam's coat front. He nodded, swallowing the lump in his throat. "Yes. I'll see to her. Thank you."

The man nodded, placed his hat on his head, and left. Adam guided Samantha into the house, shutting the door against the curious neighbors. A rocking chair sat near the stove, and he eased her into its smooth seat. Kneeling in front of her, he kept a grip on her icy hands. She kept her head down, refusing to meet his eyes.

A cold shaft of fear whizzed through Adam's middle. Did she blame him for her father's death? His heart pounding, he gave her hands a gentle squeeze. "Samantha, I'm so sorry about your pa. I didn't want to hurt him." He gulped, fear making his throat dry. "You know that, don't you?"

Her face lifted. Fresh tears spurted into her eyes. "Yes, I know." Her chin quivered, her face crumpling. "Pa, he . . . he's always . . ." One harsh sob escaped. "It was just so awful. . . ."

"I know, honey, I know." Adam smoothed the tangled hair away from her tear-stained face and stood. "Let me get you something hot to drink. And a blanket." His gaze searched the small space.

She reached out and grasped his hand. "No, I don't need anything but . . ." Tears rolled down her pale cheeks, her luminous eyes beseeching. "Please, Adam, just hold me?"

Without a moment's hesitation Adam scooped her into his arms. He slid into the rocker, cradling her in his lap. She nestled against him, and his arms curved around her to provide warmth and comfort. They remained in the rocker until the coals in the stove burned themselves out and the sun slipped over the horizon.

Chapter Twenty-Seven

*F*our days later Adam assisted Samantha from the train at the Mountain Lake depot. Arms outstretched, she moved directly into Ma's waiting embrace. She clung, the tears that had plagued her constantly since her father's death flowing again, but she smiled through her tears as she said, "It's so good to be here."

Adam stood back, observing as Samantha moved from Ma to Pa and then down the row of assembled brothers and sisters assembled, hugging each in turn. Would he have ever imagined her entering willingly into an embrace? She'd changed so much.

He hadn't mentioned locating David. She'd been so distraught about her father, and then her focus shifted to the memorial service, which was attended sparsely by neighbors, mostly out of compassion for the daughter left behind. Wishing to spare her, he'd made all of the arrangements for burial and care-taking of the grave.

Adam had telegraphed his parents to inform them of Burt O'Brien's accident, so David was aware of his father's death. If David had come to the funeral, the separation would have reached a natural conclusion. But he'd remained in Mountain Lake, waiting for Adam to bring Samantha. She'd have to be told about her brother soon.

Liz kept her arm around Samantha's shoulders. "Do you want to come to our home or go on and stay with Mother?"

Samantha looked from Liz to Laura, then back again. "I— I'm not sure." She shook her head and released a rueful chuckle. "The simplest decisions just seem beyond me these days."

Ma reached over to cup Samantha's wind-reddened cheeks in her hands. "That's fine, Samantha. Why don't we all come to the farm for our evening meal, and then you can decide where to go from there."

Liz offered another quick hug. "You are welcome at either place."

Adam caught Samantha's elbow, steering her toward Pa's wagon. No matter where she was welcome, she'd be staying close to him if he had anything to say about it.

Samantha allowed Adam to lift her into the wagon. She flashed a smile of thanks before settling into the mound of soft hay meant to protect the riders from the January cold. Josie and Becky wriggled in on either side of her, forcing Adam to the opposite side of the wagon. Although only a few feet separated them, she missed his presence. He'd been such a comfort in the past difficult days.

The girls chattered cheerfully all the way home, and Samantha found herself joining in despite herself. How wonderful to be carefree and laughing again. A twinge of guilt stilled her laughter. Shouldn't she be despondent? Pa lay dead. Sorrow pressed on her—she couldn't deny it—but most of her unhappiness was regret for what could have been, but wasn't. She'd prayed so hard for Pa to change—for him to become the loving father she'd always longed for him to be. Now he was gone, and with his death the chance for a loving relationship was forever gone. That was her deepest sorrow.

As they gathered around the table for the evening meal, Samantha looked around at her surrogate family. Her heart swelled. What a gift she'd received when she'd met the Klaassen family. She had so many people to love now—people who loved her in return. Tears stung the back of her nose as she thought of everything they'd given her.

Her gaze traveled to Adam, seated on her right in Josie's usual place. He'd traded spots with his sister, as if afraid to let Samantha out of his sight. His nearness made her feel protected and secure and—her heart pattered wildly—even loved. What would she have done these past days without him?

The Klaassen family held hands around the table to pray, and Samantha placed her hand in Adam's firm, warm grasp. When Mr. Klaassen said, "And thank You, Lord, for bringing our Samantha safely here again," Adam's fingers tightened on hers. Samantha peeked at him. He peeked back. They both smiled.

Ah, it was good to be home.

⁓◌

Adam paced in the parlor, his ear tuned to the kitchen where Samantha helped Ma with the breakfast cleanup. The younger children had trooped off for school in a thunder of footsteps, so other than Ma and Samantha's soft chatter, the house was quiet. A perfect setting for a serious talk.

His mouth went dry. He'd gone over in his mind a dozen different ways to tell Samantha he'd found her brother, but he still wasn't sure how to approach the subject. She still possessed hurt bitterness about the broken promise he'd made to return for her. Could she move past the bitterness and on to acceptance?

Impatience to finally let his secret loose propelled him across the kitchen floor. Samantha was laughing with Ma over something Sarah had said at the breakfast table, and he interrupted by touching her lightly on the shoulder. She turned, and the happy look of contentment on her face took his breath away.

She tipped her head in query. "Yes, Adam?"

"C-could we go into the parlor and . . . talk?" He fiddled with the buttons on his flannel shirt, unable to stand still. "There's something I need to discuss with you."

Samantha flashed a puzzled look at Ma.

Ma smiled. "Go ahead, Samantha. We're nearly finished here." She returned to sorting the silverware in its drawer.

She shrugged, her shoulders hunching in a jerk. "All right then."

Adam guided her with a hand on the small of her back, gesturing for her to sit in the upholstered settee. Once she'd settled herself, he pulled a small parlor chair forward and sat, carefully to keep his trouser-covered knees from brushing her rose-scattered skirts. He ran a nervous hand through his hair, leaned forward, and rested his elbows on his knees. Head low, he stared at his clasped hands and gathered his courage.

"Adam?"

Her confused single-word question made Adam jolt. He peeked at her. She nibbled her lower lip, her brows pinching. "Is something wrong?"

He gulped. In his mind, everything was right. "No. No, not at all."

"Are you sending me away?"

His jaw dropped. He sprang upright, shooting out one hand toward her. "No! Why would you think such a thing?"

She offered a slow shrug, her gaze flitting to the side. "You've seen where I come from—my pa, my neighborhood. Everything." She swallowed, her pale blue eyes shifting to meet his. "Maybe now that you know, you don't want me here anymore."

Adam's heart ached. How could she ever think he'd hold something outside of her control against her? He grasped her hand. "Samantha, none of that matters. You're *you*, and I—" He bit down on the tip of his tongue, holding his profession inside.

"Then what is it?" Her voice held an undercurrent of fear. "Something is bothering you."

He gave her hand a squeeze then released it. "Nothing's wrong. I just need to tell you something, and it's hard to know how to get started."

A soft chuckle escaped her lips—a nervous sound. "You've never had any trouble talking to me before. Why not just say it?"

She was right. He should just spit it out. Clamping his fingers over his knees, he drew in a deep breath, and finally divulged the secret. "I've located David."

Samantha gasped. She clapped both palms to her chest. Her mouth dropped open and her eyes grew as wide as a pair of full moons. She looked like she might suffer apoplexy. "W-what did you say?"

Adam bounced from his seat and dropped down beside her, slipping one arm around her shoulders. He fanned her with his free hand, willing her white face to gain some color. "I'm so sorry. I shouldn't have blurted it out that way. But I know even though you miss him, you're still angry with him, and I wasn't sure the best way to say it, so I just *said* it." He fanned with one hand, patted her back with the other, and inwardly prayed for understanding. "I wanted you to know right away because he's here in Mountain Lake. He's eager to see you—and I'm sure you'll want to see him once you're over the shock, and—"

Pink crept back into Samantha's face. She caught his flapping hand and lowered it to his knee then placed her fingers over his mouth. "Adam? Please stop talking and take me to my brother."

David held his sister at arm's length and shook his head. Astonishment and joy mingled in his chest. "Sam . . . Sam . . . You're all grown up. And you're so pretty. All these years I've pictured you as the little girl I left behind. . . ." A lump filled his throat. He held her face with his long, narrow hands, regret for the lost years nearly strangling him. "Sammy, I'm so sorry I left you. I came back for you, just like I said I would, but Pa—he said you'd run off. I should've known he was lying. This happened a few years before you'd actually left. I should've stuck around, kept looking for you. I'm so, so sorry. . . . Can you ever forgive me?"

A tender smile curved her lips. She curled her hands around his wrist, looking directly into his eyes which matched her own. "There's nothing to forgive, Davey. I have you back again, and that's all that matters."

David pulled her tight against his chest. His sister—his sweet little sister—snug in his arms. Had he ever believed this day would come? He flicked a glance at Adam, who sat on the sofa in the corner of the tiny apartment. What a debt of gratitude he owed the man. He planted a kiss on the top of Samantha's head, battling joyful tears.

Samantha's muffled voice came from somewhere in David's shirt front. "Davey? I love you, but I can't breathe in here."

David released her with a loud burst of laughter. The sound startled him. When had he last laughed out loud? He couldn't remember. But only five minutes of having his sister back, and he'd regained the ability.

Adam rose and crossed to the pair and put his hand on Samantha's shoulder. "How about we go out to the house? Mother and Father are eager to see you two together. When the kids come home from school, there'll be no peace. If we want a quiet conversation, we'd better go now."

As much as David wanted to keep Samantha to himself for a while longer, he also wanted to thank Adam's family for rescuing her. "I would like to get to know the family who befriended Sam." He linked fingers with his sister, smiling down at her. "Let's go."

The evening that followed was one of the happiest in Adam's memory. David and Samantha's joy at being together once again was beautifully heart wrenching. The pair couldn't be separated—they stuck as close together as two kernels on a corncob. Ma prepared a homecoming feast fit for royalty, and afterward the entire family, which included Frank's betrothed, Anna, gathered in the parlor to light a fire in the fireplace, pop popcorn, and drink hot homemade apple cider spiced with cinnamon and cloves. David contributed little to the conversation, as reticent as Samantha had been upon her arrival in Mountain Lake, but Samantha joined in as easily as if she'd always been a part of the Klaassen family.

As much as Adam gloried in Samantha's delight at having her brother so near, he experienced a slight twinge of envy. He tried to squelch it—he shouldn't begrudge the too-long-separated brother and sister time together—but he'd also suffered separation from Samantha. He longed to slide in next to her on the settee, to see her sweet face tipped to him and only him in attentiveness, to experience a oneness with her.

A little after eight, Frank caught Anna's hand and drew her from the window seat. "We need to head back. I promised Anna's pa I'd have her home by eight thirty." He turned to David. "I'll drop you off at the boarding room on the way."

David heaved a sigh heavy with reluctance, but he rose and bestowed a shy good-bye on everyone. Samantha curved herself against his side and walked him to the back door. Adam trailed behind, watching as the pair paused in the doorway to exchange a lengthy hug.

David pressed his lips to the top of Samantha's head—he bent his tall, lanky frame like an apostrophe to reach her. "No more unfulfilled promises for either of us now, Sammy. This time, I'm in your life to stay."

Adam's heart caught as Samantha lifted her beaming smile to her brother. Tears shimmered on her thick lashes. "That's the only way I'll have it."

David placed a quick kiss on Samantha's cheek and then hopped off the step and ran to climb into the wagon. Samantha remained in the doorway, arms wrapped around her middle, gazing after him. Adam hesitated, wanting to draw her back inside yet unwilling to intrude.

"So when are you going to propose?"

Adam spun around, surprised when Liz whispered in his ear. He shot a frantic glance at Samantha, but she remained looking outward, seemingly unaware. He caught Liz's arm and tugged her to the opposite side of the kitchen. "You hush that kind of talk!"

Liz laughed. "Oh, nobody's listening—they're all having too much fun." A burst of laughter carried from the parlor, proving her words. She looked past Adam, her eyebrows high, as Samantha scuffed her way toward the parlor. When she'd disappeared through the doorway, Liz shifted her attention to Adam. "So . . . when?"

Adam played dumb. "When, what?"

She punched him on the shoulder. "You know what. It's as plain as the nose on your face. You love her. You're glowing, just having her back here. So when are you going to let her know?"

Adam scratched his chin. He tipped sideways, peering through the wide doorway to Samantha, who sat on the settee again, now with Sarah and Josie—surrounded by his family and obviously at home in their midst. A smile tugged at his lips. He sighed. "Soon, I hope. But her life has been full of half promises and uncertainties. I need to make sure that when I propose, I have more than just my name to offer her. When I promise to care for her, I need to have a home ready, I need—"

Liz shook her head in amused exasperation. "Adam, Adam, Adam . . ."

He didn't need to play dumb now. "What?"

"Samantha is so head over heels in love with you, she needs nothing more than *you*." Liz bumped him lightly with her shoulder as if to say, *silly man*.

Adam cocked his left eyebrow. "That's all?"

Liz laughed. "That's what I like about you, Adam. You really don't have a conceited bone in your body." She socked him again in sisterly fashion. "Yes, you silly goose. If it will make you feel better, ready your home and do whatever else you think needs doing. But I'm telling you right now, all that will be more for your benefit than Samantha's. The offer of your name is all she needs." With a grin, Liz scurried to join the other.

Adam remained in the kitchen, lost in thought. He appreciated Liz's advice, but Liz didn't understand everything. He'd listened to Samantha pour out her hurts in the old shed behind the depot. She needed security and promises that would be kept. He shook his head, discounting his sister's opinion. Liz might be right in some things, but this time she was most certainly wrong. He had a lot of things to work out before he could officially ask Samantha to be his wife.

And he knew just where to get started.

Chapter Twenty-Eight

The next three weeks, Adam was rarely at the house. The winter months were the slow months on a farm. Not having crops to attend, the men had a few hours of precious free time. So once morning chores were completed, Adam disappeared, returning briefly for his noon meal, then taking off again until it was time for milking in the evening. Although his family questioned him—Sarah nearly pestered the patience out of him—he refused to tell anyone where he spent his time or what he was doing.

The rest of the family had no secrets, though. Si and Frank spent most of their day in the barn, working on furniture for the small frame house that had been erected in a tree-laden area near the soybean fields to the west of the Klaassen's homestead. The date of Frank and Anna's wedding crept ever closer, and Frank readied the house like a mother robin readies her nest. Laura stayed busy finishing a lovely Double Wedding Ring quilt, the rings of which she'd formed from pieces of Frank's and Anna's old clothing. It was a beautiful quilt, the colorful patchwork rings showing crisply against the bleached muslin. But more beautiful than the pattern was the thought behind it. Bits and pieces of each of the couple's past, sewn together into a circle—a never-ending symbol of love. Samantha longed for the time when she, too, would make preparations for a home and family. And those longings always centered around Adam.

Samantha had taken several dress orders and kept her hands busy stitching, but her mind was restless, wondering where Adam was, what he was doing, who he was with. . . . The beautifully feminine Priscilla Koehn niggled at the back of her memory. Could he be spending his time wooing her? Priscilla would certainly welcome the attention. The green-eyed monster, jealousy, visited her often.

She sat in the parlor, sewing the hem on a new dress for a friend of Laura's, trying to reassure herself that certainly Adam wouldn't have come clear to Milwaukee for her if he didn't care for her. But on the other hand, Adam was such a caring person, he probably would have done it for just about anyone he thought was in trouble. Still, she had gotten that one kiss from him, and he had held her so tenderly after Pa died. . . . But she'd been horribly upset that day. Maybe he was just comforting her the way he'd comfort Sarah if she was hurting.

Her trembling fingers skipped a stitch, and with a huff of frustration she set the dress aside. Crossing to the window, she hugged herself and stared across the brown yard. If only she knew how she stood with Adam! He'd been wonderfully kind to her, had treated her as if she mattered deeply, but he'd never come right out and said how he felt. Was it simply brotherly affection, special friendship, or did he love her? She longed for the courage to simply ask him. That is, if she could pin the man down long enough for a conversation these days.

She searched the yard, seeking a glimpse of his familiar blue plaid shirt and thick brown hair. Where was he keeping himself lately? What could he be doing that would consume so much time? Christmas was over; it couldn't be Christmas secrets. But a secret it was. One of the best-kept secrets ever. It drove her to distraction, trying to discern what his disappearances, smug grin, and boyish winks could mean.

With a sigh, she returned to the settee to continue sewing. But her tangled emotions held her captive. She couldn't focus on stitching. David had started working at the Family Mercantile with Hiram Klaassen. Maybe she could ride in and visit with him. Folding the dress neatly, she placed it on the window seat and went to the kitchen where Laura kneaded a huge ball of bread dough. Samantha paused beside the flour-strewn table. "May I take Bet to town?"

Laura glanced up, her brows puckering. "You have an important errand?"

She needed her brother to help her sort her thoughts. "Yes, ma'am."

Laura examined Samantha for a few moments, as if waiting for a further explanation. Samantha remained quiet. Finally Laura offered a nod. "I suppose it's fine. But bundle up in my wool coat and a knitted scarf. There's the scent of snow in the air. And try to be back well before dark. I don't want you caught out in the cold."

Laura's motherly caring warmed Samantha more than the coat ever could. She gave the dear woman a brief hug. "Yes, ma'am. I won't be long. And thank you."

Soon she was on Bet's back, snug in Laura's wool coat with a thick scarf draped over her hair and around her neck. The extra layers made her feel bulky, but she appreciated the protection from the chill air. While she rode, she admired the beautiful landscape. Yesterday's snowfall coated the ground like frosting on one of Laura's scripture cakes. Fence posts wore little pointed hats of snow, and leafless tree branches were dressed up with a fine lining. A pair of cardinals flitted through the trees above her head, their brilliant red a beautiful contrast in the world of white.

"You sure created a wonderful world, God." Samantha spoke aloud into the quiet beauty, startling a small white rabbit into zigzagged escape. She laughed at the rabbit's frantic course then prodded Bet with a few bumps of her heels. "Come on, old girl. Let's hurry a bit."

Samantha hitched Bet to the wooden rail outside Klaassen's Family Mercantile and gave her nose a brief rub of thanks before entering the store. The doorbell clanged, and David looked up from a stack of cans on the counter.

His eyes widened. "Sam! Did you ride in?" He crossed the floor toward her, hands outstretched.

Samantha moved into his embrace. "Yes, I did."

"Brr, you're cold." David shivered and turned her in the direction of the potbellied stove that filled the corner of the store. "Come warm yourself."

Samantha offered no argument. She hunkered near the stove, rubbing her hands together and allowing the heat to steep into her bones. She glanced around the quiet shop. "Where's Mr. Klaassen?"

David's chest puffed. "Gone for the afternoon. He left me in charge—books and all." David squatted down next to Samantha, a look of wonder on his face. "Can you imagine someone trusting the son of Burt O'Brien to care for his property?"

Samantha patted his knee. "Davey, you are much more than just Burt O'Brien's son. The Klaassens know that, and so do you, I think."

David nodded, his expression pensive. "Still, it's hard to imagine. . . ." He brightened and asked, "So what brings you into town on this nippy day?"

"You." Warm again, she moved to perch on the cracker barrel. David seated himself on the apple barrel nearby. She fixed her gaze on her brother's serious face and confided, "I was feeling restless and decided I needed a chat with my big brother."

David's narrow face creased with a tender smile. "Got a case of cabin fever?"

Samantha shook her head. "Not that kind of restlessness. I need to . . . make sense of confusion."

David closed his long-fingered hand over hers. "What's the problem, Sammy?"

Frowning, Samantha shrugged. "I'm not sure there is a *problem*. It's more an unanswered question." She paused, chewing on her lower lip, her brows pulled into a puzzled frown. Drawing in a deep breath, she forced herself to ask the question that plagued her mind. "Davey, do you think I'm good enough for Adam?"

David reared back. His frown turned stern. "What kind of a question is that?"

"He's seen where I come from, and he knows how Pa liked to drink more than he liked anything else. If you put our family up against his, look at the differences! Sometimes I think he cares for me, but other times . . ." She bit her lip again, lowering her gaze to her lap. "I don't know what to think."

"Well, I do." David gave her hand a shake. "Look at me."

She did, seeing his face blurred by the tears flooding her eyes.

David swept the moisture away with his thumbs. "None of the Klaassens look down their noses at you—and that goes doubly for Adam. What did you say to me a little bit ago? There's a heap-sight more to you than just being Burt O'Brien's daughter. Adam sees that."

Samantha sighed. "I want to think so, David, really I do. But since I've come back here he's been so odd. He spends all his time away from the house—away from me—and he won't say where he is or what he's doing. It's as if he's avoiding me for some unknown reason." Tipping her head, she fixed David with a worried look. "Do you think he knows how I feel about him, and he's staying away as a means of telling me he doesn't feel the same?"

David sucked in a slow breath. "How *do* you feel about him?"

Samantha answered promptly. "I love him. I love him *so much*. . . . When I was away from him, I felt incomplete. When I'm with him, I feel like I'm a better, bigger person than I was before. Somehow he makes me *more* than I've ever been." She lowered her head, laughing self-consciously. "I suppose that sounds funny."

David cupped her chin, lifting her face. "No, Sammy, it isn't funny. It's wonderful, and I'm so happy you've found someone like Adam. If I could have handpicked someone for you, I would have chosen him. He's a good man."

"Yes, he is." She threw her hands wide. "I just wish I knew if he cared at all for me, too."

David grinned. "Stop wishing. Adam's got feelings for you, have no doubt. Now, I don't know what he's doing off by himself, but I can almost guarantee it's not to avoid spending time with you. That wouldn't be Adam's way of handling things. He'd come right out and tell you if he thought there was a problem between you."

Samantha considered David's words. She knew Adam to be open and honest. He wouldn't run from a conflict. The knowledge only confused her further. "Then what—?"

"Has it crossed your mind, little sister, that he's planning a surprise for Frank and Anna? Their wedding is when—next Saturday?"

She nodded.

David gave a knowing wink. "Well, my guess is he's off doing some special fixings for his brother and future sister-in-law."

"That would make sense." Samantha worried her lower lip for a moment, contemplating. "If I only knew for sure . . ."

David stood, holding out his hand to Samantha. She took it and allowed him to tug her to her feet. He slung his arm around her shoulder and walked her toward the door. "Well, don't stew about it. The wedding is only a week away. I'll wager you'll know soon enough what Adam's up to. In the meantime, try not to turn those puppy dog eyes on him at every turn, or he may end up spilling the beans and spoil a good surprise."

She laughed. "David, it's so good to have you back. It's wonderful to have my big brother to talk sense into me." Then she hung her head as another thought struck. Didn't the Bible Adam had given her assure her the heavenly Father had good plans for her? Why was she wasting so much time worrying instead of trusting His leading? *I'm sorry, God, for not asking You what I should do concerning my feelings for Adam.*

"Sam?"

She looked at David, who watched her with lines of concern marring his brow.

"Are you all right?"

"I'm fine. I won't worry anymore. I promise."

"Good." He pulled her close, resting his chin on her hair. "Then can I give you one more piece of big brotherly advice?"

"What's that?"

He bounced her against him once and ordered with mock sternness, "Get on your horse and go home before the sun drops any further. And when you get there, drink a cup of hot tea to warm up your innards."

Samantha giggled. "Yes, sir."

David followed her outside and helped her into Bet's saddle. Placing the reins in her hands, he offered a tender smile. "See you later, baby sister."

She smiled her reply and headed for home.

he evening before the big wedding day, Grandpa and Grandma Klaassen, Daniel and Rose, and little Christina and Katrina arrived by train. The house overflowed with people, chatter, and laughter. While happy chaos, it was chaos just the same, and midevening Adam observed Samantha drawing a shawl around her shoulders and slipping out onto the railed porch. The idea of a few quiet moments alone with Samantha appealed, so he tugged a jacket into place and followed.

She held to the porch railing, her face aimed upward. Stargazing, seemingly lost in thought. If she sensed his presence, she gave no indication of it. Her eyes remained riveted on the black velvet sky which wore a spattering of sparkling diamonds. Adam perched on the porch railing and watched her admire the sky. He'd been so busy lately, gone so much, that her beauty took him by surprise. Hers was a simple beauty enhanced by her modest nature and caring spirit. In his eyes, she was a perfect gemstone set in a moonlit mounting of gold. His heart swelled in anticipation as he thought of the preparations he'd been making. The time neared to tell her his plans. But for now he simply enjoyed watching her as she gazed heavenward.

At last she turned to meet his gaze. Her lips tipped into a self-conscious smile. "Did you think you were being ignored?"

He shifted his weight to lean more comfortably on a post as she turned to perch gracefully on the railing. "Maybe. Just a little."

"Probably the way all of us have felt here lately, by you."

He caught the hint but he smiled, refusing to rise to the bait.

After a few moments she turned her attention to the sky again. She released an airy sigh. "The night never fails to move me."

His gaze pinned on her sweet profile. Lit by the soft glow flowing from the parlor window, her hair became burnished copper, her thick lashes casting small shadows on her cheeks. He swallowed, nearly undone by her beauty. "How, Samantha?"

She searched the sky, her eyes roving over the millions of stars winking on their carpet of ebony. "The sky is so soft and black—like fine velvet—and the stars blink and shimmer. . . . Sometimes I pretend they're looking at me, sending me a message from heaven—maybe from Gran. And I feel so close to them, I could just reach out and put one in my pocket to save for a sad day when I need some beauty." She raised her hand, the fingers reaching skyward. Then she peeked at him, color flooding her cheeks, and she pulled her hand back to the railing. "I must sound awful foolish."

"For wanting to put a star in your pocket?"

Her head low, she nodded.

Adam chuckled. "Not at all. That's like carrying around a special wish and being able to take it out and hold it now and then, knowing that it's yours to keep forever."

Samantha's chin bobbed up, her eyes widening in surprise. "You *do* understand."

"Well, sure." Adam angled his body to face her. "I have wishes, too, Samantha. We all do. They might be different desires, but no one *never* makes a wish on a star." He tipped his face upward. "If I could put one in my pocket, I'd choose that one." He pointed to an exceptionally bright star that blinked almost blue.

Samantha followed his gaze. "Yes, that's a nice one, but I'd choose"—she pointed, too—"that one, because it's smaller and off by itself, and it looks as if it could use someone to love it." *Just like me.* The words, unspoken, hovered in the air between them.

Adam stared at the star for several silent seconds before he found the courage to ask softly, "Do you feel like that star, Samantha?"

The rosy color in her cheeks deepened. Hugging her arms around herself, she swallowed twice. When she spoke, the quaver brought the sting of tears to Adam's eyes. "Sometimes. I used to feel very alone. But now . . ." Abruptly, she turned to look him full in the face. "Now, I know God loves me. I've found people who care about me. So . . . now . . . I can dare to believe that my wishes could come true."

Their eyes locked. They leaned close. So close her warm breath brushed his cheek as she exhaled in tiny puffs. So close, he could see the reflection of the stars in her cornflower blue eyes. Adam's heart thrummed. *Yes, Samantha, I will make all your wishes come true. Just be patient with me. Let me make things perfect for you.*

Her eyes beseeched. Her breath coiled around him in a wisp of white. Her lips parted, as if ready to ask a question, and he held his breath, waiting. Then the parlor door swung open, sending a shaft of golden light across their feet and surrounding them with the laughing voices of his family.

Sarah called, "Mama says come in. We're gonna make taffy." The door slammed, sealing them once again in peaceful darkness.

The intimate moment had passed. Reluctantly Adam slid from the rail, his feet echoing against the floorboards. "Come, Samantha." He held out his hand, and she placed her palm on his. He curled her fingers around her small hand. It fit, just right, in his grip. Just as she fit, just right, in his heart. He'd tell her soon, but for now he led her back inside to join his family.

Frank and Anna's wedding day dawned bright and clear, a crisp windless winter day with bright sun bouncing off the snow and sending millions of shimmering diamonds into the air. Samantha pulled aside the lace curtains that shrouded the parlor window and looked out at the perfect day. A hint of melancholy tugged. If only this could be her wedding day. Hers and Adam's . . .

"Samantha! Samantha!" Sarah's voice intruded.

Samantha turned in time to catch Sarah, who threw herself against Samantha's middle in a boisterous hug.

"See my pretty wedding dress?" The little girl spun an impromptu pirouette in the shaft of sunlight that streamed through the bayed windows. The confection pink dress with miles of lace trim was an ideal wrapping for Sarah's china doll prettiness.

"It's lovely, Sarah. You'll make the prettiest flower girl ever."

Giggling, Sarah dashed away. Samantha's thoughts drifted to the previous evening, when Laura read the list of wedding plans, ascertaining all was ready. Sarah would be the flower girl, with Anna's youngest brother, Benji, as ring bearer. Anna's sister, Katherine, and Josie were serving as attendants to the bride. Daniel and Adam were standing up for Frank. Arn and Becky would light the candles that lined each window sill and the edge of the altar at the front of the church. Anna's brothers, Mort and Matthew, were singing two songs, and Teddy had responsibility for carrying all the gifts that arrived to a decorated table.

When Laura had finished, Frank exclaimed in exasperation, "If we'd had one more brother or sister to find a wedding assignment for, I would have insisted we elope."

Anna had leaned close and gently chided, "Would you rather have no family at all?" They'd both looked at Samantha, and Frank had ceased his grumbling, but the funny feeling that filled her stomach at their words remained like a lump of dread in her belly. Now that David was here in Mountain Lake, she had someone. One someone. Was it wrong to want more?

After breakfast, everyone climbed into the buckboard, which the Klaassen siblings had decorated with huge tissue paper flowers and crepe paper streamers in pink, yellow, and blue. Even Bet and Tick wore paper flowers on their ears, and they stamped their feet, blowing billows of steam from their noses as if to say they understood the importance of the day.

The ride to the church was raucous. Joyous jabber and playful ribbing rang from every corner. Frank sat nervous and twitchy, fiddling constantly with the perfect black bow tie resting below his chin. Samantha thought he looked particularly fine in his wedding suit of black broadcloth and crisp white cambric shirt. But not as handsome as Adam would be in such finery. She imagined Adam standing at an altar, his head held high, his brown eyes shining with love as she walked down the aisle toward him.

Sadness threatened to grip her. She must stop indulging such fanciful imaginings! She turned to Josie and joined in the conversation, determined to enjoy Frank and Anna's special day.

When they reached the churchyard, everyone spilled out of the wagon. Other wagons and buggies were already there, with people milling around outside, enjoying the sunshine. Laura herded the younger children inside. Si, Arn, and Frank unloaded the food and gifts the family had brought. Adam helped Grandpa and Grandma Klaassen down from the high wagon seat and escorted them into the church. Daniel and Rose each took a small daughter by the hand and headed inside behind them. Samantha lagged behind, feeling out of place and sorry for herself.

The service was brief considering the amount of time spent in preparation for it. Anna's mother cried through most of the ceremony, dabbing at her eyes with a lace handkerchief. What were her tears all about? Was the woman overwhelmed with happiness or filled with regret over her daughter's choice? If it were Samantha's wedding day, would her mother-in-law-to-be shed tears of regret or joy over the wife her son had chosen?

She looked at Laura who was seated next to Si—no man and woman separation on this day. Her gently lined face tipped upward, her ever-present smile soft and accepting. Would she be wearing that same expression of contented happiness if Adam and Samantha stood at the altar?

Her eyes moved to Adam, so straight and tall, flanked by his brothers. He stood with his hands clasped at his spine, his gaze on the minister as the man advised the young couple on the seriousness of their commitment. Tears stung her eyes. He was so handsome. *Oh, Adam, can't you see me as I see you?*

As if he sensed her yearnings, he turned his face slightly, his eyes seeking. When his gaze found her, his expression softened. His lips tipped into the sweetest smile she'd ever seen— a full-of-promise smile that lit him from within. Her breath caught. She sent him a timorous smile, tears filling her eyes as emotions too heady to contain swept through her. For only a few seconds, they gazed into one another's eyes, and then Adam turned his attention back to the minister.

Samantha crossed her hands over her pounding heart. Her thoughts raced. *Dear Lord, I saw something in Adam's eyes. Something different, something special. I saw . . .* She hardly dared to believe it. *I saw love.*

Adam forced his gaze forward but everything within him strained toward the lovely young woman sitting only a few yards away. His thoughts tumbled, making his pulse gallop. *It will be our turn soon, Samantha. Soon it will be you and me standing here before our family and friends, exchanging vows that will bind us together for the rest of our lives. Believe it, Samantha. It will happen. Soon . . .*

Reverend Goertzen turned the couple to face the congregation and announced, "I present to you Mr. and Mrs. Frank Klaassen. Frank, you may kiss your bride."

Frank's face flooded with color as he leaned toward Anna and she lifted her face for his kiss. Their lips touched briefly, and as they separated, a whoop resounded. The people filling the pews came in a rush, flooding the newly joined couple with well-wishes.

Adam stood to the side, watching the throng swarm his brother and sister-in-law. He needed to get out of the way, and he sidestepped, placing the heel of his boot on someone's foot. He spun around, an apology forming on his tongue, to find himself face-to-face with Samantha. The secret he carried trembled in his throat, and a smile broke across his face without effort.

People continued to mill around them, causing them to shift and move with the tide of bodies. But her eyes remained locked on his, as if unable to look away. He caught her arm, drawing her from the throng. Once safely in the corner, he brushed her arm with his thumb. "I'm sorry I stepped on you."

"It's all right." Her words came out with little huffs, as if she'd just run a footrace. Her cheeks bore bright streaks of pink, and her eyes shimmered. "You didn't hurt me."

"I'm glad. That's the last thing I'd want to do." Remembering the evening in Liz's yard when he'd frightened her so, pain pinched Adam's heart. He leaned close, hoping she'd read the sincerity in his eyes. "You believe me, don't you?"

She nodded slowly. "Yes, Adam, I believe you. More than I've ever known anything, I know you wouldn't hurt me."

At her reply, his heart lurched and fluttered, rising up into his throat. He wanted to say more—to offer other assurances—but the wedding party was moving toward the double doors, Frank and Anna in the lead. He'd have to wait. With a gentle nudge, Adam turned Samantha toward the others.

She remained close to his side as they stepped out into the churchyard. Together, they cheered when the others cheered, threw wheat kernels when the others tossed handfuls into the air, and even chased the buggy that bore the newlyweds toward their new home until it rounded the corner and headed out of town. But when their steps slowed, and the merrymakers had turned back to the church for the after-wedding celebration, he caught her arm and held her back, and within minutes they were alone, side by side, in the middle of Main Street.

Adam grinned and couldn't help teasing, "Remember the last time we ran down Main Street?"

She blushed prettily, but she laughed. "Yes. You tackled me."

"You deserved it."

"I did." Her eyes sparkled with laughter.

But something other than humor simmered beneath the lapels of his jacket. "Samantha, I'd like to show you something. Would you mind skipping the party at the church and going for a ride with me instead?"

She shook her head, the movement barely discernible. "I'd love to go for a ride with you." The simple reply seemed laden with meaning. She leaned toward him—so without guile or coquettishness he believed the gesture was done unconsciously. Her face lifted, her blue eyes speaking volumes without words.

Adam's heart read the unspoken message shining from her face. And he responded in kind. He leaned forward, his movements slow and deliberate. He watched her draw in a breath, her eyes slipping closed as his face came nearer, nearer. Their noses bumped lightly, and hers was cold. But her lips were warm. Their mouths brushed once, twice, then they pulled back slightly, foreheads pressed together lightly, and he sensed her smile even without looking.

They opened their eyes at the same moment. Brown eyes met blue, and he discovered he'd been right. Her face was nearly split by her happy smile. He brought up his gloved hands and closed them on her shoulders. Her hands came up to grasp his forearms, gripping hard through the layers of clothing. They stood thus, sunlight reflecting off the crystal snow and surrounding them with thousands of tiny prisms.

Adam couldn't keep the smile from his face. In minutes—mere minutes—his secrets would be revealed. He would be free to make promises that he intended to spend a lifetime keeping. It was time. Their time.

Unable to hold back any longer, he said, "Let's go."

Chapter Thirty

*H*and in hand, they laughingly ran to the waiting wagon. Samantha started to climb aboard, but Adam grabbed her around the waist and boosted her onto the seat. He jumped up beside her and placed one quick, impetuous smack on her lips.

"Adam!" She glanced around, seeking prying eyes. "What if someone sees you?"

He shrugged, his grin so boyish it stole her breath. "Then they'll say, look at that lucky guy, stealing a kiss from the prettiest girl in town."

"Oh, Adam . . ." Her face flooded with heat, and she ducked her head. But she couldn't stop smiling.

He laughed aloud as he raised the reins and flicked them downward. "Let's get movin'." And they were off.

The air was crisp, clear. It stung her lungs as she inhaled, but she wouldn't complain. She was with Adam, in a world of their own—a shining, shimmering, brighter-than-sunshine world of happy abandon. Never had the sky seemed bluer, the clouds fluffier, the birds as full of cheerful chatter as they were on this day. Hoarfrost coated everything from the tiniest tree branches to the barbed wire that ran from fence post to fence post, catching the sun and bouncing it back into millions of tiny rainbows.

She turned toward Adam and caught him staring, smiling, admiring. She smiled and admired right back. She asked, "Where are we going?"

He waggled his brows. "You'll see."

She pretended to pout. "You won't tell me?"

"Not a chance."

She tipped her head and batted her eyelashes. Had she ever openly flirted with anyone before? No, but with Adam she felt at ease and truly beautiful for the first time in her life. "Pleeeease?" She drew out the word, giving him her best pleading look.

He laughed. "Don't even try it." With a grin, he advised, "Just settle back and enjoy the ride. We'll be there soon. Why don't you tell me what you thought of the wedding?"

So Samantha and Adam chatted away as the sun shone down and the clouds floated lazily in the clear blue sky and cardinals scolded the squirrels that danced in the treetops. In time, Adam pulled back on the reins and called in a deep voice, "Whoa now, Bet and Tick." When the horses came obediently to a stop, Adam tied the reins around the brake handle and leaped off the wagon. "We'll walk from here." He reached for her, and she placed her hands on his shoulders as he lifted her down. Her feet touched the ground, but Adam kept his hands on her waist, hers remaining lightly on his shoulders.

A smile—tender, yet containing a controlled excitement— lit his eyes. "I have a surprise for you."

Her pulse began tripping in erratic double-beats. What was he up to? "For me?"

"Yes. I wanted to get it ready for you as quickly as I could, and it took longer than I'd expected. So I haven't spent much time with you since you've been back. I hope you aren't angry with me."

Angry? How could she be angry when he looked at her with his warm, brown-eyed gaze? Her heart felt light and fluttery, and her stomach leaped in happy flip-flops of anticipation. A giggle spilled from her throat. "Well, what is it?"

He smiled a reply, took her by the hand, and led her through a small wind block of scrub maples. Samantha recognized the area—the north wheat field. Puzzled, she scanned the snow-dusted landscape, seeking her surprise. Adam led her straight toward the hill where his grandfather had constructed the dugout. She sent a curious glance at him then looked ahead. She let out a little gasp that created a small cloud in the chill air.

The old dugout had undergone a transformation. A new door, painted a green as deep as the pine needles on a Christmas tree, stood in place of the old warped plank door. The shutters had been repaired and painted the same dark green. Bright curtains hung behind—was she imagining things?—real glass windows. Samantha's feet stumbled to a halt. "Adam . . . ?"

Beside her, Adam fairly twitched with excitement. He urged her forward with a tug on her hand. "Come inside, Samantha."

She allowed herself to be pulled along. Her mind raced with a dozen questions, but her tongue felt thick and dry. She couldn't speak a word. Adam turned the bright white enamel door knob and swung the door wide. When Samantha got a look at the spanking clean, whitewashed interior, she clapped her hands to her cheeks. Her startled gaze swung to Adam, her mouth hanging open.

Chuckling, he reached out with one finger to close it for her. "I could see your tonsils." How could his teasing sound so sweet?

Samantha gulped, staring around the room in amazement. Wide pine planking covered the dirt floor. Muslin stiffened with whitewash hid the crumbling dirt walls. A round claw-footed table stood in the middle of the room, flanked by two pressed-back chairs and topped with a red-and-white checked oilcloth. A rocking chair sat invitingly in front of the stone fireplace. Samantha, frowning, crossed to it and stroked it with her fingers. Why, it was Gran's old rocker!

She spun to face Adam, her heart pounding and her hands trembling. He remained planted next to the door, hands thrust deep into his pockets, a knowing smile lighting his handsome face. His eyes seemed to tell her to go ahead—explore, examine, enjoy. So she continued her perusal of the room.

In the far corner, a green enamel kerosene stove took up residence, and on new shelves mounted on the wall beside it sat a selection of turquoise graniteware pots and pans, plates, bowls and cups. Samantha moved along the shelves, fingering each item, a lump in her throat.

A blue calico curtain split the room slightly off-center. Samantha pulled it aside and peeked behind it. A bed with a tall, carved maple headboard and footboard filled the space. Her breath coming in little spurts of uncertainty, Samantha stepped over to it and pressed both hands down on the Trip-Around-the-World quilt covering the straw mattress. All these new, bright, wonderful things. What did they mean?

Adam appeared at the curtain. Dimples winked on his tanned cheeks. "Well, what do you think?"

Samantha straightened and turned an amazed circle. "It's wonderful, Adam. Why, it's like new in here. And Gran's rocking chair—how did it get here?"

"David arranged to have it shipped. He knew you would want it."

She shook her head, awed. "And this—" She gestured to the curtain, the new shelves, the floor. "You did all of this?"

Adam shrugged in feigned nonchalance, a secretive smile playing on the corners of his lips. "Liz helped a bit with the curtains and tablecloth and quilt."

Smiling but still puzzled, she repeated, "It's wonderful—a snug, perfect little home. But—" She bit her lower lip. Who was it for? For her to live there on her own? For her to share with David? Or . . . She wouldn't allow herself to consider her deepest hope.

Adam pointed to the other side of the curtain with his thumb. "There's something for you on the mantel."

Samantha sent him another seeking look, which he returned with a smile of encouragement, as she passed him to cross back to the fireplace. Next to the glowing lantern she found an enameled box with a beautiful rose on its top. Her fingers quivering, she lifted the lid. A tinkling melody poured forth. She recognized the tune—"Lohengrin," the traditional wedding song. Her heart leaped into her throat.

Adam crossed to her slowly, his steps measured and purposeful. He stopped inches in front of her. Taking her by the shoulders, he turned her and gently eased her into the smooth seat of Gran's rocker. He bent down on one knee, sliding his palms down her arms until he reached her hands and linked fingers with her. The tune continued to play as he began to speak.

"Samantha, this little dugout was prepared over fifty years ago by my grandfather as a first home for himself and his new bride. It was simple, but it was built by loving hands and was offered with a loving heart. Grandpa told me that he and Grandma were as happy as could be in this little dugout, because it was their *home*. They didn't have much in the way of material possessions. They'd just arrived from Germany—two young people far away from their family and friends. They were scared and probably lonely, but they had each other. They had a common faith, as well as a lot of love. So when Grandpa dug out the side of this hill and made a house around it, he was building on the promise of love and of better things ahead."

Love and better things . . . Yes, that's what Samantha had discovered since arriving in Mountain Lake. She held her breath, her gaze pinned on Adam's sincere, fervent face, her senses so alive the air seemed to crackle.

"It took a lot of faith in one another to make their new start a bright one, but they did it. And when the dugout was complete, he painted a plaque for Grandma which they hung beside the door." Adam released one of her hands to reach beneath his jacket. He withdrew a small, flat package wrapped in tissue and placed it in Samantha's lap.

She stared at the package nestled in the folds of her dress, afraid to touch it, afraid to speak. She dared not break the spell his words spun around them.

"Samantha . . ." He paused, and she lifted her gaze from the package to look back on his. "I've dreamed of the day when I would embark on the same journey my grandparents made—a journey of living and loving and becoming one with a special woman."

The breath she'd been holding released in little puffs of delighted disbelief. Was this moment true? Was this man—this wonderful, tender, open, loving man—truly speaking such words to her? Her—Samantha O'Brien, a nobody. She felt at once undeserving of it and full of longing to hear him continue his soliloquy.

"I'm ready for that journey." His brown eyes glowed, capturing her with their intensity. "I've met that special woman, and I know that God will bless the union." He took in a deep, shuddering breath before continuing. "Samantha, I want nothing more than to begin a new life with you, here, in this little dugout that I've made ready for you much the same way Grandpa made it ready for Grandma all those years ago."

Tears sprang into the corners of his eyes, emphasizing the flecks of green that rested in the velvet brown of his irises. He squeezed her hands. "Samantha, I love you. I am asking you to marry me."

Chapter Thirty-One

She inhaled sharply, taking in a great, choking breath of joyous disbelief. He'd said it. He'd said he loved her. He *loved her.* "Oh, Adam . . ." Too overcome for words, she covered her lips with her trembling fingers as the room began swimming through a spurt of happy tears.

He dipped his head to peek at her impishly. "*Oh, Adam . . . ?* Does that mean yes or no?"

Samantha lowered her hands. Tears overflowed to stream in warm rivulets down her cheeks. "Yes, Adam—oh, yes!" With a joyful burst of laughter, she threw herself into his embrace. "I love you so much, Adam. I can't believe it—your wife. Your *wife.* Oh, I'm so happy I can't bear it."

Her chest would surely burst from happiness. She clung to his neck as he rocked her in his arms. He buried his face in her tumbling curls, and she heard him murmur, "How I love your wild, untamed hair . . ." Her heart caught. He even loved her hair? What a gift God had bestowed when he brought Adam into her life.

Finally he set her aside and picked up the paper-wrapped package, which had fallen to the floor beside their knees. "Here . . . open your present."

She took it, her smile so wide her cheeks ached. With shaking fingers, she pulled the string that held the paper closed. A giggle rose from her chest. She felt giddy with excitement. She peeled the paper wrapping aside and revealed a nine-inch square of cedar, sanded smooth and bearing a painted image of a small yellow frame house at the top, a crude red heart at the bottom. Some sort of writing filled the center.

She frowned, staring at the lines of print. "What does it say?"

Adam cleared his throat. "*Ein Haus wird gebout von Holz und stein; Aber ein Heim bout mon von Liebe alein.*" The unfamiliar words sounded melodious when uttered in his even, baritone voice.

"Is it German?" she asked.

"Yes. Low German, the language of my heritage."

She wished she knew the language of his heritage. "What does it mean?"

Without looking at the plaque, Adam recited, " 'Houses are built of wood and stone; Homes are built of love alone.' "

She retrieved the plaque and ran a finger across the painted words, leaving it to rest on the last two words. " 'Love alone' . . ." Her voice drifted as soft as a feather floating downward. Her gaze lifted to meet Adam's again. "Our home was built with love, and it will always be filled with love, Adam." She knew the pain of broken promises. She didn't make promises lightly. Her chest swelled with conviction as she stated firmly, "I promise you that."

Tears glittered in Adam's eyes. "I make that same promise to you, my Samantha. Forever, and ever."

"I believe you." A weight seemed to fall from Samantha's shoulders as she spoke her assurance to Adam. Such healing God had brought, that she could accept his words as truth and not doubt.

Fresh tears crept down Samantha's cheeks. Adam used his thumbs to whisk them away then cupped her face with his palms, his fingers woven through her hair. "Miss Samantha O'Brien, you have made me the happiest man in the world today. I'm so blessed to have you in my life."

Samantha caught his hands and drew them downward. "Adam, the blessing is mine. You'll never know what it means to me to be loved by someone like you."

He opened his mouth to speak, but she shook her head to silence him. "Please, let me finish. I need to tell you this."

He settled back on his haunches, fixing his attentive gaze on her face. "I'm listening."

Completely confident in his love for her, she opened her heart to him. "When I came to Mountain Lake, I was frightened and filled with angry bitterness. I didn't—couldn't—trust anyone. I didn't know how. Where I came from, if you trusted, you got hurt. So I'd closed myself off. But a person all shut away inside himself is a lonely person." She swallowed, experiencing a sting of pain as she relived the past. "I was so very lonely, Adam . . ."

He took her hands, offering a gentle squeeze.

Encouraged by his understanding, she continued. "You asked me once what I was running away from, and I told you I wasn't running away. You didn't believe me, but it was true. I wasn't running *from* something, I was trying to run *to* something. But I didn't know what. I've been seeking that illusive something since I was six years old and they covered my gran with dirt."

Tears clouded her vision, but she smiled, her lips quivering tremulously. She clasped his hands between hers and lifted them, creating a steeple of their joined hands. "My searching neared its end the day you came dashing down the street after me—when instead of treating me with anger, you reached out to me with kindness. Me, some dirty little thief from the wrong side of the city. I never could have imagined being loved by someone like you—someone good and kind and virtuous. I never could have imagined deserving the love of someone like you. But because of you, I don't see myself in the same old way anymore. I'm not that same frightened, lonely, seeking person anymore."

She gulped, gratitude and love filling her so fully her throat went tight. "Adam, you've given me everything my heart ever longed for. You introduced me, through example and word, to a Savior who will ever be with me. You found my brother and brought him back to me. You gave me love and self-respect and helped me open up to trusting again. You gave my seeking heart a place to call home. I've never done anything to deserve you, but you're mine anyway, and because of the things you've taught me, I can accept you as my own without feelings of guilt or unworthiness. You've even given me *me*. I am so thankful for you."

"Ah, Samantha . . ." He withdrew his hands from her grasp and pulled her close. He lowered his head and pressed his lips to hers. Their kiss was salty and wet with tears. But only happy tears. His hand on the back of her head, he drew her into his embrace then rocked her gently, slowly, contentedly. She relaxed against him. She could remain here forever.

Suddenly he stiffened, and a huff of laughter blasted in Samantha's ear. She pulled back, startled. Adam threw back his head and laughed again, uproariously, uninhibited. She pressed her palms to his jacket front, confused. "What's so funny?"

Adam's eyes crinkled merrily. "You."

She shook her head as if to clear it. "Me?"

"Yes, you, Miss Samantha O'Brien." His voice warbled with suppressed laughter. "When you came to town, you were trying to pass yourself off as Sam Klaassen." He leaned down and kissed the end of her nose. His face close to hers, he finished with a impish smirk. "Well, now I intend to make an honest woman out of you."

She burst into happy laughter as well. He opened his arms, and she fitted herself against Adam's chest. When his arms closed around her, Samantha's seeking heart beat a happy message—*I'm home.*

Laura Klaassen's Scripture Cake

(Use King James Version for references)

1½ cups Judges 5:25
3 cups Jeremiah 6:20
6 Jeremiah 17:11
3½ cups Exodus 29:2
2 tsp. Amos 4:5
2 Chronicles 9:9 to taste
A pinch of Mark 9:50
1 cup Genesis 24:17
1 tblsp. 1 Samuel 14:25
2 cups 1 Samuel 30:12
2 cups chopped dried Song of Solomon 2:13
2 cups slivered or chopped Numbers 17:8

Preheat oven to 325 degrees. Cream together butter and sugar; beat in eggs one at a time. Sift together flour, baking powder, salt, and spices. Add alternately with water to creamed mixture. Stir in honey, fold in raisins, figs, and almonds. Mix well. Turn into two well-greased 9x5x3″ loaf pans. Bake about 60 minutes, making sure not to over bake, until loaves test done by the toothpick test. Let cool for 30 minutes in pans before turning out onto rack. Cool completely before slicing. Serve with whipped cream or ice cream, if desired.

Acknowledgments

Mom and Daddy, whose encouragement propelled me down this road to writing. And Mom, thank you for sharing your German-Mennonite heritage with me. I pray I bestow the best parts of it to the next generations.

Hulda Just, who translated the poem from English to Plaut-dietsch for me.

Jill Stengl and Beverly Olojan-Sticken, my first critique partners, whose patient tutelage gave more than they'll ever know.

My agent, Tamela Hancock Murray, for her endless efforts on my behalf.

Carol Lehman, librarian of the Plum Creek Library in Mountain Lake, for her assistance in research.

Carol Johnson, who gave me a second chance to spend time with the Klaassen family.

And most important, God, who answers the call of every seeking heart. May any praise or glory be reflected directly back to Him.